INVASIVE LEGACY

INVASIVE LEGACY

Richard Malmed

Kravitz & Sons
INNOVATORS IN PUBLISHING, MARKETING AND ADVERTISING

Kravitz and Sons LLC
1301 Farmville Blvd, Suite 104
Greenville, NC 27834

Published by Kravitz and Sons LLC.
ISBN:(sc)   979-8-89639-140-1 (sc)
ISBN:(e)   979-8-89639-139-5 (e)

Library of Congress Control Number: 2025905636

Because of the dynamic nature of the Internet, any web addresses or links contained in this book may have changed since publication and may no longer be valid. The views expressed in this work are solely those of the author and do not necessarily reflect the views of the publisher, and the publisher hereby disclaims any responsibility for them.

Table of Contents

Invasive Legacy

P eter, Digby wants to see you about something. Come on in when you can." Ms. James, Digby's loyal legal secretary and general confidante of many years, stuck her head into my office with the message. I was finishing up a few drafts of letters and briefs so now was a good time. Since I had made a big score years earlier, I was only "of counsel" to the firm. This meant I worked when I wanted to. Digby the senior partner would give me things to do which whetted my appetite for adventure.

"Is this going to be good? Should I bring Angelina?" My own version of a she wolf protecting her young was Angelina, my secretary of many years, who would want to know what was going on. She enjoyed each new matter as her own personal soap opera. I should also say that her take on these things was very valuable. She had street smarts that told us egghead attorneys what people really thought.

"Of course, bring her along." Angelina was sitting just outside my door and was standing with a note pad, before Ms. James had finished her words. She could smell a new adventure a mile away. So we went to the conference room just across from Digby's office. Digby was already walking across the hall as we approached. As usual, he looked like a character from another era.

He was wearing a heavy tweed suit in a medium brown, and a white shirt with green and yellow stripes. Best of all were the flood pants – a style from long ago. The cuffs of his suit pants stopped five inches above his shoes. His reading glasses perched on his chest from a strap behind his neck.

"'Day, Peter."

"Digby, what's up?"

"Maybe something. We'll see."

Digby was a double graduate of Harvard, undergrad and law school, but had an uncanny ability to relate to everyone. He was a regular dinner partner of the Episcopal Bishop of Pennsylvania, the local head of the Republican Party and some of Philadelphia's brightest men. He was an expert fly fisherman, and an authority on wine. His legal career had passed from a first rate litigator, through large scale corporate matters until now in his later years, he was a Wills and Estates lawyer. He had seen it all, done it all and was now our senior partner. Best of all, he could advise on anything with a touch of worldliness that combined wisdom and practical morality. I was indeed blessed to be one of his top go-to-guys. I did not come from the elite social strata he did, but we could discuss matters on a down-to-earth practical level that some of the other tight asses in the firm would never understand. He had more gossip about prominent socialites or local rich guys, but was respected for his discretion. And I could discuss anything with Digby on every point as a father confessor. So as we assembled in the small conference room, Angelina and I anticipated a nice tale with some suspense. That of course, all dissipated when Roger Humphries came into the room with several large files.

Roger was a full time estates lawyer. Basically, he represented rich people in designing their estate plans and wills to fit their personal whims. Mainly, they were confused elderly people who needed support and affection and when they sensed a slackening of interest or attention on the part of their children or other beneficiaries would redo their wills accordingly. Roger was a toadie and a suck up who put up with the hand holding, the ego stroking and the many personal attentions these people demanded. The world of the estates lawyer is often lucrative; but only pays off when these clients die or as lawyers say "when the file matures." You cannot bill very much for the many changes or personal attentions these people require in their lifetimes, but you get a healthy percentage, fee for administering their estate upon their death. Managing an estate for a wealthy client is most often an easy accounting matter usually passed on to para-legals. You collect the assets, pay any outstanding bills, pay the inheritance taxes and distribute to heirs. In the meantime, you farm out some granddaughter's divorce, some maid's son's criminal case, get some driver's license restored, and threaten some neighbor whose dogs barks at night. Often, unprofitable billable hours done by some junior associate who gets little credit for his work, while the estates lawyer cashes in big time when the file matures.

So Roger brought in nice fees, for being a toadie socialite whose nose was brown, but whose wallet was green. And he had two large files to dump on me. I looked over at Angelina; she gave me an eye roll and an Italian shoulder shrug. I was sure she was doing an Italian forehead slap mentally as well.

When we had assembled, adjusted our coffee to the right mixture of artificial creamer and artificial sweetener, Digby started. "Mr. Humphries, has a problem with the Horton Estate and needs our help. So, Roger, please enlighten us."

Roger Humphries was a throwback to another era also. He wore a yellow flowered bowtie and a blue oxford button down shirt. He wore a seersucker blue and white striped suit, with his flood pants. His speech was sprinkled with coughs, pauses, tics and old maid inflections enough to make me want to shake him by the shoulders and smack him across the face a few times. He had the speech patterns and inflections of his elderly female clients, but he did bring in nice fees and he kept the rich old ladies happy. I kept telling myself.

"Well, as you certainly must know by now, Mr. Horton appears to have suffered a most unfortunate accident at the barbecue in his retreat in the Poconos and was burned quite severely. In fact, he died under most excruciating circumstances. I am his executor along with a trust officer of Franklin National Bank which is, by the way, also a client of ours. Because of the circumstances of his demise, the local gendarmerie have pronounced it an unfortunate contretemps – perhaps accident, perhaps a murder. However, the life insurance people want an autopsy and an investigation, before we administer the estate and distribute the largesse. The county in which poor Mr. Horton met his fate, has a less than professional coroner who deems the circumstances suspicious, but the township police chief has neither the ardor, the funds nor the staff to parse out the possible misfeasors, if any. So it falls to us, to dislodge this estate from its somnolent state. Our co-executor also has premonitions of foul play and has authorized us to put our best sleuth on the matter. There are ample funds in the estate and it is wholly appropriate and fiscally sound that we undertake this endeavor. Digby?"

"Yes, quite, Roger. Quite so. I have brought in Peter Stern, as you can see, and he may have some questions. Peter?"

"Ah. Yes. Quite." I was somehow infected with Roger's speech patterns. A mental slap across my own face.

Since Humphries knew the client best and had drawn the Will, I asked, "So, Roger, who is this guy and what does the Will say?"

"Well, Mr. Stern, I have chosen to keep the contents of the Will secret at the suggestion of the insurance carrier's counsel. He feels it may prejudice the possible murder investigation. If it was an accidental death the carrier must pay double. If one of the heirs committed the foul act, he or she could not by state law enjoy the benefit of their evilness. So you see a good bit depends on the investigation."

"But Roger, wouldn't that supply a motive if it was in fact murder?" "Quite so, but I feel I have to maintain confidentiality. Besides, I only have a copy of the Will, not the original. We cannot usually probate a copy. As you know, the Will must be probated, i.e. submitted to the Register of Wills who determines that it is in fact the decedent's Will. A copy will not normally be accepted since the decedent may simply tear up the original at any time to revoke it."

"Look, Roger, we are in the same firm, this Will may give us a lead in the murder investigation. Where is the original? Don't we have to submit it to the Register of Wills?"

"I don't have it."

"What?"

"No, we have made a cursory search for the original and can't find it."

"So, the estate would be what, if we can't find it?"

"An intestacy. A distribution by the order the laws of Pennsylvania prescribes."

"So, someone might have an interest in finding and destroying the original?"

"Quite so. A disinherited lineal. Someone left out of the Will but in the family tree."

"So who gets what in an intestacy?"

"First the wife, but if there are children they get 70%, the wife 30%, then the parents, then the siblings, etc."

"So who was left out of the Will?"

"Mr. Stern, as I told you, I have been asked to maintain confidentiality on the point until the original is found, or the murder investigation is concluded."

After some thought, I seemed to see where Roger was going. "Basically, if someone in line for an intestate distribution was left out of the Will, they would have an interest in destroying the original."

"I have to admit that would be the case."

"So, who are Harry's people?"

"He had discussed a number of options with me, so I am familiar with his family and acquaintances. He was not married, having divorced his wife some ten years ago. They had no children, but he was fond of his stepson from his wife's prior marriage. The ex-wife was close to him, and is a law professor at Savonarola Law School. He had a sister, a Hermione Horton Farnsworth, some years his senior. She lives in Florida and I believe works for a casino. He had a female companion, Ms. Alicia Allende, who is the administrative assistant to the head of the Democratic Party in Philadelphia. He also had a past interest in an importing business and was friendly with its owner, a Mr. Giaconda."

"Oh, that's a start. So my assignment, should I choose to accept it, would be to figure out if it was an accidental death or murder. Also, I have to find the Will. Now, if we get the estate, we can of course bill the estate for my time. But, if we don't get the estate, and the intestate heir, now I believe Ms. Farnsworth, and she chooses not to pay us for my time, we don't get paid."

"Very perspicacious of you, Mr. Stern. We need the Will, yes. But if Ms. Farnsworth did in Mr. Horton, she gets nothing under Pa. law."

"I see. So that is why you won't tell me who inherits under the Will. They might look at Ms. Farnsworth as an enemy."

"Yes. Quite so."

"But if Ms. Horton located the Will and destroyed it, she knows who her enemies are, and they don't."

"Uh, why… why yes."

"Not good, Roger, not good. Shouldn't they know if they are an enemy of Ms. Farnsworth?"

"Sorry, Mr. Stern, I will not disclose the contents of the Will until it is appropriate."

"Digby, can't you help here?"

"Peter, let's see where this goes. If it becomes an issue, I'll decide. Now Peter, we have been told to investigate on behalf of the insurance carrier. If it is murder, they don't pay under the double indemnity clause in the insurance policy which you are about to find out about. So they have retained us to investigate and possibly prove it was murder."

"So my time is covered."

"Your time is covered."

"Can I use Carmen as an investigator as well?"

"With my blessing. Now, all of you get to work. Sufficient unto the day is the evil thereof."

Angelina had been furiously jotting down notes, and leafing through the files as we spoke. She went over the list of names, addresses, telephone numbers email addresses of every name mentioned. I could feel the energy as she was being deprived of the opportunity to do her research online. It was still midmorning and I knew the sun would not set before a dossier on every name would be on my desk. She was starting to take it personally and the adrenalin would drive her to feats of glory.

While she was going over the files, I asked Humphries for more detail about the autopsy and the police investigation. Apparently he had not ordered or seen the autopsy as yet and had only cursory discussions with the police. In short, Horton had been almost completely consumed by a fire near his barbecue pit behind his house in the Poconos – Lake Naomi to be specific. No one other than he had registered coming in or going out. In fact. The gate house did not seem to know if Horton had come in, or slipped his pass key in the owner's box.

He had apparently entered on Tuesday, October 14, but his body was not discovered until Friday by a maintenance man driving the trash truck. No one had heard the fire or Mr. Horton during that time and the houses on either side of his were not occupied that week. At first the local police just labeled it a tragic accident, until the coroner came to pick up the body. The coroner was a local realtor working part-time, but he chafed at the local cops. To be sure, he called in the medical examiner from the State Attorney General's office who ordered a number of tissue samples and said his preliminary finding was that death was "suspicious."

Apparently, both his girlfriend and sister had called several times about the estate. Humphries had no new information and said he could not do anything until the cause of death was determined. They all seemed irritated at this news. The sister, Hermione Horton Farnsworth, had telephoned from a vacation in Cuba. He couldn't even tell them what was in the Will yet until the police released the body. "It isn't done."

"Do we know when he died?"

"Not yet."

"Had he had a dispute with anyone lately?" Roger had had a number of chats with Honey in his estate planning.

"He could be a bit difficult and had few friends, I must say, but no, nothing that serious."

"His stepchild rarely saw him and his ex-wife had moved onto her third husband with whom she had lived for over 10 years."

"Do we know where everyone was during this time, about Tuesday to Friday?"

"I haven't asked, but I know Ms. Farnsworth called from Cuba on Wednesday, and I suspect Thursday and Friday, as well."

"How about the business partner?"

"I spoke to him. He was at work the whole week in South Philadelphia. Their business was in an industrial garage around there. He started calling for Mr. Horton on Wednesday but only got his telephone message saying he would be away. When he heard Harry had died, he called me."

"Do we have that message?"

"No. Is it important?"

"Yes Roger, it is. Very important. Okay. Let us review all this and we'll follow up with you later."

"Thank you very much, Peter. It has been a great worry." "Now, don't tell the heirs where I am or how I can be reached. Just tell them I am authorized by you to investigate. I don't want a flood of phone calls. That's your job. You're the diplomat."

"Yes, of course, Peter. I understand."

I was getting some head jerks from Angelina – she wanted to leave and get started. She was already wearing out her clothes from the inside.

Digby nodded in approval and we all left. A new mess was now squarely in my lap.

Angelina was halfway back to my office before I turned around. Not much later, I could hear her on the keyboard tapping away. Soon papers started spewing out of the printer. I had a day of phone calls to make and letters to dictate.

While Angelina was tapping furiously at the keyboard outside, I started to make a few phone calls to set up interviews. Many suspects, no answers. Or was it just an unfortunate accident.

I had asked the ex-wife to come into the office. She was happy to comply. I discovered that Roger had actually been wise about something. He had not disclosed the contents of Mr. Horton's Will because he believed it might have a bearing on the investigation. Good for Roger. The sister, Hermione Horton Farnsworth, was harder to get. She seemed distracted and maybe inebriated on the phone. I had heard from Roger that she was on some vacation in Cuba, unmarried and had no children. She eventually agreed to come in after many questions about her deceased brother's estate and questions about the investigation of his death.

As I passed Chris Chattington's office, I stuck my head in. "Chris, have you got a moment?" Chris was our corporate/business guy.

"Sure, Peter. What's up?" I explained briefly what I had heard about Horton's estate and death. So I wondered if Chris knew anything about Harry's relationship with his business partner in the importing business.

As with many small businesses, there was a buy-sell agreement. This usually provides that if one partner dies, the survivor buys out the interest of the other from his estate and becomes the sole owner. Basically, the partner did all the work, while Harry was an investor, and business consult for him.

"What about his business partner?"

"The buy/sell agreement provided that the surviving partner would receive full ownership of the company because the corporation would buy the decedent's partner's share for the face value of the life insurance policy which the corporation had maintained. The estate then would receive the one million dollars, and the surviving partner would own the entire outstanding shares of stock."

"Was that a good deal or a bad deal?"

"A very good deal. The company earned about two hundred thousand dollars per year, so I would expect that Mr. Horton's share could be worth maybe $300,000 at best. His estate getting $1 million was a windfall for his heirs."

"Should we suspect the partner?"

"Yes and no. Mr. Horton was the brains behind the company. His partner was at best a good chef and had a vast store of culinary knowledge. Without Mr. Horton, the company's growth and sales may diminish. These men were in their mid-forties, had a good relationship and could look forward to many more profitable years. While Mr. Horton's demise may have provided the partner with control and full ownership of the business, it is difficult to say whether it would have been beneficial in the long term to him. It was very beneficial to the estate, since Mr. Horton's share was worth far less than the insurance proceeds."

Crime Scene

I brought Carmen along to look at the crime scene photos and the autopsy. Another pair of eyes. It was a nice drive up the northeast extension of the turnpike and a main road to the community where Harry's cabin was. My plan was to kill a few birds with one stone – look at the scene of the fiery death, go to the detective's office to look at the photos and review the autopsy and talk to the detective about his thoughts. If I didn't develop any doubts, maybe I could conclude that this was just a horrendous accident and leave it at that. If I had any lingering doubts and smelled homicide or major lawsuit suing some equipment manufacturer, then plunge further ahead. Carmen was very upbeat and happy to get away from the office for the day. I always valued her street smarts. She had been a teenage client my old mentor David Magen had rescued from a criminal charge not too many years ago. She had landed on her feet after getting stashed in a Catholic girls' school for witness protection and then becoming a paralegal par excellence at community college. Somehow that academic work had not harmed her instincts for sniffing out human foibles.

First, the burn scene. As we had the story, Harry had been using the grill on his back deck at his cabin. At some point, the grill erupted in a puff of fire which caused him to fall backwards. In the fall, he struck the back of his head on a heavy metal outdoor table and he fell unconscious to the ground while spilling the contents of a lighter fluid can on himself. The ensuing flame severely burned his body from his knees to his chest and consumed all the organs in between down to his spine. The initial pictures showed a man flat on his back with a huge black burn from his knees to his chest cavity. The death was attributed to shock, or heart failure from the burn. Thus, a tragic accident. Carmen and I would have to doubt all of this.

We parked in the driveway of the cabin on the scattered gravel, and walked into a very nice, well maintained cabin. It was extraordinarily neat and decorated in a very sophisticated manner. There were wall-to-wall carpets in an expensive woven Berber design. The furniture was arranged in a neat conversation style with mixed hues of beige, chocolate and brown around a chrome and brass glass coffee table. The walls were not paneled but covered with sheetrock from which hung paintings which looked to be all collectible types of frontier early American style, neatly framed. There was a large oak antique side board with a beveled mirror which served as a wet bar along one wall. The conversation arrangement of furniture faced a fireplace with a large mantelpiece of stamped brass and an immaculate set of fireplace tools in brass and chrome.

The master bedroom had an immense king size bed with a duvet and cover in a mauve with embroidered elements of angels, unicorns and stars. At the foot of the bed was a large TV screen and a library of videos – all unmarked except for a system of numbers and letters. Three sides of the room was painted in a deep purple and one side was a rosy beige.

The other bedroom was set up as a den with a desk, and an entire computer layout. The desk was an antique polished chestnut in a French style, probably named after some French king. On the floor was a fine old oriental rug laying on a dark walnut floor.

The kitchen was all modern chrome and glass with the finest stove and refrigerator on either side of a marble countertop – all of which looked out on the woods at the rear of the property.

The entire place was squeaky clean and in perfect order. A man's clothes recently cleaned and pressed hung in the closet or were in a large chest of drawers in a walk in closet. Clearly, the owner was extremely neat, had a distinct taste, and had created a sophisticated urban environment in the midst of the Poconos, in a gated community.

Here and there, there were smudges of luminol and graphite powder as some local detective had sprayed the area for fingerprints or blood residue. On close examination, it did not appear that any of these smudges had yielded a print or any blood samples.

In short, our visit to the cabin was like flipping through the pages of Architecture Digest, before we went out to the rear deck to examine the accident scene.

I could hear Carmen mumbling, "gay" I had similar thoughts but wanted to hear what Carmen had to say.

"No man who is hetero lives like this, and it"s his second home. And decorated to the nines. No. This guy was way too OCD and too fuhpitzed. This house was his second little hobby. I've got to see his condo. I mean most single guys have a few weeks of pizza boxes and cheesesteak wrappers, some NFL posters, and..."

"OK, I get it Carmen. I have to agree. We need to learn more about him to see who might want to do him in."

We went out to the deck. As advertised, the grill was on the left side and was open. There were some charcoal briquettes unlit but with a few singe marks. The tape marking the body was perpendicular to the grill with the hands up. Sure enough, a heavy metal table was just behind the body marks. It might be possible to conclude the back of the head struck the table, and the entire body fell on its back to the floor of the deck. Burn marks were on either side of the chalk marks but not inside. The burn area including the body was about three feet by three feet in a rough circle. A chalk mark on the bodys right side had an outline of a probable lighter fluid can. It might be that the concussion from the puff back of the lighter fluid ignition shocked the decedent backwards so that he hit the metal table and spilled the lighter fluid contents on himself. He might have been unconscious after striking the table or froze from the shock of the lighter fluid flames covering his torso. Plausible. Plausible. But something about this man didnt ring true. He was a perfect, careful, meticulous guy. I didnt like the lighter fluid puff back theory. He probably would never have used lighter fluid. Maybe briquettes already permeated with it. Why not a gas grill? And he was probably an exacting chef. He never would have wanted his food to taste like charcoal fluid. No. Something wasn't ringing true.

We'd have to look at the crime scene photos and the autopsy report.

Carmen at Lunch

e had completed most of the reason for our trip and our appointment with the coroner was not 'til this afternoon. On the way, we passed a decent looking restaurant and Carmen was already hungry. From David Magen I had learned of Carmen's prodigious appetite. She stood about 5' 1" and weighted about 105, but she, I was told, could pack it away.

We went into the restaurant which had a full four page menu. I ordered a tuna sandwich with unsweetened ice tea, and Carmen was deep in thought as the waitress stood. Carmen turned to me.

"Is this meal on the firm?"

When assured that we were on an expense account, Carmen in rapid fire, ordered a chicken parm sandwich on an Italian roll, French fries and a strawberry milk shake.

"Carmen, aren't you going to eat for the next three days?"

"Yeah, I amazed Mr. Magen too. I can pack it away."

When the food arrived, she sprinkled hot sauce liberally on the sandwich and the fries. When she saw me staring, she looked up challengingly.

"Yo! I'm Latino, I need my spice." I held up my hands in surrender. As we ate we went over what we knew. The initial idea was that Mr. Horton died in a tragic accident. If that were true, we were on a wild goose chase, or a snipe hunt. But we agreed, something was strange here. A very circumspect, very careful guy dressed in a very nice casual outfit was up in the Poconos grilling a steak for himself. Somehow, he carelessly oversaturated the charcoal briquettes, and caused a huge flame which caused him to stumble back, bump his head to the point of unconsciousness so that he poured the rest of the lighter fluid on his midsection while he was unconscious and charred his entire body down to the spine. It could have happened, but we had questions. Why was he so well dressed alone up in the forest? Well, he was pretty fastidious and his cabin showed careful attention to detail and style. But if he was so careful, how could he allow the barbecue fluid to ignite so explosively?

But facts were creeping in. There were no splatter marks from the burning drops of lighter fluid on his face or arms, or for that matter on the deck. The fire was concentrated on his stomach and spread only slightly to his thighs and chest.

All good questions. Now who might have done it? His sister would be his heir if he had left no Will. A look at the Will might answer some questions. We weren't sure which side of the plate he batted from yet. Could the sister have killed him and destroyed the Will? Or was he involved in drugs? Was this a drug deal gone bad? Or was it something else? We needed to verify a few issues. Where was the video of him entering the gated community and who might be in his car as he entered? Was he a junkie? A blood test might tell. Was he gay? Were we looking for an angry male or female lover? I mean he was in his forties and divorced. Could it be an angry client? Had he screwed up somehow? Many, many questions, few answers. Carmen was now finishing her sandwich and fries and milkshake and had wandered over to the pies shown in a glass cabinet.

"I'll have the Boston Crème and a root beer float," I heard her order. My veins were already shriveling at the thought. As soon as her dessert order arrived, it was gone – inhaled as I sat shaking my head.

"Come on, Pete. Let's move. We've got a body to look at," she chirped cheerfully. I might have needed a serious nap after that meal, but she was on the move. I paid and we left.

Trip to Local Police

We left the diner and went to the local police station. En route, we mused over what we had seen at the cabin.

"I have to agree the place was neat, compulsively neat, and decorated with a very distinctive style. My guess it was his own style. He had planned and decorated the whole place himself as a very high style get away," I thought out loud.

"Like I said, 'gay.' This was a secret lover's den. A place to impress someone, but a little over the top. Real men don't decorate like that."

"True. But not necessarily gay. I mean it is a cliché that gay guys have great taste and love to decorate. But sometimes, guys are just plain compulsive and like everything just so. I mean he was a lawyer – somewhat successful from what I hear. Maybe he liked society women or shall I say fancy dames who are impressed with taste – especially if it looks expensive. I mean I'm talking martini class, jet set, that kind of thing."

"OK, I can buy that. Not my kind of guy. We need to dig a little deeper. Could we be dealing with a dumped lover? Hell hath no fury. But gay ex-lovers can be pretty vindictive, too. Could go either way."

"Or both."

"Or both."

The two story standard brick building for the local constabulary appeared along the main road just off to the left. I pulled into the parking lot and we both went to the front desk.

"Detective Hinson, please."

"Is he expecting you?"

"Yes. Peter Stern and my paralegal Ms. Jacinto. We called earlier." "Ah, the crispy critter case." Some police have this annoying habit, perhaps to steel themselves from devastating emotion when confronted with awful crimes. They make light of the event. Sometimes, this shallowness comes out uncensored. Do they mean to be so disrespectful or is it an act to show their macho distancing from true emotion. It is not a nice quality.

"Yes. Mr. Horton's unfortunate demise." The severe tone seemed to stiffen up the desk man and he shouted over his right shoulder for Hinson. From one of the side offices, Detective Hinson leaned out.

"Come in, Mr. Stern." Hinson was a lanky gawky man with a balding scalp and an absurd collection of a wardrobe – a plaid shirt, with a patterned silk tie, and a loose pair of baggy pants, and black sneakers. He motioned us into his office where the files already sat. "You can look to your heart's content, but nothing leaves the room. We can copy anything you need. Oh and very important, anything you find goes through me first – no newspapers, no lawyers, no other investigators. Got it."

"Seems fair enough." Hinson was protecting his turf and wanted to look good on anything that might help him with this matter. He was about to go for the okey-doke and write this off as an accident. He was afraid we might find something to prove otherwise and hold him up to ridicule. I could care less about who got credit. Everyone would know anyway since I logged everything on my computer with a time signature. But why upset the schnook. He wanted credit, we would let him have it.

Carmen and I pulled out different sections of the file and began to read it and make notes. It dawned on me that there was no surveillance footage from the entrance gate at the Pocono gated community. I stuck my head out the door for Hinson who was chatting amiably with the desk sergeant.

"Any tape for the camera at the entrance before the date of death."

We don't know the date of death, so we didn't get the footage."

"But you could review several days before he was found."

"Yup. We could. But why waste the time?"

"That's okay. We'll look at the footage. I mean it's October. There can't be too many cars and we could fast forward."

"OK, I'll set it up with them in an hour." The man's been dead at least 24 hours and they hadn't bothered to get the tape at the entrance gate. We were definitely in the sticks here, not too many brain cells working.

I went back to the file when I heard Carmen snort. She was looking at the autopsy pictures. They were pretty gruesome. Another snort.

"Pete, look at this."

I could see what remained of a man lying on his back with his arms back and the lighter fluid can lying off to his right side in the crime scene photo. Only a small portion of his right hand was burned. The autopsy showed the man in the same position lying on a steel table. There were photos of his heavily charred mid-section. There were close-ups of his head, shoulders, the burned out area of his torso, his arms, etc. It struck me that there were few spatter burn marks on his upper body. The fluid had apparently not caught fire until it was on his lower torso, but not his chest. Could that be what Carmen had noticed?

"No, Pete! He has a needle track. Like with drugs. He might be a user." Sure enough there were two small but distinct miniscule puncture marks on the inside of his elbow. Time to ask Hinson again.

"Yo, Mr. Hinson. Were any tox screens done of his blood?"

"No, not yet. Is that important?"

"Absolutely. He might have drugs in his system, or some fatal disease. All that blood work is important."

"I'm not the coroner, maybe he has that information. Maybe it just didn't make the file yet."

"Would it be possible to see the body and talk to whoever did the autopsy?"

"Sure, knock yourself out. I'll call him. When can you see him?"
"Today would be great."

"OK, today it is."

We went over the rest of the file. Nothing jumped out. Prints were searched. The only prints were the decedent's. Strikingly enough, there were none on the car, the car's steering wheel, there were none in the kitchen, none on the grill, and none even on the can of lighter fluid. The absence of something could mean something. The prints could have been wiped clean. Or our guy was just a neatnik or he wore gloves. But gloves in October. The temperatures were in the 60s and 50s now.

We made copies of everything and went to the car. The coroner held the body some 30 miles away but he would be in. He was not a doctor, he was simply part of the local political machine who had been elected for the past three terms.

Autopsy and Body View

After lunch, Carmen and I drove to the county coroner's office to review the autopsy and view the body at the morgue. We were greeted by Mr. Bembury, the coroner. He was not a doctor and in fact had no medical training. He was a local realtor who was popular with the local party officials. He had a pleasant round pink face with a balding forehead, was short and plump and anxious to please. He wore a yellow button down shirt, a red bowtie and khakis.

"How may I help you, Mr. Stern?"

"We would like to review the autopsy report and take a look at the body." We had already left word we wished to do this when we set up the appointment. Maybe he was hoping we had changed our minds because he did not want big city types looking into his business. In any case, he directed us to follow one of the ladies in the office to a room in the rear of the building and down some steps to the basement. Although we did not ask, he followed us closely and sat at the table where we reviewed the autopsy file.

Carmen spoke up first. "Mr. Bembery, were any blood tests run on the decedent?

"Not that I know of. Why?"

"A number of reasons. He may have had some drugs in his system. He may have had some disease or health indicators.

"Why is that relevant?"

"Frankly, there seems to be some needle pricks in his right arm. He may have been on narcotics. That might have something to do with cause of death."

"Ah, I see. But he was burned in a bad fire."

"Someone may have set the fire."

"Ah, I see. Well, we may have some blood taken from him, maybe we can send it out for tests. But these are expensive. And…"

It was time for me to say that we would pay for the tests, but I asked about the injury to the rear of the skull, and the condition of the man's shoes.

"It looked like he bumped his head on the metal table that knocked him out and caused him to dump lighter fluid on himself. Why would his shoes be relevant?"

"He may have been hit on the back of the head by someone else. He may have been dragged to the scene."

"Ah, I see. Well, you can certainly look at both."

So we were taken over to the morgue area and the body was rolled out. A bundle of his clothes – such as they were – were brought out as well. Interestingly, the very nice soft leather Italian loafers were in pristine condition. There was no mud or even dust on them. We also took a closer look at the marks on the inside of his right elbow. While quite small, they were definitely some type of puncture wound with no blood or scab at the site. Of course, it was a few days after the incident. Carmen took a few pictures of the punctures.

"Well, what do you think?" Mr. Bembery was anxious.

"Nothing yet. But it is interesting that the man was walking in the Poconos and yet had no dirt on his shoes. And there certainly are some needle marks. But nothing conclusive on either."

"What are you suggesting?"

"He may have been carried to the scene. He may have been administered something by needle. Like I say, may have."

"Well, I certainly don't want to write up a report until you have ruled out any foul play."

"Thank you for indulging us, Mr. Bembery."

"Oh, glad to help." Since Mr. Bembery was not a medical professional or even had any forensic training, he relied on one of two local doctors to do the examinations and do the reports. Both doctors were paid on a case by case basis and worked part time in their spare hours. Going into exhaustive examinations was not in their best interest unless they thought they might be embarrassed by contrary findings later on. Obviously, they thought this was a simple matter, and put in the minimal time. Carmen and I were now a threat to their reputations. Their reports were not in yet, so they would want to be sure we would not stir up some problems.

After Carmen and I jotted down our notes and took a few pictures of the inside of the right forearm and the back of the head, we thanked Mr. Bembery and left. The day was over. Time to return to Philly and mull over what we found.

Next on the schedule was to ask his friends and co-workers what he was like. Was he gay? Why would somebody want him dead? Who would inherit? Was he into drugs? Did he have any angry ex-lovers? A number of things to rule out.

Funeral

Harry Horton's body was released by the county and sent to Philadelphia for his funeral. I thought it a good idea to attend, something might turn up. I got there early before the 10:00 a.m. published time. I walked up to an elderly woman and introduced myself. She had her hair up in a gray bun, had an ample bosom and wore a purple blazer over a pink shirtwaist. She looked friendly.

"Good day, ma'am, I'm Peter Stern from the law firm for Mr. Horton's estate."

"Oh! I'm Aunt Jane, Jane Felder. I've known Harry all his life. I was his mother's sister."

"At this point, we're investigating his death."

"Oh! I've heard about that. He was quite young. Such a pity! He was a very nice young boy. Always obedient, always neat and clean, and so smart. We were very proud of him. Such a shame!"

"I wonder if you could point out the people who are coming to the funeral."

"Of course. Of course. He didn't have many relatives. My husband died and we didn't have any children. My sister, his mother, was in a nursing home. She fell ill and died a few years ago, too. So she won't be here. I guess I am taking her place. Her husband also died some years back."

"I hear he had a sister."

"Oh yes. Hermione Horton – we called her Honey. I don't think they were very close. Honey was a good bit older. She's had a tough life. She was into rehab a few times, and had a few husbands. I'd say, let me see, she's about 10 years older than Harry. She was a wild one in her day."

"Is she here yet?"

"Oh, no! I heard she wasn't coming. She's on some kind of vacation for some kind of medical problem I heard. Probably drying out. She's done that before."

A few people trickled in. Aunt Jane didn't know them. They were dressed in business suits, both the men and the women and were carrying brief cases. I would guess they were lawyers. Not many others showed up. The minister walked up to the podium and we all sat.

I have always felt vaguely insulted by a religious man giving a eulogy for someone they don't know. Of course, they had met a few close acquaintances or relatives for a half hour or so and would get maybe a half dozen facts and then spin them into praise of the deceased. Then, they shift to some comforting but false theological premise that they are now in heaven. I listened in half consciousness to the expected and continued to survey the attendants. Aunt Jane had been helpful with the family, but the best I could make out were the lawyers in suits, of course Alicia Allende – in a very smart silver suit with a short skirt, pearls, and a black shawl. The ex-wife was there, and what I thought may have been his partner in the Italian importing business. Check and check. Maybe I could get a decent interview here today. The brief ceremony was over. Such is the mark of man. A brief remembrance by a somewhat hypocritical minister who never knew the man, and an obligatory appearance by family and acquaintances. Harry had obviously been a private, solitary man – by choice, by psychological make up and had sunk beneath the surface with just a few ripples. But his death was suspicious. Was he rich? I'm guessing not. Who were his heirs in the Will? Was he envied? Or hated? It wasn't getting a strong vibe on motive yet.

Since the ex-wife was from out of town, I decided to sidle up to her first. She had a teenager with her. I would have to be delicate with this.

"I say, could you be the former wife of Mr. Horton?" She had an exquisite little doll face, pale, blue eyed with straight blond hair, cut with bangs and a neat pageboy, a turned up nose and a perfect little figure. Yes. Harry's choice.

"Why yes. I could."

"I'm a lawyer with the firm that will be involved with estate. My name is Peter Stern. Could I ask you a few questions?"

"Of course. Our plane doesn't leave 'til tomorrow and I'm staying with old friends."

"I am looking into his death, I have to tell you. So some of these questions may be a bit off-putting. I hope you don't mind."

"Well, Harry was basically a good man, but our marriage just didn't work. He was a perfectionist, and made many demands which made life for me very difficult."

"Yes, I understand he was a bit compulsive."

"Yes, you could say that. In spades. I was not the woman for that partnership. He needed a perfect housekeeper dressed up with perfect makeup every day. But he was always kind, gentlemanly. His support was generous. I've remarried and live in Ohio. While we were married he was a good father to my son from my first marriage."

"If you don't mind, can I ask where you were last week?"

Oh, I understand. Yes. I teach law in Savonarola Law School in Pittsburgh, I was busy from 7:30 until 3:00 every weekday and then I made dinner for the four of us – I have one child with my third husband – a very nice man himself. My name is Fisher now, Sally Fisher."

"Do you know if you get anything in the Will?"

"No. I haven't been told yet."

"Well, if you will give me your contact information I will let you know as soon as possible."

"Is that all I can do to help?"

"Not unless you had seen Harry in the past year."

"No. We haven't spoken in some time. We had a few squabbles over money in the divorce, but everything was civil. Frankly, we never had a fight. Harry seemed to recognize he was a bit difficult and often expressed his guilt that our marriage hadn't worked."

"Well, I'm happy to hear you landed on your feet."

"Yes, I feel lucky to have come out alright."

By this time, Roger – her son, about eight years old, had grown tired of running through the cemetery stones and had come back to us.

"Thank you, for your time. And please contact me at the office to find out about the Will."

"Sure, Mr. Stern."

Most of the guests had left already, so I started for the exit.

I was stopped by another lady in a dark suit. Maybe fortyish. She looked tired, worn out. Once attractive, now non-descript.

"Mr. Stern."

"Yes. Can I help you?"

"I am Mr. Horton's step-sister. The younger one. His step mother remarried and had me by her second husband. I'm not really related, but lived in the same house as Harry. He was like an older brother."

"Ah! I saw that in our records."

"I am Jeanine. I ran away from my parents when I was 17 with a guy. I haven't seen the family much since, but I had to see Harry off."

"Sorry for your loss."

"Not really a loss. Harry was a nice older brother, but like my parents very strict and demanding. I couldn't take it so I left."

"Had you seen Harry much lately?"

"Not much. He sent me some money a few years ago to get out of a financial scrape, but he gave me such a lecture. I don't know. I didn't want to face him again."

"Where do you live now?"

"Florida, near Orlando, I manage the golf shop there."

"Have you been up to Philadelphia lately?"

No. There's nothing here for me. Oh and by the way, am I in the Will?"

"We don't know yet. We haven't found the original yet."

"If I am in it, could you call me?"

"Sure. Here's my card. Check into the office, tell them who you are and we'll put you in the file. So it's Susan…?"

"No, still Susan O'Day. We never married. Just lived together all these years. Put Susan O'Day from Kissimmee, Florida in the file – youngest sister. Just let me know if I'm in the Will."

"Sure thing, Susan. Just leave your information with the office." She turned and left. Probably an attractive woman in her day. But very time worn now. A life of bad choices.

I would have to check on the Will. Of course, we had copy in the office, but only a copy. Not a valid document. We needed the original. That meant a Will search through Harry's office and apartment. A copy is not usually valid for Probate because the testator – the one making the Will may always destroy it or revoke it. Only the original is absolute proof. Of course, if someone steals the original, then we have a Will contest. Which is valid? No Will at all, the missing Will or something else? And there was some decent money at stake here, or at least so I was told. So back to the office to take a look at our copy.

At the Bar

The autopsy and trip to Harry Horton's cabin in the Poconos had given us more answers that we had questions for. It seemed that the few clues we had raised doubt as to the accidental nature of his death. We were tipped by a few of his friends from the legal profession that he hung out on Wednesdays at the Borgia Bistro. (Could it have been named after Lucretia?) This was currently a popular hangout for the bottom feeders of the legal profession. Those that got high marks in law school went into the big firms – i.c. and represented the big corporations and wealthy individuals. Their interests included large decedent's estate, corporate mergers, real estate development and major litigation. Those lesser lights did minor accident cases, criminal work, minor domestic disputes. They worked with the minor judiciary. What they lacked in book knowledge they often made up for in street smarts. When I say lesser lights, I do not mean they were not as smart. Usually those with higher marks had gone to better schools all the way through and came from wealthy suburban backgrounds. Often these so-called lesser lights were the first college graduates in the family and had come from families that had little background in verbal skills and from underfunded school districts. So, to adapt, while fighting their way through college and law school, they developed a compensatory skill in a knowledge of the streets. Their clients also came from the streets and to them the lawyers were their guides through the bewildering complexities of the modern world. Such was our decedent and so were his compatriots from the Borgia Bistro. They were following what was an Italian tradition of taking Wednesday night with the guys, and not their families. The mixture of backgrounds however was by no means solely Italian, but Greek, Irish, Jewish, Polish – what have you. But in other words, ethnic, street smart and far less stuffy than their big firm counterparts.

So Carmen and I decided to drop by the Bistro to see if we could pick up any gossip on our man. The lawyers were starting to filter in about 6:30 when we arrived. I delighted in explaining to Carmen the many peccadilloes of those beasts at the water hole. Many minor politicians, quite a few members of the minor judiciary and a variety of many others. Some represented small drug dealing organizations, some were ambulance chasing accident lawyers, many did criminal defense work, some had government patronage jobs. Mixing with the minor judiciary had benefits for both. Need I say more?

By the way, that is not to say that they did not make a decent living. Big firm lawyers spent ferocious amounts of their income on overhead – fancy and spacious office space at the best addresses, receptionists with pseudo British accents and smart outfits, oriental rugs, secretaries, paralegals and PR. They also were expected to make large charitable donations and belong to fancy clubs to hobnob with potential wealthy clients. Small time lawyers shared office space, secretaries, and were not engaged in the production of vast amounts of paperwork. While two-thirds of the big firm income went to overhead, only about a quarter went to overhead for the sole practitioner. As a result, they often took home as much or more than their big firm counterparts and frequently in cash.

The guy who had the most vicious gossip would be Albert Oppenheim. A rough cut Jewish criminal defense lawyer known for his withering wit which he used very effectively cross-examining opposing witnesses. He was part of a tradition of criminal defense lawyers who relied on their ability to make juries and usually judges laugh at the absurdity of situations. In person, he could be cruel and vicious with his put-down humor and was feared and hated by most of the lawyers who had felt or observed the sting of his jibes; but he was popular because he was, after all, funny – a comment on humanity that art overcomes morality.

Before talking to Albert, I had to explain to Carmen that she should be careful not to come too close less she be singed. I gave her the rumor about Albert himself. The story goes that Jews simply cannot hold their liquor, and Albert tried to keep up especially on these Wednesday nights. It was a source of amusement to the Irish, Italians and Poles. On one occasion, he successfully made a pass at an attractive woman and managed to bed her at a local hot pillow in South Philly. Unfortunately, she turned out to be the girlfriend – poo-kyak – i.e. occasional girlfriend of an only distantly connected member of the local mob. On finding his temporary squeeze in Albert's arms, he came into the room wielding a baseball bat and severely crushed Albert's right femur. The Mafiosi wannabe left with his girlfriend in tow, his love sufficiently proven, but Albert remained for a few hours in exquisite pain until the desk man stopped by. Albert was transported naked on a stretcher to the local ER and was on crutches for many months thereafter. His wife immediately took hold of Albert's habits and he became a member of AA and a teetotaler ever after. He was standing by the bar nursing grimly a glass of seltzer.

So I sidled up to Albert and casually mentioned Harry Horton and his untimely demise. Albert brightened up with a new subject to keep his unseemly comments on. We got a full description of our guy as a dandy and an anal compulsive personality, replete with embarrassing anecdotes. This we had already surmised from his Pocono hideaway.

"So, Albert, was he gay?" This was a dangerous question. In the macho ethnic culture to which many of the males in this Bistro subscribed, being gay was an anathema. Although many in the population may have harbored full or partial gay tendencies, it was still necessary to hide them absolutely. Jokes and jibes about gay men and women were the daily, nay hourly, conversation traffic in these quarters. But Albert would know, he sniffed out human weakness and preyed on it.

"Doubt it. But maybe. Dunno." Either he was or successfully hid it. Either his extreme dandy-hood, his overbroad predilection for neatness and order, was just a personal fixation or he hid his gaydom very well. If Albert hadn't teased it out of him, no one could.

"Does he have a girlfriend?"

"As a matter of fact, yes. Now that you mention it, she is a tall blond goddess type with an exotic name. But I mean drop dead gorgeous. Made up. Like a model. But nothing permanent. I think they were both into themselves too much. She was not the hausfrau type and he was most definitely not soiling his tailored shirts birthing no babies."

"Interesting. Thanks Albert."

"Why you interested anyway?"

"My office is handling his estate."

"Ah." The maleficent wheels were beginning to turn. "Ah. So, maybe he didn't die of natural causes."

"We're just checking it out. Why? Would someone have it in for him?"

"Can't say. But he was partners in a business with a buddy. Maybe, he knew something."

"Got his name?"

"Yeah. An Italian guy. Garibaldi. Garofalo."

He was naming every Italian name beginning with G.

"Ah. Giaconda. Joe Giacondo. Imported stuff from Italy. That's it. He used to hang out here."

"Whoa, good pull, Albert. Thanks."

"Nothing, Pete. By the way, who's the squeeze?"

He was eyeing Carmen, who was staring at something else in the room. I mean she was young and hot and Albert could not fail to pick up on this. "Smooth move."

"Albert, she's my paralegal."

"Yeah. I'll bet. She work under you?"

"Now, now Albert."

"I'll tell you what she got a para."

"Be nice Albert."

"She legal?"

"Yes she's legal – both in immigration status and of consensual age. But she's my assistant."

"Yes. Smooth move." As we pulled away from Albert, I could hear the wheels clicking as he made up delicious stories about me and Carmen. I should sic Carmen on him. But no, she might destroy him.

At this point, we had gotten two leads to chase down, so Carmen and I decided we should split up and ask as many people while they were still sober. My next choice was George Hinklebach. He was on his way to inebriation with the third of three Cosmos."

"George," I said. "Cosmos? Isn't that a girl's drink?"

"I feel pretty," he said with an exaggerated flip of the wrist.

"So George, let me ask you some questions about Harry Horton." "Oh yeah, he got burned up in the Pokes. Sad. Very sad. What do you want?"

"Our firm represents the estate."

"So you're investigating his death?"

"Yes."

"Ah, so somehow there's skullduggery afoot."

"Easy, Sherlock, this is just a preliminary investigation."

"Oh, I got it. Wink, wink."

"Now, George."

"OK. What do you want?"

"Just some background. Did anyone hate him?"

"No, he was a decent guy. Stuck to himself mostly. Very well dressed. Usually a showpiece."

"Did he have a girlfriend?"

"Not really, he took out this super model type – also a showpiece. What was her name...? Wait it's coming. Got it. Alicia Allende. A Spanish name but she was a Polish princess – tall, blond, great cheekbones and a great cleavage."

"Were they an item?"

"Somehow, I feel they were arm candy for each other."

"Anything else about him?"

"He had a business interest with an Italian guy. They brought in cheeses, and pastries, that sort of thing from Italy. He was always taking buying trips over there. I think the business was an excuse for a write off. But he brought some to the Christmas party this year. Very good." The conversation tailed off with George as he began to get more glassy eyed and repeat himself. In fact the next few people I talked to were becoming less coherent, so I signaled to Carmen and waved her over to the door.

"So Carmen, anything new?"

"Nothing startling, what we already know. The girlfriend. The importing business. I got a little talk about the family. Not much else."

"OK, let's call it a night."

"Good idea. I gotta say these guys do not know the meaning of inappropriate touching. My butt has been squeezed so much and my tits are sore. I'll take a week for the black and blue marks to fade. Don't these lawyers know the rules?"

"Sorry Carmen. You are a definite babe and these guys are from a different generation."

"Well, if I wasn't working here, there'd be a few in a full crouch on their knees, believe me."

"You deserve hazardous duty pay."

"Yeah, well. This better be worth it."

"I got a good feeling about this."

"Yeah, well, I got felt plenty. See you tomorrow." She was taking the El out to her place in the Northeast. I was walking to my condo.

Alicia Allende

That afternoon, I picked up Carmen so we could interview Alicia. Because Horton's sexual makeup was a bit strange, but as yet undefined, I hoped Ms. Allende would shed some light on his lifestyle. I also knew that I needed a feminine point of view. Carmen was all about street smarts and could see beyond what women appeared to be to men. I had called Ms. Allende and managed to meet her after her work as secretary to the head of the Democratic Party in Philadelphia. She wielded great power and knew everyone of political substance. So at 5:30 p.m., Carmen and I rang the buzzer for her apartment in a new high rise condominium in the Old City section of Philadelphia. The building was sleek, all glass and steel rising up five stories with a view of the Delaware River. Angelina had been busy on the computer and tracked Ms. Allende from Google and beyond. On my desk before I left to pick up Carmen were a stack of printouts. There on top of the pile was not Alicia Allende, but Mary Ann Malinowski in her senior picture from Scranton's St. Agnes Catholic Girl's High School yearbook. I imagine if everyone could hide forever their senior yearbook picture they would. Mary Ann was a pleasant looking girl in a white round collar shirt and long, blondish hair. Somewhere in that face were nice cheek bones buried in some teenage baby fat. But the smile was stiff and a bit shy. She had taken an academic course curriculum but didn't seem to have joined many clubs, no sports, just a minor part in the school musical. But her prediction did say she would be in some part of the political world. Carmen glanced through the stack in the car and on the way up the elevator. She sniffed "a small town mouse" and closed the file.

At the apartment 5C, we buzzed and as the door opened, we gaped. Before us was a striking woman. She was wearing five inch platform heels and stood over six feet – well above Carmen and me. She had on a shimmering silk dazzling silver wraparound dress with a slit at the right thigh that displayed a shapely leg which invited, nay, demanded further inspection but at the same time forbade it. As my eyes traveled upward, I saw the points of two firm high breasts, unbound, outlined in the silk. My eyes reluctantly scanned further upward. There, a carefully made up face with brown lipstick, heavy eyeshadow and mascara, and severely plucked eyebrows. Her hair was short and severe and styled into streaks of ash blond, silver and black and closely cropped. No more Mary Ann from Scranton. She was a city girl now.

"Ah Mr. Stern, please come in." A mixture of some English accent and some vague European accent of unknown origin. As she turned to lead us into the living room, Carmen turned to me and shrugged her shoulders with a puzzled head shake. We were in for a real performance. The living room as stark. There were several Bauhaus chairs and a chrome and glass coffee table over a black and white area rug of geometric design.

"Ms. Allende, I'm so pleased you would indulge us in a few questions about Mr. Horton."

"Oh, no bother. He was a good friend and I'm sorry to lose him. We were close, confidantes."

"In that case, may I ask a bit of a personal question?"

"I knew you would ask this. No. We were not intimate. We dated occasionally, and very much appreciated each other's company, but no, we were not lovers. He was not very much into sex, and, if I may admit it, neither am I." I tried to hide my disappointment as I struggled to force my eyes up from the delightful breasts in the silk to her face. Somehow, I didn't quite believe her, she was hiding something and too willing to offer up this explanation.

"Did he have any other love interests?"

"I would have to say no. And before you ask, I would also have to say he was not gay. He liked to look at women, especially well-dressed, carefully coiffed, and with a well thought out makeup and color selection." A little too quick to offer up this as well. She knew we would ask.

"OK?"

"He was neat and clean, and did not like to be mussed.

"He shaved twice a day, frequently moisturized, and was well manicured. As you can see, he took good care of himself. And if I may say," turning to Carmen, "you could use some fashion counseling as well. No offense intended. I am a professional."

Carmen was wearing a very short skirt, her heavy black hair hung about her shoulders, and her clothes were an odd mixture of purple and lime green. "Really, Ms. Allende, I could use some help."

"Well, I have made an effort to learn these things, but in memory of Harry, I could give you a few tips. A short layered pageboy and a little mascara. Your natural colors are pink and tan. I could help you shop." Before this talk descended into a girl to girl talk, I had to get some answers. But she seemed to want to befriend us. Why I don't know.

"Excuse me, Ms. Allende."

"Call me Alicia." She lingered on the c, and rolled into the i and slowly. I was in mind of an elegant cat.

"Thank you, Alicia. Would Mr. Horton have left you anything in his Will?

"Oh. Could be. We were friends. He was a wonderful looking man and always punctilious in his fashion sense. I think he liked showing me off in public. But no. We were friends. Safe friends."

"He never ventured…"

"No, Mr. Stern, he never ventured. I don't think he liked to get dirty and he abhorred kissing. He was a bit of a neat freak. I must admit so am I. He was good company and safe."

"Do you know anyone who would wish him harm?"

"I've thought about that. I would guess no. He was very polite, did his legal work carefully. I doubt he had any disgruntled clients."

"How about his family?"

"He had a sister whom he rarely saw or talked to. He didn't seem to be mad at her, only distant. He had an ex-wife and a stepchild, but he rarely mentioned them. He seems to have assumed the blame for the divorce and usually spoke civilly about her. He was not paying child support, and the child was apparently not in his life. His ex had remarried and did not live near here."

"Have you ever been to his place in the Poconos?"

"No. I couldn't see myself tromping through the mud, and dealing with mosquitos. I am a city girl now."

"Did he know how to cook?"

"Absolutely. He loved it."

"Could he operate a grill?"

"Oh yes. He loved the taste of grilled fish and steak. I am sure he taught himself how to master the grill. I cannot. So he often cooked for me and every dish was a masterpiece."

"Did he drink?"

"Yes. Mostly good wine. He taught me how to order wine. But I don't think he drank much hard liquor… No, wait, he did like martinis, yes… martinis. But I never saw him drunk or out of control."

"How about drugs? Cocaine?"

"Never, he didn't like to lose control."

"Where were you this week?"

"I'm at the democratic headquarters about 12 hours a day."

"Do you own a car?"

"No. I use a zip car when I need one."

"Do you know how he died?" For the first time, I saw a smidgeon of a break in her composure.

"I heard he was burned in a dreadful accident by the lighter fluid at his grill in the Poconos."

"Do you know why he would be there midweek?"

No. I can't say. We usually only saw each other on the weekends. I have a fulltime job. So, no. I can't say."

"Do you know why he had a charcoal grill instead of a propane one?" "Oh, I wouldn't know anything about that."

"Did he ever have guests up there?"

"No. I don't know. I never went there and he didn't talk about it much with me. I'm not an outdoor person."

"Do you know what he did up there?"

"I knew he liked to walk. He did have binoculars to look at birds. That's the best I can say."

"Do you know if he had any friends or acquaintances up there?" "No. I wouldn't know that."

"Well, thank you so much for your time, Ms. Allende… Alicia." "Anything I can do to help. He was a nice man, Mr. Stern."

As she stood up to her full height, she was indeed a statuesque beauty self-made from Mary Ann Malinowski. I took fleeting looks at the marvelous leg peeking through the slit in her dress, and at a few bobs of her breasts nestling unbound in the shimmering silk. I hoped Carmen had a few more observations than mine.

As we walked out the condo and down the hall, Carmen grinned at me. "Put your tongue back in your mouth, you hound!" Carmen was quick and knew men.

"Sorry, did I miss anything?"

"No. You covered it, in spite of your impairment. What is it with you guys? She was untouchable. Way too cool and way into herself."

"Are you going to take her up on her fashion tips?"

"Well, I guess so."

"Aha. You women are all into that stuff."

"Well I am a girl and I would like to be a bit more sophisticated. She escaped her Polish roots, I wouldn't mind being a little less immigrant Latina."

"Well, what did you think of her?"

"A total narcissist. They were both arm candy for each other. They would think sex was just too dirty, it might mess up their hairdos."

"I can see that."

"Is she a suspect?"

"I doubt it. She has her own money and she was just an object to him and he to her."

Double Indemnity

Ms. James, Digby's assistant, rang me. "Digby's finished his conference. He'll see you now."

Digby was his usual sage like self peering over his bifocals at me. "Well, Peter, what have we on the Horton matter?"

"Well, Digby. Not much. I mean the crime scene was a bit suspicious but we got little from the locals and I have to rule out a few options." I then went into detail on what we'd found. Digby nodding asking questions, always on point.

"Peter, it sounds like our Harry was a compulsive narcissist. I mean that in the best sense. Maybe he was a bit unhappy because of it, but his life was always neat and tidy. So we might rule out Alicia and his ex."

"I would have to say so. This would have been a complicated well planned crime. They would have to have been at the scene. Their alibis are awfully strong.

"I'd like to hear what's in our copy of the Will. Maybe, we get a motive from that."

"That's an interesting point. Between you and me, he left a large bequest to Alicia Allende, some to his secretary, and some in trust for his step-son. Nothing spectacular. Don't tell Roger I told you."

"So I figured. He wasn't close to any family or friends. His female companion was just a friend. So maybe money wasn't a factor."

"I did hear he had an insurance-funded buy-sell agreement with a business partner. Try to look into that."

"Yes. He had a business he was involved in. I'll give the guy a call."

"What was his sister like?"

"She's older – apparently needs to dry out once in a while. She had a good alibi – lives in Florida, was in Cuba at this time. She has some kind of medical thing. Sounds like she was drying out again."

"OK, Peter. Check them all out. Oh and by the way, there's in insurance guy who wants to meet with us about the buy-sell insurance policy. Can you be here after lunch, about 2:00 p.m.?"

"Sure. Ring me when he shows up."

I managed to catch up on some old paperwork and plow through a stack of phone messages. I assembled a stack of files and memos for the junior associates. About 1:00, I was finally able to stick my head out the door. Waiting for me, Angelina had anticipated my lunch and there in the inbox was a ham and swiss on rye with brown mustard and a Dr. Brown's black cherry. Angelina had gone off to mass and left a sticky note saying "Mange!" No further urging was required. I dug in and listened to Mozart's 21st piano concerto. Total euphoria! Elvira Madigan always did that to me. Shame she had to die eating grass. The music was great. Then, I could dole out to the associates the files and memos as they peaked in after their lunch. Then Ms. James buzzed, "Digby has the insurance guy. Come on in."

"Thank you, Ms. James."

As I came up to Digby's office, I could see a very nervous suit sitting in the chair in front of Digby. As I came in, Digby said, "Peter, this is Mr. Pollack of American Business Life." Mr. Pollack, this is Peter Stern, our man on the Horton death matter." We shook.

Pollack turned to me. "Mr. Stern, as you may have been told, we hold a policy on Mr. Horton. He had an agreement with his partner in the importing business which required a life insurance policy on the life of the first to die. At that time, the company would receive the proceeds and was obligated to buy the shares of company from the decedent's estate and make the survivor the sole owner of the company."

"Thank you, Mr. Pollack. We are familiar with the standard buy-sell agreement for small corporations."

"But, Mr. Stern, there's an added wrinkle. It is a double indemnity policy. That means if Mr. Horton died an accidental death as defined in the policy we paid his estate twice the face value. If he was murdered we only pay the face amount. If he died of natural causes, we only pay the face amount."

"Hmm. So if I can prove his death was not an accident, your company saves the second half of the payment of the face value. Of course if the slayer is the heir, he or she would get nothing."

"Yes. You've got it."

"So my investigation might benefit you."

"Exactly. I don't have to explain very much to you."

"No. I get it."

"So, Mr. Stern, I would normally hire an investigator for this file, but if we can agree that there is no conflict of interest, we propose to hire you."

"I see. What are the terms?"

"We would fund you out of pocket costs, and pay $400 per day. Our normal investigator rate."

"Well, Mr. Pollack, my hourly rate is far above that."

"Oh, we assumed that. So there is a bonus – if you can prove it was not an accident, you save us $1,000,000. We will pay you one third of that if you can prove it – less the amount of your out-of-pocket expenses and my probate costs.

Digby after a moment thought, staring off into space began, "So if we are one of the executors of the Will and the death was accidental, the estate receives the insurance payment of $2 million. If the death was an intentional homicide, the estate only gets $1,000,000."

"Right so far."

"So if Mr. Stern proves there was a murder, he is operating against the interest of our client, the estate."

"On the other hand, under the Pennsylvania Slayer's Act, if the murder was a beneficiary of his estate, he or she could not inherit anything."

"That's also true."

"So it appears we are adversaries. You must prove murderer, we must prove accidental death to increase the value of the estate – which is our client."

"Not exactly. You see we reinsure the accidental death provision. That means we get a different insurance carrier to cover the accidental death provision and pay them a premium to do so."

"Why would you do that?"

"First of all, we make a slight profit in doing so. But also, we feel the accidental death – double indemnity provision is an attractive selling point for younger, healthy businessmen. The odds of dying by natural causes for them is still low and the odds of an accidental death are relatively high. As they get older, natural causes increases substantially the older you get. From our point of view, we do not like the idea of investigating against the interest of our client. We are purely a numbers company. We play the odds. If we sell enough policies, the odds prove out and we make money. We get a death certificate, we pay. Simple as that. We don't expect to do any investigation. Let the reinsurance carrier do that."

"I see. Well, Mr. Pollack this has been most enlightening. Thank you for coming by to explain this."

"Let me know when the Will is probated, send me a death certificate and I will pay the estate either $1,000,000 or $2,000,000. We like to make our payments very public. It's good publicity."

"Thank you again, Mr. Pollack. We will certainly notify when we probate the Will."

"Here's my card. Please call me directly." Mr. Pollack was shown out, but Digby beckoned me to stay.

"An interesting quandary."

"Yes. If I prove murder, our clients lose big time. There is no reason to pursue this further, it would seem even if we would get a bigger fee by proving it was murder."

"I agree. Let's find the Will and get the estate started."

That seemed to be that. So I left, and called Mr. Horton's secretary to locate the Will. I arranged to stop by his old office late that afternoon. I also arranged to call on his partner in the Italian importing business the next day to get a copy of the insurance policy for the file.

My investigation of a possible murder was over. So I assembled the file I had collected and put it in storage. It was now time to find the Will.

Last Will

We started our search for the lost Will with Harry's secretary. He had been in a small office where he shared space with five other lawyers – all independents like himself. He also shared a secretary, Mary Hughes. We called Mary before and told her we were coming to look for the Will. When we showed up, Mary told us that Harry kept personal files locked up in a drawer in his desk. We hoped to find either the Will itself or some keys to a safe deposit box. As we came in, Mary took us to the desk and showed us the drawer. Keys in Harry's possession when he died, did open the drawer, but there was no original Will. Only the same copy of the same Will we had in our office. A copy, by law, is of no value, only what we call the "ink" version is valid. A will may be revoked by simply destroying the original or by a new Will later in time. A copy then does not prove that the original was not destroyed. Of course, where the original never appears, it is possible to try to prove it is the same as the original by other means: it conforms to his stated wishes, it logically favors a close relative, etc.; but it is usually opposed by an intestate heir – one who inherits by law when there is no Will.

A complete search of the office revealed no other clues. There were no safe deposit keys, no letters advising family members of his burial wishes and speaking of where he had put the Will. There was simply nothing to lead us any further.

Mary Hughes did tell us two men had come by the previous week to measure Harry's office for drapes. Now having been in Harry's office, we had seen as expected the immaculate setting of a law office designed in very fine taste. The walls were hung on one side with Harry's diplomas and pictures of Harry with many politicians. The wall was covered with fine grass wallpaper in a light beige. Behind Harry's desk was an impressive piece of dark walnut furniture containing bookshelves, a small TV screen, and a liquor cabinet. On the other wall were Old English prints of lawyers and judges. The floor was covered in a dark bamboo imitating a dark walnut and on top was a large ivory oriental rug. The drapes appeared to be brand new and were in a silk design of maroon and beige. Mary could only describe the workmen as tall Hispanic-looking men in overalls. This led us back to the office and a closer look at the desk. Sure enough, we could see small pry marks around the desk drawer – not normally visible to the unsuspectingly, but clearly showing marks in Harry's exquisite desk. We took pictures of the pry marks. Mary was told to collect Harry's mail and send it to our office. She agreed. While we were there the other lawyers stopped by. They wanted to be appointed as a successor to Harry on the files he was working on. They agreed to pay a one-third percent of the fee to the estate. Since we were not officially the executor of the estate, we could not really agree. They nonetheless winked at us and patted Mary on the back.

As we left, we took a copy of a blank check to the bank around the corner Harry used for his personal and professional banking. We showed the death certificate and the blank check to the bank manager. She dutifully looked up Harry's name and found both accounts on which she placed a hold. There had been no activity for a week. She also told us unfortunately that Harry had not kept a safe deposit box at the bank. Another dead end. We had run out of obvious places to look: his apartment, his office, his bank and his cabin in the Poconos.

On my way out of the bank, I received a call that Harry's sister, Hermione, had called in to the office and inquired once again about the estate. Time for a little lunch, then back to the office.

Business Partner

I dropped in on Mr. Horton's business partner at a small garage in South Philadelphia which was the warehouse for the importing business. Anthony Giaconda sat at a beat up desk with a few steel file cabinets behind him. He was dressed in khakis and a fleece jacket, the garage was not heated. As I walked up, he was giving a truck driver a list of instructions and a series of lists of items to put on the truck.

"Hello, Mr. Giaconda, I'm Peter Stern, the lawyer for Harry Horton's estate." (Not quite true since we hadn't found the Will yet, but at least I'd get his attention.)

"Yes, Mr. Stern, I've been expecting you." He had a slight accent of some kind. I couldn't tell what.

"I'm sorry for the loss of your partner."

"Yes. Thank you. He was a big help to me and a good friend."

"Would you mind if I asked a few questions?"

"No. Anything to help." Giaconda was a very polite and accommodating fellow as if he was used to service.

"There was a buy-sell agreement in place funded by life insurance." "Yes. That was Harry's idea. You see I have a wife and two children. I needed life insurance. At the same time, Harry felt that if I died, the business would need a new manager and fast, or it would be worth much less. He said I was a key man. When the life insurance salesman came to talk to us, he explained the buy-sell policy. Since it would be on the life of either of us, it would be cheap to add Harry for his shares.

Since we were both in our forties, the chances of death by natural causes was low and by accidental death was high in comparison, we agreed to the double indemnity for accidental death. The policy overall was pretty cheap and it ran at the same rate for 20 years. It was a good deal."

"So I understand. Mr. Giaconda where is that very slight accent from?" "Ah, you noticed. I am from Trieste. I learned the restaurant and food business over there and in Florence I was the manager of a nice restaurant there and met a few Americans there who wanted to open a restaurant in the U.S. So they made me a nice offer. Unfortunately, we got into a dispute after I was here a few years and they were skimming money off the top and not paying me the bonus I had earned. So I went to Harry who was a good customer at the restaurant. He took on the case, threatened to expose their skimming to the IRS and the state. I got a nice settlement but lost my job. It was little comfort that after I left, that the restaurant went under. So I asked Harry what I should do. I had a few offers to be a restaurant manager. But I thought I knew enough suppliers in Italy, Croatia and Greece that I could import and make a nice living without the bad restaurant hours. Harry agreed. He lent me the money for an initial inventory and startup costs and I knew all the local restaurants and specialty shops so we did fairly well. My deal with Harry was we each owned 50% of the company, but I got the first $50,000 of profit and then we split the rest. We are doing alright now. I go to Europe to buy three or four times a year, and once a year Harry comes to enjoy himself on the company tab. He was happy with the deal."

"Is the business doing so well that it is worth $2,000,000?"

"No way. Between you and me, it makes about $150,000 partly in cash per year."

"So Harry was getting about $50,000 per year."

"Yes about. Give or take. On an investment of about $25,000." "So when you get his 50% when the insurance proceeds bought out his interest, you didn't profit that much?"

"Oh, I see where you are going. Yes, Mr. Stern, I did not kill Harry to get his 50%. First, he was a good friend and a very wise adviser. He did our accounting and taxes, and he was very shrewd in business matters. I knew good food and was a good salesman. He was the brains and kept me out of trouble. No, his 50% was something I was happy to pay, believe me. I'm sorry he is gone."

"Where were you last week?"

"I am here at this desk, sometimes in the area making deliveries. But I am here from 8:00 a.m. till 6:00 p.m., and I am on call by the customers at night and weekends. That comes with being your own boss. I have a closed circuit camera that confirms all this."

"No, I get that. I needed to eliminate some of the suspects."

"Did I pass?"

"Absolutely. You were a good friend to Harry and he to you. I regret having to ask these questions, but I needed to know the answers for sure."

"No problemo."

We shook hands as I left. He handed me a tin of almond macaroons and said, "Tell the office to enjoy."

"Thank you, Mr. Giaconda." "Tony, please."

"OK, Tony."

Ms. Horton

I was told by Angelina that Ms. Farnsworth, Harry's sister, was in town and would like to meet with us concerning her brother's estate. I asked Angelina to arrange for Digby and Roger Humphries to sit in on this meeting after lunch, maybe, late afternoon. She might or might not be our client depending on whether the Will was found. She was the sole sibling and it did not seem that there were other intestate heirs around. So she might be the sole intestate heir. She would need a law firm to administer the estate in that case, and I would be campaigning to be that law firm. So I wanted a full show of force to impress her at our meeting. I had somewhat pictured Ms. Farnsworth from her official documents, as if she were a female version of Harry – neat, circumspect, probably compulsive and cultured. Our firm was used to handling these upscale clients and we could talk the talk and walk the walk. So I went out to lunch and asked Angelina to look her up on Google and elsewhere on the net.

When she showed up, she was not something I expected. Digby and Roger Humphries exchanged glances and Angelina rolled her eyes. Ms. Farnsworth wiggled her way into the room followed by two male companions. She wore black and gold tights with large gold coins sprinkled here and there, and a tight gold top with a deep, deep neckline. She had gold bangle bracelets atwinkle at her wrists and large gold hoop earrings. Her cleavage was deeply tanned, with a few ominous freckles thither and yon and a swelling on each side that betrayed that "some work had been done." Not unattractive, her face was actually rather pleasant, but the tanning and injections of collagen over the years must have erased her wrinkles. The deep set of her eyes, and the tightness over her nose and jowls also betrayed the fine hand of "some work." Compared to Harry, I was careful not to gape.

One of her male companions, introduced as Vitez Vargas, was a small stocky man in a shiny blue silk suit, with black well-shined shoes and a high white collared shirt. The other was dressed in a track suit with the design of one of the Mexican soccer teams. His head was shaved, and his head, neck and shoulders all appeared to be one large formation. His eyes were dark and stared expressionless straight ahead. He was introduced as "Shorty." Ms. Farnsworth said that Mr. Vargas was her "adviser."

"Call me, Honey, please Mr. Stern. I dropped Farnsworth years ago after a bad divorce. Now I'm Honey Horton. Back to my old self," she said breathlessly. As I introduced her to Roger, Digby and Angelina, I could see Angelina already tapping away on her laptop.

"Sure, Honey. What can we do for you?" I explained the status of the case – Harry's death and homicide investigation, the Will search and the condolences from Alicia Allende.

Mr. Vargas with a strong Hispanic accent, broke in. "Meester Stern, how mooch is the estate?"

"At this point, I can't say for sure. I would guess Mr. Horton's personal assets were about $300,000, but a life insurance policy could be another $1 million or $2 million depending on whether his death was accidental."

"His death was not accidental?"

"We are not sure. The police are investigating." I had not gotten into the details, only that he died at his mountain cabin.

"Huh!"

"How mooch Honey get?"

"We don't know until we find the Will."

"And what if no Will?"

"As we now believe, she may get it all as his sole sibling."

"Uh-huh. So maybe a mill ploos, or two mill ploos."

"About right, depending on fees and taxes."

"So how long you look for Will?" This sounded ominous. The obvious answer was until we find it. He might be implying that he wanted to know how long we would look until we gave up looking.

"That would be up to the courts. We have filed a caveat, telling the court we have a copy of the Will, but cannot reveal its contents until the original is found. So there is no one appointed to handle the assets yet."

"So who is in charge of estate?"

"At this point, no one, but if I may. We drew the Will and in it, we were to be "in charge" or what we call the executors. If the Will is not found, the intestate heir appoints who is "in charge" or what we call the administrator. So if you agree that our firm acts and Ms. Horton is the sole known intestate heir, the court would appoint our firm to administer this estate."

"So you handle the money until we figger out who gets it."

"Yes. If you agree." Vargas turned to Honey, but Honey said, turning to Angelina who was still tapping at the laptop, "Dearie, can you take me to the little girl's room?"

Angelina looked up a bit startled. "Of course, Ms. Horton."

"Call me Honey."

"OK, follow me, Honey." Angelina held the door. Without Ms. Horton, the meeting was silent for a second.

"So what if you steal the money?"

Roger Humphries breathlessly said, "Well first we lose our license to practice law, then we are insured so you get your money back, and last we go to jail. But I can assure this firm has been in business for 75 years and we have never lost a dime of a client's money."

"So tell me about this double pay thing."

"If the decedent, Mr. Horton, died an accidental death, the policy pays double. If he was murdered or dies of natural causes, it only pays the face amount."

By now, Honey and Angelina were back.

With no prompting, Honey started to ramble. "Forgive me, I'm a bit nervous. Everyone calls me Honey, since high school, except the boys called me "Honeysuckle." You see Harry was a goody goody. He always studied and got good grades. My parents loved him. I just liked to play and I was popular. I tried some acting and modeling at first, but then I danced in some casinos. They liked me, so I got to entertain the whales. You know, the high rollers who get all the comps. Well, I was like a comp and got a piece of their action. I did pretty well until I got into gambling myself. That and some drinking. I mean I was a good party girl so what was I supposed to do."

"What do you do now, Ms. Horton?"

"I work for the casinos in Florida and the Bahamas."

"We tried to reach you before, but they said you were on vacation."

"Oh yes. I was in Cuba. Not much Email there…"

Mr. Vargas coughed and looked menacingly at Honey. She bowed her head and looked sheepish. I had to ask.

"Mr. Vargas, are you an attorney representing Ms. Horton?"

"No," he croaked. "I'm an adviser."

"And, Mister?" I said looking at the husky fellow to her right.

"Oh, him," Vargas croaked. "He's my assistant."

"May I have his name for our records?"

"Sure. Joe Don… Joe Don Tell." Mr. "Tell" just sat there. Very funny. Joe don't tell. I got it. An old police maneuver after arrest.

I nodded to him and said, "Please to meet you, Mr. Tell."

He nodded. "Ditto!"

By this time, I was getting some headshake from Angelina as if she had something she wanted to tell. By this time, some coffee was brought in and Roger began to explain the whole estate process with taxes et al. I left with Angelina just into the hallway.

"They're mob or almost."

"What do you mean?"

"Both guys have some arrests but no convictions for guns, drugs, and assault. It looks like they work for the casinos as muscle and enforcers. Is she his girlfriend or what?"

"I think "or what" They're here to keep an eye on her money if she gets it. I don't like it." So we went back in.

Roger was finishing up a long pedantic explanation. So I said, "So we need to clear up a few things, Honey. First, it may be some time before we figure out who is the executor or administrator, but in the meantime the assets have to be collected and some of the bills paid. The funeral, the rent, etc. We have to sell the cabin and the condo, etc. If you are with us, our firm should handle it, we would be happy to do so and hold the funds for whoever is supposed to get them."

"Oh, you seem nice. I vote you should do it." Vargas had started to speak up, but sat back.

He then rumbled, "If you collect the money, do we get an account?" "Oh yes, Mr. Vargas and we will ask Ms. Horton before any transaction as if she were our client. She will hear about every bill we pay, and every asset we sell."

"OK, suits me. But I want to hear about this Will business as you go. Do we get that?"

"I will keep Ms. Horton informed about everything. By the way where are you staying in Philadelphia?"

Vargas broke in, "We're at the Marriott by the airport."

"What are your room numbers and telephones?"

As Vargas told this to Angelina so she could put it in the computer, it was obvious that Honey was not in the same room as Vargas, who shared a room with Mr. Tell. (Who didn't)

"May I suggest that you move into the extended stay hotel, it isn't as nice, but you may be in Philadelphia awhile."

"Got it," Vargas croaked.

"In that case, if you can wait, we will type up something authorizing our firm to act as administrator of the estate until either the Will is found or the estate is declared an intestacy. Can you wait?"

"If you could deliver it to the Marriott?" Honey said.

"Of course, when will you be in?"

"Let's say after 5:00 today."

"OK, Honey. I'll see you then."

I escorted Honey and her two "advisers" to the door, but Angelina followed us with a look of someone carrying a secret. As I said goodbye and turned toward her, Angelina began.

"You know when I took Honey to the bathroom, she seemed to have a swelling in her pelvic area. She put a ton of pills on the vanity in the bathroom and began taking them. She looked at me with a kind of guilty expression. I don't know. It was just a feeling on my part. I couldn't tell what she was taking, but my son takes Prednisone and one of them looked like it. Just saying."

"OK, we'll file that away for the future. In the meantime, type up that form we used to be appointed administrator, and the one where the intestate heir declines to act. I'll have to doctor it up to plead the facts in this case. I'll need to see her at 5:00 today to get it signed and notarized." Angelina scurried off. Digby waved me into his office as I walked past.

"Peter, this estate has an odor to it."

"I have to say I agree. I did not like these two "advisers" and Honey was not at all like Harry."

"I mean combined with a murder investigation and a missing original Will. Let's dig a bit deeper."

"I have a detective looking for the lost Will, and this guy from the AG's Office, Hackett, is re-opening the homicide investigation. It's kind of out of my hands."

"We're earning a fee now for administering the estate, so we can afford to have you dig. Follow these investigations. See what turns up."

"Will do. Can I use Carmen?"

"Of course." Carmen was our very street-smart paralegal. I had represented her in the past, gotten her out of some trouble and she had gone on to be a paralegal. For me, she could see things I could not.

On my way back to my office, I stuck my head into her cubicle. "Carmen, that Horton matter is back on. Come into my office when you can and I'll give you an update." She was sitting behind two mounds of paper, which she slapped with great vigor, and said, "I'm ready now. Let's go."

I caught her up to date on the visit by Honey and Vargas and friend. "Let me see this Honey tonight. I live in South Philly now and it's on my way. I'll be your notary. When is it, five? I'll be there. The Marriott, fine."

I went out to lunch and found a telephone message from Honey on my desk. I called her cell, and she spoke in a low voice, "Mr. Stern make it 6:30 today. Don't make any phone calls. Just come up. Room 565, 6:30, okay?" I told Carmen, she was happy to finish up her paperwork for an extra hour. We'd be there.

Honey at the Marriott

Since Honey had changed the time for me to come and get the papers signed to renounce her right to act as administrator of Horton's estate pending probate, I arrived at 6:30 by myself and went directly to room 565. She opened the door at my knock. She was wearing a short bathrobe of bright yellow silk over a pair of black and gold tights. I hadn't noticed before, perhaps because I had been looking at her cleavage, alas I am only human, but she seemed to have a bulge at her abdomen. My eyes reverted once again to her ample cleavage which was heavily tanned with a few freckles. I could go into more detail, but might lose the thread of my narrative.

"Hello, Honey. I have the papers for you to sign."

She pulled me quickly through the door and sat at a small table with two chairs near the window. "You know, I didn't want Vitez to see you. He really doesn't like me signing these papers and wanted me to get someone else, but I trusted your firm right from the beginning." On the table was a pitcher of some lemony-orangey drink. "Oh, Mr. Stern, can I call you Peter? Please, I made up some golden dream." She said nodding at the pitcher. "Let me make you one. It is, after all, cocktail hour. "She seemed a bit tipsy already. "Are these the papers?" I had spread the sheets out in front of me. She poured some of the pitcher into a glass with ice and came around to my side of the table and put the glass into my hand while leaning over my shoulder to look at the papers. A brief glimpse, perhaps not so brief, over at her robe which now gaped open, and displayed her quite nicely as one who often sunbathed topless. More freckles.

"Uh yes." I gulped as she put her hand on my shoulder and leaned closer to the papers. "Why don't you read them over?"

"Oh I trust you." She turned toward me and breathed some golden dream my way. "This lets your firm collect the money until we figure out who gets it, right?" More golden dream breath.

"Yes. Why don't you sign these then?" Angelina had put two colored tabs where her signature was required. She went back to the other end of the table. I took a sip of golden dream. Sweet, fruity and strongly alcoholic.

"You know I was a good hostess at the casinos. I got the high rollers – the whales – all sorts of comps. I like you as my lawyer and I can get you some nice comps just on my signature. A room, a dinner – we have lots of women. Just name it."

"Well, Honey, I'm not really your lawyer. I represent Harry and his estate."

"Oh, I get that. But I feel I can rely on you to do the right thing. But is there any way I could get an advance on the estate? I'm a bit short."

"We don't' know who will get anything out of the estate. I mean it could be you if we don't find the Will or we could find the Will and you might not be in it."

"That's what I mean." Some more golden dream was poured into my glass. "If the Will doesn't show, I get everything, right. So, if you don't find it, and you are the only one looking, I get everything, right?" I was definitely getting the feeling I was being hustled.

"We have looked most places so far and not found anything."

"Do you have to look so hard?"

"I'm not actually doing it, we hired a detective."

"Ah, very interesting." This was a hustle. "But Peter, you know I don't have any money if I don't get the estate. I owe the casinos some money and they'll want some of it. That is what Vargas is doing here, to protect the casinos' interest. Unfortunately, I got too deep into gambling so I have some markers around. I wonder if I could borrow a few bucks until the estate comes in."

"I can lend you a few dollars. What do you need?" "How about $50 for now?" That wasn't too hard to do. I mean, she signed out the administration of the estate which would mean a middle five figure fee. So the firm could do this. Then I heard a light rap on the door. Honey got up and welcomed in a gorgeous young woman, dressed very nicely in a black cocktail dress and pearls. "Oh, Peter, this is Jean. She came up from Miami with me and hasn't been to Philadelphia before. Could you show her around? You're not married are you?"

"Uh, no." I mean this woman was gorgeous and classy. A black bun, a black cocktail dress and pearls. Who wears pearls these days? "Jean, is it?"

"Yes, Jean. Nice to meet you Peter." What was this? A fixup, a high class escort, a comp? Was I being set up? Of course I was. Go with the flow.

Honey motioned Jean over to the Golden Dream pitcher, and poured her a glass. Did Jean have a last name, or a real name? Was this from Vargas? What was going on? Jean sat on the bed and sipped her drink. Another rap on the door. Honey let Angelina in.

"Peter, I'm a bit late. Sorry." Angelina surveyed the room. Two women. A pitcher of some drink. What was going on? "I brought the notary things," she said, still taking in the scene.

"Yes, Honey. Angelina needs to notarize your signature." Honey got up from her chair, and Angelina sat and started to fiddle with the papers. "Ms. Horton, I need to see some ID, to verify who you are. I need to make this official."

Honey got out a Florida drivers license. Angelina wrote down all the information in her notary book – not usually required – but Angelina smelled something and wanted all the details for the file. After a few minutes, Angelina was finished, packed up her stuff and took the file with the papers. On the way out, she gave me a smirk. She knew something was up, too.

"So where can I take you two ladies for dinner?" I said as innocently as possible. A knowing look from Honey, she had played this game before.

"Oh, Peter, I can't. Vargas and I have some other business. But you two run along and have fun." Jean had a smile, but I couldn't make it out. Did she think I was naïve, or stupid? Did she think I was suspicious? She just smiled.

"OK, so Jean, what do you like? Seafood, French, Italian, steak, you name it."

"I like French if you can still get a reservation." I was impressed. French. And a nice voice, low. The accent? Hard to tell. Maybe California. I know of a great French – Asian fusion restaurant. I usually reserved for those who would appreciate it. I pulled up the number on my cell. It was about 7:00 p.m. now so maybe at 8:00. Yes. Reservation for two. An intimate French – Asian fusion restaurant. Honey stood up, and patted me on the back, "Now, don't stay out too late," like a mother sending her teenage daughter off on a date. At least, I could get more background on Honey and Vargas, and dinner might not be too bad. And the firm just might pick up the tab.

Jean seemed happy to accompany me out the door. I had selected a nice French restaurant in a neighborhood where I was known. Of course, it was partly because Jean was go-to-hell gorgeous and would impress the local gentry, but, because I wanted to be as public as possible in the event someone accused me of an improper relationship with Honey on the estate. If I was out and open, at least I was not hiding anything in some discrete cheaters' hideaway. So I chose "Hue Bistro" in South Philly. They had a cellar where cool jazz was quietly played and we could talk.

We sat and each ordered a glass of wine to start, then perused the menu. It was pretty standard French. Then she said what women say that always irritates us but strokes our vanities. "Why don't you order for both of us?" This social ploy not only irritated me because the choices were expensive and I did not want to waste money on a meal she might not eat, but also it was such an obvious appeal to my supposed male vanity.

"Look, Jean. You're an attractive intelligent woman, and I don't need to be treated like someone who likes to control women. Order what you like."

She sniffed. She was probably used to entertaining "whales" at the casino whose egos needed stroking. I hoped mine didn't. I could see us drawing a few stares – mainly at Jean. Then I noticed a friend of one of my old girl friends. In the scale of male rating of one-upsmanship, having a girl friend of an old girl friend report that my date was stunning rates near the top. Yes. We are a shallow lot. Forgive us.

Jean ordered the cassoulet. I was impressed. This is basically a stew of beans and meat, but to call it that is an insult to the French who treat this old peasant dish with loving attention as the French do and it is heavenly when done right. To make this choice was not only risky in an unknown restaurant, but showed a knowledge of fine food. I would have been enthralled with her anyway if she ordered shrimp cocktail and a steak well done. Even if she poured ketchup on it. I would have been enthralled, lowly and base that our male appetites are. I had the trout amandine. We split a nice Caesar salad.

"Jean, you know I have to ask. Please don't be insulted."

"Oh, I'm used to this question. Yes, I work for the casino, I'm a hostess." I stared into the face, white flawless skin, dark brows, a pouting lower lip and deep blue eyes, her hair pulled by into a bun. Yes. She was something. "I'm not a hooker. I don't sleep with the whales."

"I stammered, "I… I… I didn't mean…"

"Yes, you did. I am Honey's present to you for the evening. That is covered. Anything else is just between you and me. That's how I work."

"I… I…"

"Look, Peter. Let's just enjoy the evening. OK."

"Yes. So what do you do otherwise?"

"I am studying art and architecture at Miami and I'm almost done. Then I can quit the casino. My funds are invested safely and I live happily ever after."

"OK, that's good. Do you expect to marry and have kids?"
"Of course, most women want that. I haven't been on a date-date in so long, I won't know how to act. Sometimes the boss takes me out, but that's it."

"Who's the boss?"

"Scuzzy. John Scarramazza. He prefers Scuzzy."

"You know Scuzz means…"

"Yes. But he seems to like it. He identifies. He is very rough around the edges and tries to act possessive of me, but I keep it all strictly business."

"Forgive me for asking. But if you do this for a living, don't you disassociate. Suspend yourself from the so-called action and become immune to intimacy."

"I've thought about that. My parents were California hippies who raised pot in Mendocino County. They were stoned most of the time, so I kind of raised myself. Someone saw me on the University of Nevada Las Vegas campus and recruited me for the casinos. I can't say I'm unhappy. I pay my rent, I pay my tuition and I sock some money away. Most of these guys are older and are very nice to me. So that's me. How about you?"

"Me. I'm divorced. It was my fault. I had to work too hard. I see my daughter, she's seven now, and I pay support."

"So do you disassociate from the world of living to tend to your profession?"

"Ah, very clever. Good question. I'll have to think about that."

The conversation was getting too sticky, so we agreed to move on. We discussed art. It happened that there was a traveling Cezanne exhibit at the Art Museum. I bragged about our museum.

"So, what kind of art do you like?"

"Of course, like everyone, I love the impressionists, but I really like the Renaissance and gothic best."

"Our museum has a terrific permanent collection from the period. How would you like to go tomorrow?"

"Well, I'm kind of stuck here in Philly with Honey. So, yeah. Let's do it. "I'll pick you up for breakfast at, say, 9:00?"

"Good."

"Besides, I want to tell everyone we had breakfast tomorrow."

"Ha, ha, very funny."

"So anyway, what is Honey like and what are you doing here?" "Honey is very sweet. A little daffy. She is way into booze and pills, and is way in debt to the casinos. They own her now. Unless this inheritance comes in. I'm here to be her watchdog – keep her out of trouble. Vargas is here to make sure the money she gets is used to pay off the casino and her medical bills."

"What kind of medical bills? Drug rehab?"

"No. Something else. I don't know. But she went to Cuba for it." "She seems street smart enough to take care of herself."

"Not from the casino guys. She's in deep."

"She wants me to kill the murder investigation and the search for the Will."

"So I heard. You look like an honest guy. I suggest you don't get into it. You could get hurt."

"Oh, I know that. After all, I am a lawyer."

"A smart guy who let us say, might help her, would get a percentage, and then if it turns out the guy was murdered or the Will is lost, then you collect. If it turns out the other way, you don't. But you didn't help it one way or the other."

"I don't operate that way."

"Well, Vargas does. He may push you more than you like."

"I get that, too."

"So don't say anything one way or the other."

"You know for a pretty girl, you've got some brains."

"I hope the rest of the feminine movement didn't hear that. Would it help if I told you I was a softball player, too?"

"No, wait, a girl who likes baseball?"

"No, a woman who does."

"Very good" We went on like this for a while and the waitress was looking like she wanted to clear the table, and collect the bill. I signed everything up.

As we walked out, I passed two lawyers from a competitor firm, Stapley and Hochmeister, something and something. They were sitting with their dowdy wives at a cocktail table. All four eyed Jean copiously and thoroughly. One of the men, an asshole when sober, stood up to pat me on the back while still looking at Jean. "Very nice.

Wonderful stuff." I probably should have smacked him, but I wrote it off to being the better man. Besides, I should have said, "Eat your heart out, motherfucker." But lawyers are passive aggressive guys so I simply shook his hand and left him to the dowdy wives. She looped her arm inside of mine in a sufficiently intimate way. Take that! It was only 9:30, but I dropped Jean off at the Marriott.

Art Museum

About eight the next morning, Jean called, could I pick her up at the Hyatt rear door instead of the Marriott. She also did not want to have breakfast at either hotel. No problemo. So I picked her up, she in her jeans, sneaks and a loose pullover but hair down. Still beautiful. I decided to give her a taste of Philly, so we went to the Melrose Diner in South Philly – usually a mixture of all walks of life. A pleasantly plump middle aged woman in a uniform, greeted me as "Hon and the missus" and waved me to a table.

Jean ordered the standard – scrambled eggs, bacon, toast, orange juice and coffee. I mean there was no white egg omelet, no gluten free stuff, no complicated omelet, no croissants. Plain Jane. I have to say with all due respect to the ritual food faddists, just the basics.

"So, Jean, I don't even know your last name."

"No, you don't."

"Uh, you don't give it out."

"Sorry, no." A little distance then. Apparently I was not to be trusted.

"Did I do something wrong?"

"No. Just professional caution."

"Are you really Jean?"

"Oh yes. I trust you that much."

"Yahoo for that."

"No, Peter, don't be upset. My life is complicated."

"I can tell. You wanted to avoid anyone seeing me pick you up, but you still wanted to go with me to the Art Museum."

"Sometimes I am watched."

"By whom?"

"Vargas on orders from Scuzzy."

"What is it with Scuzz?"

"He has a thing for me and gets jealous."

"But he's not your…"

"No. He's married. I think he messes with the other girls in the casino. Not me."

"I see. Are you in danger?"

"Not really. I get what I want and most of the time he leaves me alone."

"That doesn't sound too healthy. I mean suppose you want to leave and start a career or a family?"

"Then there's a problem."

"Not good!"

"Well, I have some money stashed and I figure out a way to arrange things."

"I hope you do. Does he get upset if you… you know… with the whales?"

"Oh, no that's business."

"What about me and this unpaid-for hostessing?"

"Don't be so literal. He doesn't know about this. I went through the Hyatt and out the back door."

"Would I upset him?"

"No. I sized you up pretty quickly. You are too proud to ever pay for this, and you are a professional. You wouldn't make that kind of a move on me. He's only helping Honey because she owes so much money for her casino debts and her operation."

"Was Honey his girl friend?"

"I heard she was at one time."

"What was this operation?"

"I don't know. She went to Cuba for it. She seems ok now." "He paid for it."

"Yes. Most of these guys go to Cuba because they have great medical facilities, they're extra cheap and then there are no medical records."

"Whoa! I hadn't thought of that. Yeah, it makes sense." By now, we had finished breakfast, so I and Jean (last name unknown) went to the Art Museum. We left the details of her life alone since she seemed to tense up when we got to issues she didn't want to share. I have to say that Cezanne was in his usual good form, the museum staff did an excellent job with the exhibit, the portable electronic guides were very well done and, although crowded, the lines moved along at a decent pace. We had lunch at the museum, and then went to tour the permanent collection. As usual, it was great. She was enthralled. She had no local art museums she could compare it to, and was overwhelmed that we had such culture in Philadelphia.

I drove her back to the Hyatt and let her in the back door. I got a peck on the cheek and a very sincere thank you. Did I see a somewhat wistful look in her goodbye? Was it me and my ego, or was she just a good professional? Who knew? Anyway, on to another day in my life.

Alicia's Conference

The day began as usual. Angelina had stacked a pile of letters and documents for me to review. So I read over what I had dictated and signed them in between telephone calls. Roger Humphries stopped by to say the petition for our firm to serve as interim administrator of Horton's estate had been signed. He was sending out letters to every possible heir telling them that he was listing Harry's condo in the city and his cabin in the Poconos for sale. So far, the insurance carrier had no word as to whether the death would be considered accidental so they would provide no proceeds.

Towards noon, I got a telephone call from Honey. She said the hotel was too expensive and wished to move into Harry's condo pending its sale. Generally, I thought it might be a good idea to have the place occupied but a nagging idea came to me. If there was no Will, Honey would inherit everything. So I held off for a few days so that we could make one last thorough search in the condo. I told her she could move in Thursday, and asked Angelina and Carmen to help me do one last search.

I then got another phone call, this time from Alicia Allende, could we meet after lunch. She would be in all afternoon at the headquarters of the Democratic Party a few blocks away. I agreed wondering what this was about.

After lunch, I stopped by Alicia's office and was escorted into her conference room. She was as usual dressed to the nines in a silver silk suit and dazzling white blouse.

"Mr. Stern, I want you to now that I know what is in the Will and that I am a substantial beneficiary."

"Ms. Allende, as you know, I can't confirm that one way or the other."

"True enough, but Harry gave me a copy some time ago. I think he wanted to show me his gratitude for our friendship. I have it here if you want to see it."

"No, that's fine. What do you have in mind?"

"Two things. First, I got Harry appointed to the board of the Delaware River Port Commission. It paid well and Harry got considerable clout from the power it gave him. As you know, I am close to the Governor and he looks to me for advice."

"Harry's position is now open and the Governor wants me to suggest someone who will be loyal to him. By loyal to him, I mean loyal to me. Someone I can depend on to support our political agenda."

"I assume you mean your political agenda."

"Very good. You see where I am going. I was considering you for the job."

"Me. I'm not political."

"No. Just as well. Not objectionable to anyone."

"So what kind of loyalty might you want?"

"The original Will is missing, am I right?"

"Yes."

"So Honey Horton would get everything as his intestate heir."

"So far. It looks that way."

"That seems very unfair. I mean Harry intended to do things a certain way, and then someone came in and took his original after he died. I suspect Honey and her thug friends from Miami. Clearly, a crime has occurred if the Will was stolen."

"That remains to be seen."

"Well, maybe not."

"Suppose a duplicate ribbon copy of the Will existed."

"You mean one with the original signatures and notarial seal?" "Yes. Would a duplicate original be probated as the original?" "Theoretically, duplicate originals are not supposed to exist."

Now, here's where loyalty comes in. If I were, say, to create an exact duplicate original and submit it to probate, there are a number of problems, I would have to ask you about. If you can help me, I could see to your appointment to Harry's seat on the Commission."

"Whoa! Are we safe talking here?"

"This conference room belongs to the Democratic Party and many deals are done here. Believe me it's clean. Now, first question: If the original – the real one – shows up, does it harm the validity of the one I create?"

"I doubt it would show up if it was identical. Obviously, the one you create is a forgery, but the real one is not and it says the same thing. So it would be probated in its place and accomplish the same thing. So no harm, no foul. But if it came out that there was a forgery, but of the same original, I don't know what would happen? On the other hand, I don't think the people who might have stolen the original would be all that anxious to speak up about it. On the other hand, if your forged version just showed up through some innocent source, so that it could not be traced to you. Probably nothing would happen and we would have the same results in each Will. Since we have our copy of the Will in our office, no one could say it was not Harry's intent. Interesting problem. A forged duplicate of the original corroborated by the copy in the lawyer's office. Yes, it could be done."

"Your firm would then be the administrator still?"

"Actually, we would become the executor since there would now be a validly probated Will."

"Would you keep your mouth shut if suddenly the original should turn up?"

"I'd have to think about it. I am not sure if this is a crime or not. I can see I am not doing anything morally wrong since it comports with Harry's wishes."

"OK, next issue and this is a big one. Harry came to me with some documents about the Commission. They seem to show a fairly large embezzlement was going on by the New Jersey part of the Commission. As you know, Pennsylvania and New Jersey each have five seats on the Commission. As it works out, New Jersey figures out what to spend on the New Jersey side, and Pennsylvania on the Pennsylvania side. The funds come from the tolls over the various bridges. There is a substantial amount of excess money over the regular expenses and the maintenance and repair of the bridges. As a result, there is a large slush fund each state gets to spend on projects on their side of the river. This money is totally outside the states' budgets and is not held to much accountability. More often than not, it goes to patronage jobs and whatnot directed by the governor of each state through their representatives on the Commission. Through some anonymous source, Harry however, found a secret fund that was going directly to a New Jersey representative and his cronies. I have his file here. He was going to give it to the Governor but he died. This file is pure gold politically. If you get it, you will make a name for yourself in the press as an outsider in the political arena who has blown the whistle on a multimillion dollar fraud. If you help me, I help you.

"So I get credit for doing good and actually do good at the same time."

"You got it."

"Hmm. Interesting. So basically I do nothing, I get the appointment, I get the file, and I get credit for crime busting all at the same time. Can I think about it?"

"Don't take too long. I have to fill the seat on the Commission soon." "It's a lot to think about."

"I agree. Get back to me." We shook hands.

I took a long slow walk back from Democratic headquarters. What had I just heard? Definitely a bribe offer. She knew she could get a major portion of the estate as Harry's let's say companion if we could find the Will. It was also clear that someone had stolen the original, someone who would profit by an intestacy. That someone had to be Honey, who was also offering me Jean somehow. Now if Honey had stolen it, it certainly would be improper for her to inherit. On this other hand, forging a copy of the original to pass an original would take some doing. There were signatures of two people witnessing

Harry's signature on the Will and the signature and seal of the notary. A good forger could copy the signatures and the seal and stamp of the notary would not be hard to duplicate. Yes, it could be one. Would those signatories admit or deny they were their own signatures? Good question. But would it come to that? Honey, who may have stolen the original Will, would contest it, and would know it was a forgery. If she contested it, she might get a handwriting expert or she might cross-examine the signatories to see if they could agree that this was a forgery. Would all this hold up in court? A risk. But to whom? If Alicia did not actually present the forgery herself but simply had an innocent third party drop it at the law firm, no one could be blamed if it was later proven to be a forgery. But more important, the copy our firm had retained would have identical provisions in it. So the court, if it was a close call, might decide that, since the possible forgery expressed Harry's true intent, it would be possible to overlook the possibility that it was a forgery and rule that it was valid. A neat series of problems. Where did I stand on this? Could I ignore the possibility that a forgery was in progress which would have the effect of righting the wrong of a stolen Will? And should I profit from all this passively? I wrestled with the issues. I knew the answer was to talk it over with Digby. Digby would be rabbi and father confessor all in one.

Government Appointment

On my way into my office this morning, I got a series of congratulations. I hadn't done anything spectacular or noteworthy and couldn't fathom my newfound success. Angelina of course beamed and was clipping out a newspaper article to put in a file.

"Look, Pete. You're on the Commission." I looked. Sure enough there was a short blurb in the local news announcing the Governor's appointment of me to the Delaware River Commission. Needless to say I was surprised. I certainly hadn't accepted Alicia's deal concerning her intention to forge the Will. Had I not made myself clear? Thoughts filtered through my brain. One sure move to make – tell Digby. At least, talk it out with him.

Digby was in, as usual sitting at his desk peering over his bifocals. "Ah, Peter, been waiting to hear what this is all about."

I explained Alicia's proposition. "Digby, I haven't talked to Allende since we talked last. I didn't tell her I'd go along with her plan."

"I figured that. She may be trying to box you in. She may think if she gives you this plum, you can't refuse her later. She's trying to force your hand."

"But, if I decide to prevent this forgery, she may claim I helped or knew about it all along."

"Let her claim. There's nothing in writing and no one else knows about this but you and she."

"True. But if I stop her, does she get me thrown off the Commission?"

"I'd say no. She can't undo this unless she really wants to look bad."

"I guess that's true. But I haven't agreed to do anything. I have to tell her that."

"Do it in person. Her phone may be tapped. And don't do it in her office."

"I get that!"

"Just tell her you haven't made up your mind and you're waiting for more facts."

"Seems like a good plan."

I went back to my office and called Alicia. "Oh, Peter. Congratulations."

"Alicia, we have to talk. I didn't…"

"Oh, I know, I had a very small window to get this appointment in." "Alicia, can we meet?"

"Sure, Peter. How about coffee?"

"Great. Where? On Chestnut Street, there's a nice little coffee shop, about 1506."

"Good, see you when?"

"Now, is a good time."

"OK, now."

I wasted no time going to the coffee shop. Alicia strode in a little later. Eyes were drawn to this tall stately woman.

"Peter. Glad we could meet." We were sitting in an isolated corner of the shop. "I didn't mean to rush you into anything, but I had to move before the other politicians starting advancing their buddies."

"Alicia, this doesn't mean I've…"

"Don't' worry, Peter. I understand that."

"I mean if the real original turns up."

"I've got that covered. Don't worry."

"You don't have to vouch for anything except that it contains the same terms as the unsigned one your office prepared at his request."

"I can do that."

"Now, I've got something else. Here's the file on that embezzlement. The stuff in here was collected mostly by an anonymous whistleblower on a guy named Newberry, the New Jersey Governor's buddy. He may be kicking back to the Governor. Read it over and tell me how you want to play this." She pushed an envelope containing a mound of paper across the table. I took it. Thoughts ran through my head. What had Harry been doing with this file? Was he sharing it with Alicia? Was she playing some political game, maybe blackmail with it? After I'd reviewed the file, I'd have to talk to her about it. Maybe, I could always say that she got me appointed because of my reputation as an investigator and know I'd pursue it. I'd have to read it first. I wouldn't know what had fallen in my lap. I thanked Alicia and got up to leave. I had a vague sense someone had photographed our meeting. At this point, I was not hiding anything and had a good reason not to contest the appointment. I would have to get back to the office and do some serious reading.

The file seemed to sketch out an embezzlement scheme involving a charter school in New Jersey. What does a charter school have to do with the Commission which collects tolls over bridges to maintain and repair interstate bridges? This particular political boondoggle is one of those hidden pockets for slush funds. The Commission collects far more than it needs to maintain and operate the bridges. You would think that the tolls would be set to cover current operating costs and set aside funds for future repair. But, nooo! It decides to use its excess funds – not to lower tolls – but to spend on an unaccounted for basis on pet projects without interference by the state legislatures or the governors – unless the governors don't get their own pet projects some of the money. So these unelected, appointed political cronies have free rein to share funds with their own friends and family.

I called Alicia to meet for coffee again. She was OK the next morning at 10:00. Fair enough.

As she sat, I just jumped in. "Alicia, who knows about this file?" "As far as I know just me and the whistleblower."

"How did the file come into Harry's possession?"

"It was on his car seat one day."

"So he didn't know the whistleblower?"

"I don't think so."

"Did he just give you the file?"

"Yes. He wanted me to have a copy in case something happened to him."

"Was he concerned about something happening to him?"

"I would say yes. But the file was most important, he was not."

"So whoever left him the file had to have the keys to his car?"

"He left his car in a garage. Sometimes, he left the keys so they could move his car."

"Did you have keys?"

"Me, no."

"So someone may have taken the keys from the garage key holder?"
"I would guess yes."

"If you had the file, you might have great political leverage on the people involved, wouldn't you?"

"You mean political blackmail?"

"I suppose so, but it is a dangerous game."

"Yes. Could be."

"So would you care if I simply gave the file to the FBI?"

"I would want to play a few games first."

"Well, I have some more investigation first, but then I'll contact you if I decide to call in the FBI."

"That would be nice."

"Well, thanks for the appointment. Do I understand I only meet once a month and get paid $80,000 a year?"

"That's it."

"This is certainly a major opportunity."

"Enjoy it in the best of health."

I was already going through in my head what to do with the file as I left. I had been given a golden plum, and without strings. At least, not enforceable strings.

First Commission Meeting

As the second Wednesday of the month came around, I anticipated my first commission meeting. As the new guy, I would of course be heavily scrutinized. I was to the other members an unknown quantity. I had no known political affiliates, had been appointed out of the blue and did not appear to have any loyalties to anyone. I was simply a young trial lawyer with a past which displayed an ability to conduct sound investigations. This of course made me someone to be feared. The rest of the Commission were a collection of people known for undying political loyalties and little else. A few union leaders, a few career politicians, a few former close business associates of the respective governors. Almost no business or budgetary talent or desire for strong reform. Actually, the Commission was run by the staff – all political appointees themselves who owed a duty of loyalty to their political bosses. However, the staff had to be mildly competent. They had to assemble the figures of daily receipts from the bridge tolls, compare that to the images on the cameras which were computerized to render counts of the coins in the toll booths.

With the advent of technology, the E-ZPass counters did most of the work. They registered the car going through the transponder, deducted the toll from the E-ZPass account, put it into the general account of the Commission. Only the dwindling number of cash payment lanes needed some oversight. The E-ZPass technology had been a huge financial boon to the industry. Formerly, union toll takers collected nice salaries during three shifts each day year in year out. The transponder mechanisms cost far less, were more accurate and certainly, less temperamental. However, despite the savings achieved, the tolls somehow remained the same or increased regularly over the years with the blessing of the legislative committees designed to oversee this money making operation.

The supposed watchdog over the income and expenses of the Commission, was an auditing firm of public accountants hired once again on the recommendation of the political bosses. To be fair, auditors are credited with abilities they do not possess. Human fraud, embezzlement and other crimes are often difficult to detect without some human whistleblowing. Mostly, auditors just verify income in, and expenses out. Phony supplier payments, unapproved disbursements, ghost employees are hard to detect as long as the paperwork backing them up is in place.

So the meeting each month, for which I was to be paid $80,000 per year was a formality. Ten men – and I do mean men – no women on this board – sat, had a nice catered lunch, chatted about politics, went over numbers briefly, and reacted to a few staff memos or suggestions. They were done often no later than 3:00 p.m.

As I walked in, the men were gathered in friendly groups. As the newcomer I drew their attention. I already knew one of their number from New Jersey was to be watched. I had to detect any "tell" or hint that he may have known something about the file Alicia had given me implicating him and his wife and her friend in this charter school. The main question would be why donate Commission funds to a very profitable non-profit who had the Commission member's family as ghost employees.

I shook hands as I was introduced to the members, and some key staff. From my handshake, I have to say I could not detect a tremor, a grimace or a "tell" from Artie Newberry at all. He was a plump, round faced, pink cheeked little fellow with a perpetual smile on his face. He ran a funeral home in a blue collar neighborhood in Trenton, had no college education, and had inherited the funeral home from his father and uncle. He had a substantial interest in a large cemetery, and the ear of the Catholic diocese for burials and funeral matters.

Angelina had been busy on the Internet. Newberry and wife owned a nice house in a nice section of suburban Newark, and a nice beach house in Mantoloking – neither spectacular, merely comfortable family houses for a large Catholic family. They owned a medium sized boat docked in a yacht club not far from their shore house. Three of the seven children had graduated area Catholic colleges and two more were in process. Two lived at home and attended St. Stephen Martyr High School. In family pictures the children were short, stocky, had normal pleasant faces. Nothing spectacular there.

The school Ms. Newberry ran had high admission standards and was mostly white. There were optional Catholic education classes that were well attended. The students all wore uniforms – khaki pants or skirts and blue blazers with light blue shirts. In short, the school looked like it had been a traditional parochial school recreated as a public charter school and eligible for public funds. Two of the college students received full time salaries from the commission.

Angelina had been busy in my absence. On my desk were paper clipped files of printouts from the Internet of everything Newberry Properties owned, newspaper articles, kids' report cards, credit reports, Facebook pages, cell phone tweets. I took them all home to go over at leisure. After a thorough review, I got nothing. Bupkas. The guy on the surface at least was clean. He was a politician, pillar of the community. Lots of kids. Dumpy wife. Where was all this money going? He certainly was not spending it in any overt way. Of course, a smart guy could find dozens of ways to hide ill-gotten gains. Buy gold or gems, offshore bank accounts, limited partnership interests, straw name ownership. What could it be?

I had stopped by the Commission offices after the meeting and asked for a list of all the "economic development projects." – Another term for the recipients of the grants the Commission members doled out to their friends. I said I wanted an idea of what kind of projects we supported. I didn't think this would attract much attention, but I'm sure it was reported. Some newspaper would defiantly like this list and would do proper research. I thought it also might send a message to this anonymous whistleblower to contact me. Maybe I was being contacted now by someone else.

I stared off into space from my condo window and ran through ideas randomly. Alicia had given me this Newberry file. Was it for a specific reason? Some agenda of hers? Why hadn't Harry turned over the file to the FBI before?

Maybe Harry was planning a big splash in the newspapers so he could get all the credit and be a hero. I certainly could do that now. Had Alicia handed me an instant ticket to major publicity? Good questions all. What to do?

As I walked home from the office one day, I passed a corner pizza shop and heard a woman standing in the entrance say: "It was my file, Mr. Stern. Please, it was my file." She had on a baseball hat pulled over her forehead, otherwise, she was a black woman dressed pleasantly in a flowered shirtwaist dress and heels. I of course turned.

"Mr. Stern, it was my file." Was this a set up? I was in public, just the usual pedestrian traffic along a commercial strip in the city.

"May I help you, ma'am?"

"My pastor says I can trust you. Can I tell you something in private?"

"Of course. What can I do?" She seemed nice enough and serious. Not a panhandler or a conman.

"If I tell you something, can it be private, like a lawyer?"

"If you give me a dollar, I can give you attorney-client privilege, at least for our conversation. Step into the drug store and let me hear what you have to say."

We went into a local Rite Aid and she fiddled with her purse and pulled out a dollar.

"My pastor says his lawyer knows you and you are an honest man. I should trust you."

"Oh, what's on your mind?" Customers bustled up and down the aisle. She took off her baseball hat. She was a pleasant looking middle aged black woman with an earnest look on her face.

"Mr. Stern, that file you got from Harry Horton. It's my file. I did it."

"Oh I see. Very important stuff. How did you get it?"

"I work as a clerk at the Commission and I happened to see

something. So I started to dig. Everything I got was in the Commission files or in public records. I work in the 'Economic Development Section' where they file the applications for grants. We can ask any kind of questions from the applicants. So I did. Mr. Stern, I'm a God fearing woman and I got this job because I know the ward leader and he knows my pastor. I was a legal secretary before. So I know things."

"This file is very impressive."

"Now that you know me, you can't tell anyone, I like this job."

"Mrs…? You have attorney-client privileges. I can't reveal anything you tell me without your permission."

"OK, my name is Ernestine Hughes. This file makes me sick. I feel I am doing the devil's work and I don't like it. What should I do?"

"Come back to my office and let's talk about this."

"Will this cost me anything?"

"Not now. I don't charge for an initial consultation. Only if I accept the case."

"I can't afford much."

"Don't worry about that. I already think I can get paid by someone else, but I'll explain all that. Don't worry about the money, just tell me what's on your mind. Here's my card. Go to this address now and I'll meet you at the building entrance. I don't think we should be seen walking together yet."

On my way back to the office, I was flooded with thoughts on this new development. Of course, the file should belong to the one who assembled it. It was not my property and it would be wrong to claim the extensive amount of work it involved. That certainly solved my dilemma. It was up to the creator of the file to determine how to use it, but it created a new issue for me. This lady was now a client, I owed her a duty of full loyalty. On the other hand, as a board member of the Commission, I owed it a full duty of loyalty. I had a clear conflict of interest. I might have to choose. To represent the Commission when I had full knowledge of its participation in wrongdoing was wrong. I might have a duty to report this at the next meeting of the board if not sooner. That might betray this new client. I was on the board, so I owed the Commission a duty of loyalty. I did not owe the board members or officers anything. If I merely resigned and helped her alone, I could protect her identity. But if I kept for myself the benefits of a case against a board member, this might be wrong. I should advise the board of my knowledge of wrongdoing. So problem solved. I needed to resign my cushy $80,000 a year, much-sought-after, directorship just after I had gotten it. Definitely a newspaper item. I mean it was like a man bites dog issue. If the news simply said, as it did, that a lawyer was appointed to the Commission it would be ho-hum. But if a lawyer newly appointed to the commission resigned, it was news. A sure sign of smoke, begging the question, where was the fire.

Now what to do with my new client. I was sure she had a claim under the Federal or New Jersey Fraudulent Claims Act. If she found a fraudulent situation where someone was ripping off the federal or state government, the ripper would owe the government involved triple the amount of damage incurred plus attorney's fee. I like the ring of that "plus." She would collect somewhere between 15% and 25% of the amount collected. This was called a Qui Tam action. Now we would have to start the action and give the state or federal government time to decide whether to take it on themselves or leave it to us. If the government took it on, we would have the advantage of having the full weight of the government behind us. They could discover things we couldn't – bank accounts, tax returns, insider criminal plea bargain deals, - lots. We would be outsiders going back and forth to court to force people to give up documents or answer questions. If the government took over, the court and any jury would be behind it.

My head buzzed with anticipated strategies as I walked the two blocks to the office. My client was waiting just outside with her baseball cap on. I took her inside, signed in at the desk, and went up to my office. We sat and I got out the ubiquitous legal pad to take down notes.

"So, who are you?"

"I'm Ernestine Hughes, I lived at 5946 Ogden Street in Philadelphia, Pennsylvania. I've worked seven years at the Delaware River Bridge Commission in the Economic Development section."

"I've seen your file. How did you get these materials?"

"It is part of my job to keep files on all these organizations we give grants to. They submit large questionnaires and financial statements. Most of the time, these are thrown in the file and forgotten since the politicians on the Commission have already approved them. But our section can always ask for more information from the applicant, and we can also have access to any other government filings in any other state government agency. Since we are not a federal agency, we cannot ask the other federal agencies. But we get payroll information, audits, and state income tax returns which usually contain federal returns."

"Well, I smelled a rat. I saw the Newberry children on the charter school payroll. I saw Ms. Newberry on the charter school payroll. I had proof they never worked there. They were ghost employees. This is a no-no. I dug a little further. I saw the landlord of the school was owned by the president of the school. This was something to look into, since it was a potential no-no. Sure enough, the building permits and the deeds show the school buildings cost about $800,000 while the school was paying $400,000 a year in rent. So the rent was used to siphon off profits of a supposedly non-profit to the President. As a result, the charter school filings were all totally false, as were their tax returns, as were their grant applications, and so were dozens of other grants they got as well. Newberry, his family and the President were ripping off what was supposed to be a non-profit and getting grants from the Commission."

"So these things in the file all come from public records to which the Commission was legally entitled?"

"Yes."

"No secret burglaries, no forged documents to obtain them."

"No, my boss signed all my request for documentation."

"So why didn't you tell your boss about this?"

"I did, but he said this was all political and not to rock the boat."
"Did he warn you about pursuing this?"

"Not really. You see all of us in the Commission are all appointed or recommended by some politician who is like our godfather. My politician is an African-American ward leader who is buddies with my pastor. Most of the rest of the Commission employees are white. So no one touches the black employees and no one goes against the black ward leaders. Besides I have a good work record."

"So you're like in West Philadelphia. Do you commute every day?" "I take the El and the PATCO to Camden." It was sizing up to be a federal lawsuit I could bring in Pennsylvania. The best of luck. If I brought it in the New Jersey state courts the New Jersey politicians could take over the case and whitewash the deal with the blessing of a New Jersey judge. Federal judges are not usually very political and, in Philadelphia, not disposed to let a New Jersey miscreant off easy. I was already drafting the complaint to start the action in my head.

"Now, Ms. Hughes."

"Ernie."

"OK, Ernie. If I bring suit on your behalf, your name will come out. You may be fired. But you have two protections. One, the government, if it or we win the case, gets treble damages. Three times the amount of the fraud. You get 15% to 25% of that. Two, if you are fired and it turns out you had a good case, you get back double your lost salary. And in all cases, you get your attorney's fee if you win."

"So I might have to get another job until the case is over?"

"That's a possibility."

"On the other hand, I can just drop this file off with the FBI and let them take it. Your name would probably never pop up although your name on some of the correspondence may but, most often, the FBI will protect your identify. So you have to decide: Whistleblower with good financial payoff with a risk of being fired, or a confidential informant. You need to think this over."

"No, I don't, Mr. Stern. God guides my steps. I am ready to go forward. I want you to represent me and start suit."

"Alright. Two things. First, I will handle this on a contingency fee basis. That means you don't pay me anything unless you win. If you win something, I get one third of what you get. And that will not include any back salary you would be owed."

"One third. That's fine. I'll be more than happy with anything you get."

"Can you get a job if you are fired?"

"No problem. My old firm will always take me back. I'm a good legal secretary."

"In that case, you have little risk. Now, about Mr. Horton. What happened between you two?"

"I offered him the file same as you, but he said he was thinking about it."

"Did he tell you about the money for you as a whistleblower?"

"No. He never told me anything like you just did."

"What was he going to do with the file?"

"I don't know. He was sitting on it for a month before he died."

"Do you think he told anyone?"

"Not that I know of, for sure. I was getting some looks around the Commission. But that was it, 'looks.'"

"Alright, Ernie. I'll prepare a contingency fee agreement, and a complaint to be filed in court. At some time, I'll have to tell the Attorney General of New Jersey, and of federal government. Then your name will come out."

"Let's do it, Mr. Stern." We shook hands. I could tell her hand was shaking. She was nervous. She put the baseball cap back on. An interesting end to the day.

Meeting with Alicia

I had to call Alicia. This file on Newberry et al. was way too hot. She had given it to me and I now had to make a choice between representing Ernestine, or keeping this political job which she had so freely given me. Either was an enormous gift. But did I really intend to stand by while she concocted a forged Will which even though it named the true heirs of Harry, was nonetheless a fraud in the courts. As a lawyer, I was always presented with these difficult moral or philosophical choices. In other jobs, you often have clean, easy choices. Does a doctor provide healthcare to a suffering criminal? Of course, he has sworn to do no harm. His punishment is a question for another element of society. My choices each bore some justification. I had not made up my mind yet. To be fair there was no proof of anything yet. Sometimes the best move is to do nothing, something may happen. So I felt I had to meet with Alicia. Again, we met at the coffee shop around the corner from her office.

As usual, this tall elegant woman drew stares as she strode into the shop and greeted the waitress as Tess. The prototype waitress – the middle aged somewhat plump woman with a motherly air of nurturing about her – was long gone. Tess was a goth. Tall and skinny, black hair with bangs, tattoos up and down both arms, and a provocative hitch to her hips as she stood to take an order. I ordered coffee with cream. This drew an exasperated look from Tess as she looked at Alicia. Apparently this was no longer available in a coffee shop. Alicia interceded, "He'll have an Ethiopian, with steamed milk." Tess looked relieved and turned to fill the order.

"Ethiopian?"

"You'll love it. It's strong but has hints of chocolate. So you've been busy."

"I guess so. That file was dynamite. Did you ever meet the whistleblower?"

"No. Harry gave me a copy of the file in case anything happened to him."

"Do you think the file may have been the cause of his death?"

"Good question. It does roast a few important people. Sorry for the expression."

"This complicates my situation. I mean if I represent the whistleblower, I can't stay on the Commission board. It's a conflict of interest."

"Do you have to be her lawyer?"

"I have knowledge now I can't unknow which is against the Commission. So if I stay on and just keep quiet I might have to take action to protect the Commission."

"I get that."

"So I had to talk to you. I'm grateful for the appointment and the file. But I can't keep both. I didn't want to make you think I was acting contrary to what you may have wanted politically."

"Oh. That. No problem. My people are all Pennsylvania. This file only incriminates the politicians from New Jersey. As far as we're concerned, do your worst on them. No skin off our nose."

"But will you be embarrassed by my resignation from the board so soon after my appointment?"

"Look, we appointed a guy with a reputation as a tough anticorruption independent. For us, that was all good. So if you do what you have to do, God bless you. Another opportunity for an appointment to pay off some political debts. Handing out a plum job is always good for the Party."

"Now, sometime else. I'm not sure I can support your idea to create a copy of the Will. It's basically a fraud."

"But if it brings about the right result?"

"To me it's a fraud. Let me suggest you give us some more time looking. Maybe something will turn up."

"I can wait. But $2 million is $2 million, even for a hard working girl like me."

"Thanks for that. I'll keep you posted." We shook hands and I left the coffee shop.

As I reached the corner of the block where my office was, a rough looking guy started to keep pace with me. He was wearing a Pittsburgh Steelers jacket, a black baseball hat and loose jeans. His keeping pace was beginning to be irritating. I stopped and tried to go a different direction. He blocked my way. He was only about 5' 10" but a good 240. He was a bit swarthy and had a tattoo of some kind on his neck. But here I was in public, in a suit, in the middle of the business district, what was he thinking?

Looking me in the eye, he said, "Back off." What did that mean? Back off what? So I coolly chose the brilliant retort.

"Back off what?"

"We mean business!"

"Who are you? What do you want?" He just turned and walked away. I had just been threatened. The adrenaline was pumping through my system and my heart rate was up. Who was this guy? Was he talking about the Horton homicide investigation? Or the Newberry file? I was threatening someone somehow. Was this what got Harry killed, if he was killed? The Ethiopian coffee did not help me calm down. So I took a walk around the office building and then took the elevator back to my office. What was going on? This puzzlement energized me to start the paperwork for Ernestine's False Claim lawsuit.

At this point, I did not have to reveal her name. The State of New Jersey and the federal government each would have the right to take away the lawsuit. The sooner I started that process in motion the better. As I started sketching out the scope of the lawsuit, ideas came to me. I certainly could use more information on all the "economic development" projects and their recipients. It dawned on me that Alicia was as powerful as anyone, so I would submit a list of documents and questions to her. With the stamp of her boss, the governor, she could get some staffer to begin collecting all the data. I wanted to know all the recipients, as well as their employees, their salaries, their contractors, everyone they did business with. I was sure there would be more of these recipients with ghost employees, false payments to contractors, conflicts of interest. If Newberry could do it, anyone could. So I had a long letter typed up for Alicia. I couldn't risk an Email.

But then the question of who was threatening me. Who knew what? Honey certainly knew I was questioning the death of Harry. Honey had some ugly associates in this Vargas character. I would not be surprised that this guy in the Pittsburgh Steelers jacket was one of his. I mean who wears a Steelers jacket in Philadelphia – an idiot or a very tough guy.

And Newberry. This file was dynamite. It would implicate far more than he and expose a lot of the slimy stuff under the rock of New Jersey politics. But to threaten a lawyer. I mean we are just paper pushers with file backups on our computers. What was I to guess? They were too stupid to know that an attack on me would focus my interest in my investigation. OK, wait and see. Oh and back up my files. Memo to file about the Steelers guy with full description. I had a long talk with Carmen – my diminutive Latina pit bull – and laid out the case for her. Angelina was enjoying every page of the paperwork she was preparing. I could hear her chuckling as each juicy tidbit was typed onto the page. Surprisingly, when I am wound up, the words flow more easily. Ernestine's file was falling neatly into a compact package for a complaint. I left for lunch with the last few pages on Angelina's desk.

Honey to Hospital

The dilemma Alicia had put me in caused me a great deal of pain. On different levels of thought I was reaching different conclusions. As a lawyer, the falsification of evidence went against everything I had held dear in my profession. A strong point in the structure of law was the faith people had in the reliability of our ability to discover the truth. On the other hand, the Bible often had worked ultimate justice in many strange ways. The choice of who should receive the inheritance was between Alicia and Honey who not only did not deserve it but was not Harry's intended choice; Alicia was.

I explained all this behind closed doors to Digby, who sat quietly listening, peering over his reading glasses as I alternately sat or paced the floor in his office. When I finished, I looked at him. He had been trained to be a good listener as any lawyer should be listening for that one false note, that one fact that might reveal the meaning.

"At this point, you don't know if Honey stole the original copy. It might simply be mislaid, or Harry may have revoked it or destroyed it himself."

"True enough."

"So you could be supporting false testimony by your inaction. You have knowledge of the possible act of forgery in the future for now. Yet it has not occurred."

"True."

"So my advice is to do nothing for the time being. If you are expecting divine intervention, maybe it will come, maybe not. We never know. Patience is a virtue."

As always, a few minutes with Digby was enough to calm me down and get me thinking clearly. So I went back to my office and buried myself in the mounds of paper and telephone messages. I lost my sense of time. Fortunately, Angelina had not and ordered a corned beef special with a Dr. Brown's black cherry soda by about 2:00 p.m. I went into the lunchroom and sat eating and reading at the same time. Hopefully what I was reading would not disturb my digestion, but mostly it did. After finishing lunch, and tidying the lunchroom, I went back to my office to find a curious phone message. "Call Penn Hosp., re: Horton." I called and was directed to a floor nurse.

"Mr. Stern. Ms. Horton has been asking for you. She was brought in this morning."

"What's the matter?"

"I'll leave her to tell you. She wants to see you as soon as possible. Room 465 at Penn Hospital."

"Of course, thank you." Penn was not much of a walk from the office so I strolled down there after 5:30 p.m. What could this be about? I checked in on the fourth floor, was on Honey's visiting list and walked back to 465."

As I walked in, I saw Honey in bed with a number of tubes sticking out of her and a wan smile on her face. "Ah, Peter, good you could come."

"My goodness, Honey, what's happened?"

"I had a kidney transplant some time ago and my body's trying to reject it. It's a frequent problem I'm told and the doctors think I'll be OK, but I'm still worried."

"I am too, Honey. How do you feel?"

"A bit weak and drowsy. I had this opioid pump I can push to give me something. But I've had problems with drugs and I don't want to end up an addict."

"Is there anything I can do?"

"I have good insurance, but I may need an advance from the estate to cover the excess, I don't know. But if anything happens to me, and I die, who gets the estate?"

"If we don't find the original, and you are the only intestate heir, it might go to the State of Pennsylvania. It's called in escheat. I'll look it up to be sure."

"Suppose I live long enough to inherit, but die later."

"That depends on whether you have a Will. Then it's whoever you say." "So I need a Will."

"Everyone should have one. But, we didn't know you had a kidney problem."

"Well, I've been reckless with my life. I think I have been too rough on my kidneys. I was on dialysis for a while, but I couldn't get a donor for a kidney. As a single women with no dependents I'm pretty far down the list. So I went to Cuba and got one. My insurance didn't cover Cuba so Scarramazza put up the money. I owe the casino a ton anyway, and, if I die, they don't get anything."

"So that's why you were in Cuba?"

"Yes. The mob uses Cuba for a lot of medical stuff and it's cheap."

"So they got you a kidney in Cuba."

"Yup. But now it's giving me problems."

"I hope everything works out."

"The doctors tell me it's no biggie, but I wanted to let you know. You can't do a Will for me?"

"I'll ask the office. I think it might be a conflict of interest but I'll see." "How did you like Jean?"

"Jean? Oh she was great… But I've got to ask, was I supposed to… uh… sleep with her?"

"Oh, deary. That was up to her. It always is. So you didn't do it."

"No."

"Well, look, if the original turns up and the murder investigation is over, I'll see to it you get a lifetime comp on me."

"Can you do that?"

"Well, I may owe the casino plenty now, but I know a lot too. So we get along. See?"

"Oh, I got it. So a lifetime comp, but the sex is on me."

"We never interfere in the arrangements the girls make. Only the introductions."

"I see. OK, Honey, let me see if we can do your Will. I'll check in on the murder investigation for you."

"That would be great." I could see her taking a pump of opioid as her eyes closed and she drifted off.

Curiouser and curiouser. So Honey got a kidney transplant while she was in Cuba. That explained her whereabouts at the time of Harry's death. I had to check this alibi out. I would lose out on a lifetime comp at the casinos but I would be making myself more secure in what my job was.

The next day I called Hackett. Of course he wasn't in and didn't answer his cell, so I called the local police in the Poconos. I asked them to check the airline's information about Honey's back and forth to Cuba. This had to go through the FBI, but they'd get back to me.

I also knew we could not take Honey on as a Will client as long as we possibly represented the Estate of Harry Horton. So I knew that was a dead end.

Attorney General Meets with Stern

I had not expected much from the Horton Estate until we found the lost original Will. At this point we were in a state of limbo along possibly with poor Honey. With no Will, there was an intestacy which meant the State of Pennsylvania law applied. In order of distribution, there were first, the spouse, of which there was none, the children of which there appeared to be none, then the siblings of which there was one. However, if there was no Will, our firm was not to be the executor. So we then had no standing to do anything. Without a Will, the heir – probably the sister would become the Administratrix and we would be out, and she would get the entire estate after taxes. So our firm invested in a reputable firm of detectives to find the Will. I gave Howard Cassini, the head of the detective firm all of my notes and interviews and sent him on his way. Of course, we still had a copy of the original, which while not proof of actual Will admissible in court, still good evidence of Harry Horton's intent. Our firm kept this copy's contents secret as so not to prejudice the investigation. And so things sat. The proof of whether Harry had died by something other than an accidental death was contrary to our interests as a firm so I was no longer pursuing that issue. Of course, Carmen was disappointed – as a good bloodhound, little Carmen had a decent scent of murder and did not like to be denied the opportunity to prove it. But Digby ruled. No more time or money to be spent on a cause that was contrary to the interest of our possible client – the Estate. So we went on to other things.

And then, the receptionist rang on my office phone. "Some men are here to see you. They say they are from the Attorney General's Office." I met them in the small conference room.

"Joe Hackett, sir, Deputy Attorney General; here is my card." Sure enough, looked official.

"Harlan Jones, Mr. Stern, special agent for the A.G." Another card and a flashed badge.

"What can I do for you, gentlemen?"

Joe Hackett was a rather unkempt man in his sixties in a rumpled ill-fitting polyester suit of some kind of blackish brownish hue, with a light green shirt, and an orange tie. I was guessing a retired former District Attorney from one of the rural counties working on a second career job and a second pension. His card had Esq. after his name.

Harlan Jones was a trim black man also in his sixties. He was nicely dressed in a trim blue suit with a dazzling white shirt and a striped tie.

So, what we called a salt and pepper team.

Jones spoke first. "Mr. Stern, I am a former homicide detective with the Philadelphia Police Department. We have been asked to look into the death of Harry Horton."

"Ah. I see. How did this happen?"

"As you certainly guessed, once the insurance carrier realized it was a double indemnity accidental death policy, they were not happy to pay out an extra million dollars. So they insisted the Attorney General take over the investigation."

"Got it. Makes good sense."

"We know you and Ms. Jacinto had been doing some investigation and we would like your notes and interviews."

"I see. Do I have some attorney-client privilege on these notes?"

Hackett spoke up, "We have done the research. First, this was not a communication between you and a client. Secondly, you don't have a client until you find the original Will. So may we see your file or do we need a warrant."

"May I speak to our estates lawyer about this, briefly?"

"We don't have much time. Please make it quick or we will come back with a warrant." Hackett was not a pleasant man. He was obviously used to being a political appointee and never felt the need for manners.

I immediately left the conference room and rounded up Roger Humphries and went to Digby's office. I explained the situation to both. There was no actual evidence of a crime we were withholding, it was true we did not yet have a client except possibly Harry Horton who, if asked, would be interested in the circumstance of his death. All we had were some interviews and a few speculations by me and Carmen. Something the Attorney General's men could get if they traced our footsteps. OK, what the hell, let them have the file and find out if Harry was murdered.

I returned to find the two A.G.'s men drinking our coffee with our office manager, chatting politely with them. Carmen had also been summoned to the conference room and had the file in hand.

"OK, gentlemen, here is our file. You may watch while Ms. Jacinto runs off a copy for you." That seemed to satisfy them so Mr. Jones followed Ms. Jacinto out of the room to the copier.

"OK, Stern, what do you now and what do you think?" This Hackett was a jerk and getting on my nerves. I didn't like being addressed as Stern by this rumpled clown.

"Isn't that for you to determine? Why do you want my input? I was just collecting evidence which you will now have. You would be following in our footsteps anyway."

"Are you obstructing justice?" This was a bit much. What I thought was not evidence, it was merely attorney work product – which by the way had not been paid for, and an attorney's speculation. If I may say so, by an attorney who was several notches above this troll. He wanted to pick my brain to make himself look better.

"No. I just thought I should not prejudice your own thought process."

"OK, we'll do it this way." Apparently the country bumpkins he had questioned got intimidated by this tactic, I did not. "Was Horton gay?"

"We thought not. Just a very neat guy who was not interested in sex."

"Did you find any possible evidence of murder?"

"I think you have seen that we asked for a blood analysis because we found two pin pricks on Mr. Horton's arm. We don't know if he was a user, or what."

"Where did you ask for the blood test?"

"You mean you haven't read the local police file or the coroner's record?"

"Not yet."

"So you started with me?"

"Yes. You seemed more professional. What else did you note in your records."

"Mr. Horton's shoes did not show any marks that he had been dragged. No scuff marks on his heels or accumulated dust."

"What does that mean?"

"Look, Mr. Hackett, have you ever done a homicide investigation before?" At this, he sat upright and glared at me.

"I was the elected D.A. of Cardinal County for 12 years. I have seen a thing or two."

"Well, it means Horton if he was killed, was carried and not dragged to the spot where he was found. Otherwise his heels would be scuffed."

"Now, I see that Ms. Jacinto has a juvenile record."

"Those records are supposed to be sealed after she reaches her majority. And what does that mean anyway? The case was dropped."

"We'll keep an eye on her."

"That was 10 years ago. She has a degree as a paralegal now."

"Even so, she was arrested."

"She also helped convict a number of people."

"Even so."

"You know, Mr. Hackett, you can take the file and leave. Draw your own conclusions. Don't ask for my help." By this time, Harlan Jones had the file under his arm, and he and Hackett got up to leave.

I had a bad feeling about this. The insurance carrier had a loose cannon on deck. I felt the need to alert them. The law was my profession and I had a high regard for the facts. This Hackett, the political hack, had been sent out to find murder by the insurance carrier and he was going to do that willy nilly. I called the insurance men we met earlier.

"Mr. Pollack, can we talk?"

"Of course, Mr. Stern. What's on your mind?"

"I just met this Deputy A.G. Hackett. I have a very low opinion of him. I believe he has been sent to find murder, over accidental death. If he makes faulty findings, he could put you in expensive litigation for years. You need someone who can get you a solid factual basis for any conclusion."

"I can see that, Mr. Stern. What do you suggest?"

"Hire a good ex-homicide detective and let him consult on the investigation. If you already have the clout to get the A.G. involved, you can get this Hackett to consult with a knowledgable outside guy."

"Good idea, Mr. Stern. We'll look into this. Any suggestions?"

"Well, Mr. Pollack. I want to stay as far away from this as possible. If we represent the Estate and if we help prove murder, we could be sued for malpractice. I just want to have a strong evidentiary basis by a professional to support your conclusions, and so do you."

"I see. Yes. I can see your point. Thank you for your time, Mr. Stern." Wonderful, I didn't have a client and here I was giving out free advice. Somewhere the God of Lawyer's Hourly Billing was aghast.

As I came down the hallway to my condo, I saw what looked like an odd lump just outside my door. Someone in a black raincoat was lying stretched across my threshold with their head or something that looked like a gym bag. I approached somewhat timidly and could see the feet with brightly colored women's sneaks, then a pair of striped tights. I tapped the person lightly on the shoulder and a woman slowly sat up. She had on a baseball cap and sun glasses.

"Oh, Peter. It's you," she said taking off the cap and touching her hair – black and shiny. It was Jean – asleep on my doorstep.

"Jean, what are you doing here?"

"I drove up from Florida all last night and today." She removed her sunglasses. An awful black eye and a bruise on her right cheekbone.

"My god, Jean. What happened?"

As she stood up, I could see her start to tremble and tears fell down her face. I took her in my arms and held her as she shuddered and cried. I opened the door to my apartment and maneuvered her in.

"Ew… Ew… that hurts." I was hugging her around the rib cage. She had some kind of injury there.

"What happened?"

"Scuzzy." More tears, more shivers. "What had he done?"

"He beat me up." This beautiful creature, someone had used force on her.

"How did this happen?"

"He gets jealous every once in a while."

"Was he your boyfriend?"

"He thought so, but I never did."

"So he beat you."

"He didn't like my trip to Philadelphia with Honey."

"Oh, I see. So he beat you up. Where do you hurt?"

"All over. My ribs, my butt, my cheekbone."

"Anything serious. Do you need a doctor?"

"No, no, it's just humiliating. I had to run. You were the only person I thought of who could protect me."

"Sure, sure. What do you need?"

"Some aspirin and a place to spend the night."

"Sure." I went to get some aspirin and a glass of water. She gulped it down and flopped on the couch. She had her gym clothes on.

"Do you mind if I just fade off for a few hours? I left Miami last night and drove all the way through."

"Do you want something to eat?"

"Maybe a bowl of cereal. My stomach feels a bit off."

"Got it." We went into the kitchen area, she had a bowl of Cheerios and a glass of orange juice.

"Do you mind if I sleep for a bit?"

"Of course, Jean. Take my bed" I hate to say my bed was not made, but she almost staggered into the bedroom and fell on the covers. I pulled the shades and turned off the light. By the time I left, I could hear polite feminine snores as she lay face down on the pillow. I brought her gym bag in and put it near the bed. I had some lasagna left over from the night before, I heated some up and ate on the kitchen counter. Something had caused this beautiful creature to be wounded and land on my doorstep. Who beats up women? I turned on the Phillies game in the living room and watched. The game was just not interesting enough to absorb my full attention. Like most lawyers, I went through my cases in my head, and came back again and again to Harry Horton and his Will. So far nothing had broken. No facts I overlooked jumped out. But it certainly was exciting. I would hear in a few days if the State of New Jersey or the feds would take over the Newberry fraud case. Somehow it had leaked out and I got some nice press coverage. And now, Jean. When the last Phillie had failed to come through with a man in scoring position, I peaked in on Jean. She had rolled under the covers and had her back to me now. OK, let her sleep. I rolled out the sofa bed, made it up and discretely put on my own gym clothes and turned out the lights.

I awoke to some sounds in the kitchen. The light was coming through the blinds. Jean was cooking something. She had on my robe and her hair was wet. She turned as she heard me stir.

"Peter, I remember you like them over light, right?"

I got up and came over. "Yeah, Jean, over light."

"And white toast. I found some Jimmy Dean sausage."

I poured myself some coffee and sat at the counter.

"So how do you feel today?"

"Bruised and embarrassed."

"OK, the usual. What are you going to do?"

"Hide out for a while. Scuzzo will have his thugs looking for me.

I'm never going back to Miami. I know that. I have to transfer my college credits and get my degree. No more casinos. I got that so far."

"I guess Temple and Drexel would be good for you if you want to stay here."

"That would work. "She turned. She did not have her sunglasses on and her eye and cheek were badly bruised. She held her left arm stiffly at her side. I guessed she had some serious pain in her side. She wasn't very big, but she was young and athletic. How had she gotten into this? I know I'm supposed to listen at times like this, but my lawyer-sense to collect facts was churning. But I had to be quiet for now.

She brought the plates for breakfast to the counter. She had rummaged through my drawers and had on a tee shirt and shorts under my robe. Even with the black eye and swollen cheek, she was beautiful. Her long shiny black hair hung in curly waves, her bright blue eyes in the pale face, and now, a smile. I guess most of the storm had passed. We ate and I waited for her explanation.

She was just staring off into space as the words started to flow. "Why do I feel guilty? I guess I let it happen. I mean I was supposed to be his favorite. He'd hit me before, but then he made it up to me. I was in some sick situation where I expected it… Not this time… I need help… I am sick. I can't let this happen." More staring into space, then she turned to me. "You know Honey was his favorite years before. He beat her, too. But she was into booze and drugs. When she got older, he made her the den mother of us… Kind of the mother superior. We kept the big rollers happy, she got taken care of and she took care of us. I was recruited off the UNLV campus and later sent to the Miami Casino. I made good money. Got lots of benefits… Trips, modeling assignments. Most of the girls got into drugs. I knew that was a dead end. I mean dead. Some are already dead. I got an education. But I got to get this beat-up thing out of my head."

"You know Scuzzy paid for Honey's operation and picked up her gambling debts. Now he owns her."

"So what operation?"

"Honey went to Cuba for an operation. She'd been on dialysis for years. He paid to get her a new kidney in Cuba."

"Where'd they get the kidney?"

"Who knows, this is Cuba, right? No medical insurance, no records."

"So Scuzz took care of it?"

"Yup. Sent Vitez along as a bodyguard."

"Yeah, now man what is this Vitez?"

"You know, enforcer, thug, body guard, sheep-dog. He keeps the herd in line."

"What does he do with you?"

"He follows me around. Makes sure I don't run off with rich guys." "Does he hit you?"

"Vitez. No. He just reports to Scuzz. Scuzz hits me."

"So did he tail you here in Philadelphia with me?"

"Of course. But we lost him when we went to the Art Museum. Remember?"

"Oh yeah. So that was Vitez we lost?"

"Yes. And he reported us back to Scuzz and Suzz didn't like it. So he beat me up."

"Because of me?"

"Well yeah. You're a threat. You're not some rich whale with a wife back home who couldn't get a girl on his own. You're young, good looking and independent. So you threaten him."

"So why did Honey set me up with you?"

"Partly to get you on her side in this Will thing, partly to piss off Scuzz. She has this love/hate thing with him. She's mad he dumped her years ago, but grateful for all he does for her. But he owns her, her gambling debts, her shrink bills, and her habit."

"Ooo! That's ugly."

"She sent me to you to piss him off. You were a nice straight guy with a job and single."

"I see. I'm too eligible."

"He didn't like that. That's why Honey stayed in Philadelphia."

"So now, what do you do? What about your apartment, your clothes, your college credits?"

"Well, my apartment was paid for by Scuzz. No. I never paid rent. My clothes. I can replace them. My money. I was always careful to stash it somewhere they didn't know about. My credits should transfer. So I'm a free agent."

"So what do you want to do, right now?"

"Hide out from Scuzz. Apply to transfer my credits. And buy some clothes."

"It looks like you've thought this out."

"Driving 20 hours from Florida with a black eye and bruises all over will do that."

"So what do you want to do first?"

"Get a temporary place to live. Off the grid. Then buy some clothes. I saw a bunch of stores on Walnut Street before. So figure out a temporary spot for me to crash for a few days while I check out the college curriculums here."

"You want to stay in Philadelphia?"

"That would be nice."

"Do you have enough money?"

"Oh yes. I've stashed plenty over the last few years."

"He'll check your credit cards."

"Oh I know that. I've already put them away. I'll be in cash for a while."

"Good so far. I was just thinking. Harry Horton's place in the Poconos is vacant. It's up for sale. It might be good for you to house sit for a while."

"Is it nice?"

"Harry was an impeccable housekeeper. Just keep it nice so it shows well for the realtor."

"How far is it from Philadelphia?"

"About an hour and a half."

"Sounds good. I'll check it out."

"I've got a duplicate key. The place is in a community. It has small lakes for swimming. You can check out the area."

"At least 'til l my black eye heals. I'll check out college online."

"By the way, will Scuzz come after me?"

"Maybe. Ask Honey. Better yet don't say anything to Honey. She may tell Scuzz where I am."

"Look. Is Scuzz with Cosa Nostra."

"No… No… The casinos are very close to the mob but not in it. I mean they launder money, provide hookers, lots of things. Not here. Just cooperate in business."

"Is the mob after you now"

"No. They wouldn't bother the mob for something like this. Scuzz would be a laughingstock."

"No, Scuzz has his own thugs."

"Someone came after me the other day and said "Backoff." I don't know what he meant. He was about my height, wore a Steelers jacket, maybe in his mid 40s."

"No. Scuzz wouldn't have known about me yet. It was someone else. What kind of trouble are you in?"

"Must be something else. Well, look, stay as long as you like, here's a key, bring some clothes."

"What do you want for dinner?"

"I'm not fancy. Anything."

"I grew up as the daughter of two hippies on a marijuana farm in Mendocino. I cook plain Jane."

"Sounds good. I'll see you tonight then."

"See you then." I got dressed and went into the office.

Leaving Jean in Condo

I got dressed and left for the office. After a bit of neglect, a number of routine matters had begun to pile up. Angelina could handle many of them, but a large stack of files and phone messages greeted me.

Mrs. Hockfleisch wanted her Will redone, and just had to come into the office to explain at length why. Mainly she wanted to have me listen to her complain about her children. I made sure the appointment was scheduled in the morning because she usually became incoherent on several Rob Roys at lunch. She as usual wanted to dangle her wealth in front of her children and servants by adjusting her estate. Ms. Lovejoy called several times because her ex was not paying child support and alimony in a timely manner and was arriving late to pick up their children on visitation day. Morton Flyth was continuing to steal customers from his old company, my client, and when was the hearing for a temporary injunction to stop this. Joel Tidmeyer had been put in jail once again because his ankle monitor went off when all he did was step outside for a smoke.

This list went on and I plowed through it. I got a call from the FBI because they wanted to discuss the Newberry matter with me. I set up a time the next day. Mr. Hackett, the Assistant Attorney General investigating Harry Horton's death had still not returned my three telephone calls, but Mr. Hinton, the local DA in Carbon County was mailing me a duplicate CD showing Honey Horton boarding the planes to and from Cuba. Honey called from the hospital to say her emergency admission was coming to an end and would be back in

Harry's condo soon and, by the way, had I heard anything from Jean. She wanted to speak to her. I had the usual corned beef special and Dr. Brown's black cherry soda for lunch. Mr. Gioconda, Harry Horton's co-owner called – no emergency, but when could he transfer the stock. Slowly the day wore on and it was time to go home.

I got to my condo and could smell good things in the kitchen. Jean chirped that dinner was almost ready, did I want a drink?

I'm not a big drinker, so no! But she already had a glass of wine poured for me, so we sat. She described her shopping spree – all new clothes. She had on her gym clothes – tights, a tank top, sneaks. She went to my gym and did her regular routine. She looked great even with her hair in a kerchief. I gave her the keys to Harry's place in the mountains. She said she saw little evidence of a woman around. Was I divorced? Yes, several years ago. I had one delightful daughter age seven. The divorce was my fault – too much time in the office, not enough at home. My ex had remarried and was happy – she was even civil to me now. I asked her about Honey. Yes, she had bad kidneys, had been in dialysis and, she thought, went to Cuba for a transplant all paid for by Scuzz who used to be her ex – never married. Scuzz still liked her, but was a control-freak. Yes, Scuzz tried to control her too.

The makeup hid her eyes bruises, and she said the Advil made her "hurts" all better. I asked her about her parents. They still talked, but mostly they were lost in the same, hippy, pot euphoria as before. So, no, they were not too helpful. She got up to get out the dinner.

She did make some roast chicken with what I could smell was a little garlic, some small potatoes, and a nice salad. She must have been out shopping because I had the usual bachelor kitchen with none of the above ingredients. She told me she also had stocked the refrigerator (apparently after cleaning and defrosting it).

"Where did you learn to do all this, Jean?"

"I told you. Since I was 12 I usually got dinner for us. My mother was Italian, so she taught me how to cook, and clean and all, and then she left it to me."

"Were you abused?"

"No. Far from it. My parents were always warm, but not very

attentive. I grew up by myself and watched the kids in school. I got good grades and stayed out of trouble. I was happy during high school, but the whole town grew dope and smoked it. I escaped somehow with a scholarship to UNLV. Honey found me there and recruited me."

"You mean you never did it with any whales?"

"Ah, the illusion. Honey made me keep the illusion, but I never did. Scuzz would have died if I had."

"So you never disassociated?"

"No. I'm pretty healthy. But how about you? You're what? Forty?"

"No, I'm 37, thank you very much. I just never had time for a relationship after my divorce."

"So you're practically a virgin again?"

"Very funny!"

"A nice straight guy like you. You are straight aren't you?"

"Yes. I'm not in the bar scene. I can't imagine an edate online. So I just don't have time to go on dates."

The conversation kind of trailed off then. We watched some TV and had some popcorn. I started to make up the sofa for bed, but she insisted it was her turn. I didn't fight it. I did like my bed much better. Besides, she wanted to catch a late movie and I wanted to go to sleep. I got up to leave and she came up and kissed me on the cheek. "Thanks, thanks for helping."

"And then it dawned on me. I had to act like a lawyer.

"Wait, Jean. I think you have to protect yourself from Scuzz."

"How do you mean?"

"You need to go to a doctor to document your injuries."

"Done!"

"No kidding, done, really."

"I may be stupid about Scuzz but I'm not naïve. I need evidence."
"How about photos of your bruises?"

"Done."

"You know you have a lawsuit against him. Possibly big bucks." "Oh, I know, but I don't want to think about that now. I don't want him to know where I am."

"You could get an order protecting you from abuse – we call it a PFA."

"Oh. I know. But he has ins with the cops. It wouldn't do much good."

"OK, have it your way." Another kiss on the cheek.

As I crawled under the covers, I wondered why I hadn't made a move on her. Was I being honorable? Don't take advantage when she's vulnerable. I didn't know. Maybe I was just stupid.

Anyway, Jean took the key to Harry's cabin in the Poconos and left the next day. My place already felt empty.

Call for Conference on Horton's Death

Late in the afternoon, I received a telephone call that Lt. Hinson, the detective in Carbon County wanted me to attend a conference on Horton's death. He said 9:00 a.m. on Thursday in his office. OK. Something might be stirring. But an odd request. Hinson was a backwoods detective with little homicide training. Last time we talked he was more interested in calling poor Harry's demise an accidental death, closing the file, leaving it at that and going deer hunting or fly fishing or whatever these guys in the sticks do. Then, somehow the insurance carrier didn't like the call because "accidental death" meant they paid out double for the insurance policy – an extra million or so. So they chewed on the butt of the Pennsylvania Attorney General to look into it. The AG sent Lt. Hackett in from Harrisburg, but Hackett was a lazy nasty sumbitch who could care less. He already had his pension from some local police department and was coasting on his AG salary for a second pension. But he at least knew a homicide investigation if it bit him in the ass.

The insurance carrier hired its own detective I hadn't met yet out of Jersey – a retired homicide guy who I was told had a good record. And me. They all knew me as the attorney for the estate, I was interested in an accidental death finding because the insurance payout doubled, which aided the heirs, and which, if the truth be known, increased our fee mightily. So why did they want me? Maybe because I did a nice job in the beginning getting some facts before I was touted off the case by my firm when we discovered our conflict. But they for some reason wanted me there. But at 9:00 a.m. about two hours drive from

Philadelphia, so an inconvenient time for me. Maybe even an insult. Hinson was local; Hackett got per diem and his hotel paid for so he could go up the night before. The detective from Jersey got expenses and his time paid for. Me. I was getting paid by no one. Or maybe, they didn't think of that. But, aha! I had a free place to stay – in Harry's cabin – unsold as yet, where Jean had been staying incognito, hiding from Scuzz. So I had little to complain about when I decided to stay at Harry's old place and see Jean. I didn't have Jean's new cell phone number. So I would have to drop in unannounced. My mind wandered for the next few hours to Jean.

Somewhere in high school, our personal view of ourselves starts forming. Who are we? At that time, the really pretty girls, the jocks, the cool guys seem to gravitate to the top of the heap. Others of us develop our life long insecurities – are we fat, nerdy, uncool? – whatever and we carry this image inside our heads. Of course this is false – all these shallow judgments. Smart nerdy guys get good jobs, nice suits, decent haircuts and have a few bucks to spend. Jocks and cool guys wonder where everything went. But I had to ask myself – how did I get this beautiful woman? And what goes on inside the heads of beautiful women? Do they think of their hair and nails all day? Or don't they think of themselves as just beauties and want something else? I had no idea.

I may have been one of those who lost out. I mean I was a reasonably successful lawyer, but I am divorced. It was probably my fault. When you are a young lawyer, the demands on your time are severe. Some judge wants you to be ready to try a big case on two day's notice. Some judge requires you to be on call all of August, so no vacation. Some client needs something done in two days that normally takes a month. Some emergency pops up. It is difficult to tell your wife you have to produce 2,000 billable hours a year or 60 – 70 hours a week before you make partner. She wants you to help raise the baby, she wants you home for dinner at 7:00, you just can't come home at 9:30 smelling of cigars and booze while you romance a client. She wants a social life, and you by her side at those times. No, the seven or so years spent making partner get carved out of a marriage. Mine didn't make it. So here I am making a decent buck, but a weekend dad paying child support. I still harbor some anger, but also some feelings for my ex, but that ship has sailed. She has remarried. My seven year old daughter is always happy to see me. But I have vestiges, not a real relationship.

Plus, I have some anxiety about Jean. Honey is really an opponent. If there is no Will found, Honey gets the whole estate. It is my job and that of our firm to find the Will we prepared and had Harry execute. The rule of law demands that we stand by our client – even if deceased. If Jean is kind of a bribe for me to downplay our search for a Will which would disinherit Honey, I am in an ethical dilemma. If I accept the gift, I have put myself in a conflict of interest of sorts. Not actually. I mean Jean is a free agent, Honey doesn't own her. But fraternization with the other side in a legal conflict rouses the specter of something inappropriate. Lawyers in a way are supposed to be like medieval knights with a code of conduct that requires us to protect our clients "zealously" and avoid even the appearance of conflicts of interest. Was Jean such a conflict? I was a fiduciary, a trusted person whose loyalty was owed to a deceased client and his will. We knew the executed Will existed, but could not find it. This question of my ethics may have been holding me back from Jean.

So I drove up to the Poconos for my meeting the next day, and knocked on the door of Harry's cabin. Jean came to the door in a tank top, Daisy Dukes and flip flops. The TV was on and she had been watching a baseball game. I didn't know God made women that watched baseball by themselves. As usual, even in casual dress, Jean looked great. Wavy black hair in a bun, that pale white skin and blue eyes and a long straight nose. Yes, beautiful.

"Hi Jean. I have a meeting tomorrow on Horton's case at nine so I thought I'd stay here tonight."

"That's great. I was a bit lonely and, as beautiful as these woods are, it's nice to hear a human voice."

I set my overnight bag in the spare bedroom, and changed into jeans and a pullover. "So, Jean, what would you like for dinner? There are a few decent spots around here."

"Are you sure? I mean there are good restaurants up here."

"Look, Peter, I'm not a fancy girl. I like it simple."

"OK, there's a take-out place not far. Do you like onions, oregano and oil?"

"However you Philly people eat it."

"OK, two Italian hoagies coming up." I moved to look at the TV to see which game she was watching. I put my hand on the small of her back, and she turned to face me. Suddenly out of the blue, some urge took over me. I pulled her to me and kissed her full on the lips, and held her there. Her lips were warm and soft, and somehow, I couldn't let go. A long deep kiss. Eventually, I pulled away and looked at here, somewhat embarrassed. Any hint of my ethics was long gone. Just busta move!

I… I…" was I trying to mumble out that I was sorry, embarrassed. That I'd broken some ethical canon by fraternizing with a gift from the opposing party.

"Boy," she grinned. "What took you so long?"

"I… I…"

"So you said. Boy! Third date I had to wait."

"Jean, it's… it's…"

"Yeah, I get it. I'm Honey's property and you can't touch me."

"Well, it's just…"

"Look, I'm my own person. Especially now that Scuzz has hit me once again. I don't owe a thing to him or Honey."

"How did you figure all this out?"

"Oh, Peter. You are such a goody-goody. I knew you were holding back."

"But why didn't you say something?"

"I don't do that. Guys always hit on me. They come on strong and try to impress me. I know they just want to bag a trophy. But I don't want that. Now, come here and do that again!" I did. What was I getting into? Oh, well. What the hell. Maybe it was time to take off the governor in my life and let things happen. I mean she definitely seemed to like me. At this point in movies, there is a fade to black. My mind had a fade to black. Next thing I knew we were driving to the local hoagie and pizza place, got a few to go with a few beers. We ate heartily and snuggled watching some dumb movie on cable. My overnight bag stayed in the spare room, I did not.

The next morning when I was awakened by the smell of coffee and bacon, I floated out of bed for my nine o'clock. I was still floating as I drove to Hinson's office for the meet with all the detectives. I slowly pulled my mind back into reality and went over the file and what I knew. As I pulled onto the driveway to the police station, I was fully engaged. Someone had put a pot of coffee in the conference room. I tried to sip as the other men trundled in. The coffee was just awful! What is it with cops that they can't make decent coffee? I heaped in some creamer to drown the taste and spread out my file.

"So, Stern, nice of you to come." Hackett by his snarky tone already seemed to be calling me out. I found he was from upstate Pennsylvania, had not had a distinguished record, but was securely in the back pocket of the local Republican boss who got him his AG job to serve out his years in restful peace. But why the attitude? Maybe just a dislike of lawyers. We are not friends of cops because it is our job to show them up in court, in public. But he didn't know me. Was something up?

"Yes. Hello. Mr. Stern." Mr. Hinson was at least glad to see me. "This is Joseph Sparano, a private detective hired by the insurance carrier." Sparano and I nodded. I already knew he had been hired and reviewed his résumé – a decent career as a detective in North Jersey, but not much homicide experience. He was a burly man with thick salt and pepper hair and a pleasant smile. I would have to reserve judgment on him.

So Hackett took charge of the meeting – laying out stacks of paper. He went through the crime scene photos, the autopsy and a few other things – most of which I had already seen. He concluded that it was probably an accidental death. Horton was about to barbecue a steak, he was negligent in pouring charcoal lighter fluid on the broiler, which created a big puff back fire which caused him to fall or jump back. He lost his balance, hit his head on his fall, spilled lighter fluid on himself which ignited. The lighter fluid burned through, his clothing and his torso, while he lay unconscious from the fall. So, basically no progress and no new information. He wanted to close the cae and move on. "Questions?" he said looking around the table. Silence at first.

Hearing nothing and hoping someone else would speak up, I waited a bit before plowing in.

"When was the time of death?" I turned to the coroner, who turned to the local doctor he hired."

"We figure he died about two days before he was found. So, we believe either late afternoon or evening on Tuesday, October 17."

"What was the state of lividity?" Lividity is the rate at which the blood flows to the lowest lying level in the body by force of gravity as a result of the heart no longer pumping.

"Uh, we didn't check that."

"Was the back of the body black and blue, or had the blood settled along the back, buttocks or the back of the legs?"

"It was mostly blue on his legs, not much of his back."

"Well, that would mean he was standing or sitting after he died, not on his back."

"It was hard to tell, he had been burned so badly."

"Uh-huh. How about where he hit his head? Was there blood around the wound?"

"Not much."

"So the blow to the back of the head may have been post-mortem, after death?"

"No, I wouldn't say that."

"Did he have any drugs in his system?"

"We found benadryl in his blood. Some, not much. You can see the lab report."

"Benadryl? Was he on any medication or prescription for that?"
"His doctor says no, but benadryl is over the counter."

"Did he have any allergies he might have taken it for?"

"We couldn't find any evidence of any."

"How about the pin prick in his left arm? Any drugs or medications around them?"

"Around what?"

"The pin pricks on his left arm."

"We didn't know about that. When did this come up?"

"When we were up here last time, we asked about the pin pricks."

"You did? We didn't hear about that."

"Did we check the Turnpike to see when his car went through the toll station?"

"Why would we do that?"

"That would tell us when he came up here. It may even show us if he had people in the car with him. I mean the turnpike is just five minutes from here. I'm sure he took the Northeast Extension. There might be a photo of the car going through."

"Now how about this whistleblower at the Delaware River Port Commission? He might have made a big enemy there."

"How do you know about that?"

"I was appointed in Harry's place to the Commission and got a file of his on this whistleblower. You read about it in the paper. This guy, Newberry, was ripping off the Commission. I'm sure he didn't like Harry if he knew about all the facts he had in his hands."

The men at the table were beginning to look tired and beaten. It was only a half hour. They had a whole list of new questions. If it was a murder, and Honey was involved, she couldn't inherit. If it was a murder, the insurance company saved big bucks. Here I was making it look like it might be a murder, and these men all must be asking themselves why is he making such a big deal when it's not to his benefit. Somehow annoying facts just kept getting in my way and I had to ask questions. I don't know why but I slid some copies of the CD they had made for them showing Honey getting on the plane to Cuba, followed by a guy carrying a cooler. I explained that Honey had told me she had gotten a kidney transplant. These trips back and forth to Cuba coincided with the time of Harry's death. Was that significant. On one hand, it gave her an alibi. On the other, maybe she could have murdered Harry for his estate.

So a jumble of facts, no resolution. We went through a variety of murder scenarios. Too many missing facts. Not enough evidence. This really bad coffee was now affecting my digestive system. We weren't getting anywhere. I suggested we parcel out the missing leads and run them down. Time was becoming a factor. We needed to lose the estate. The investigation was growing cold. So we decided to meet again in the near future with more evidence. I got in my car to go back south and gave Jean a call on the way. She was going on a nature walk at Bushkill Falls and sounded happy. I checked in at the office with Angelina, nothing much going on, so I drove comfortably south to Philly with a lot on my mind to think about. I had made a list of missing pieces of evidence at the conference and would have Carmen run them down. Then I would get to work on the whistleblower case. My mind returned to Jean and I floated again until the Turnpike exit at King of Prussia.

Vargas at the Office

I had much to catch up on at the office – stacks of phone messages, Emails, letters to dictate. It was about noon before I could stick my head out to catch Angelina up on things. Then the call from the FBI on the Newberry whistleblower matter. They wanted more time. Somehow, government always wanted more time but set difficult deadlines for us civilians. Yes, they wanted more time to review a meticulously prepared file by the informant. Of course, I could say no. It was our right. The statute gave them a very specific timeframe to take over the case. I could bring the suit myself without their help. Get in the newspapers. Set myself up for a very nice fee. But this was "the government." The FBI had access to resources I didn't – bank accounts, stock transactions, and they could get witnesses immunity or witness protection for informing on others. They had unlimited funds, and legions of lawyers, paralegals, lab technicians, detectives, forensic technicians, banks of computers, not to mention the heavy weight of credibility. But they took their own sweet time. I called my client, she said yes, so we agreed to another 30 days. When I was occasionally a criminal defense lawyer, it was always overwhelming to face the huge weight of the government and its resources against you. So we agreed, in the interest of justice to let the FBI have more time to decide whether it would take up the whistleblower case.

The rest of my daily practice details came and went. Late in the morning, I was talking on the phone with a distraught client when I heard a commotion out in the hallway, but the client needed some "client-whispering" to calm down and be reassured. The next thing I saw was Vargas – Scuzz' muscle – standing over my desk chair shouting, "Where is she?" I think I managed to get out a "Who?" I mean I know he meant Jean, but I was quickly running through my head whether I could plausibly deny whether I had seen her, or heard from her. The next thing I knew Vargas had launched himself at my throat and was trying to strangle me. His weight caused my desk chair to lurch over backwards so his weight was pinning me to the chair and the telephone to my mouth. He was shouting, "Where is she" into the phone and my distraught client. I was pinned and couldn't move when I heard Angelina say "Get off him!" I could hear a few blows hitting him and there he went limp – heavy – on top of me. Over his shoulder, I could see Angelina holding a bloody putter, giving him a few more whacks for good measure. By now, the rest of the firm had crowded into my office, and was helping to roll my desk chair over and lift Vargas off me. He was indeed out cold and head streaks of blood rolling down his back. My chair was finally righted. Some men were able to lift him off me. Angelina was receiving pats on the back, and "atta girls" from the assembled firm. My lip was bloody and swollen from where the receiver had struck my mouth in Vargas' first lunge. A number of men lifted Vargas, tied him in telephone cord, and carried him to the broom closet while 911 was dialed. Vargas was a weighty fellow, and now limp took several men to carry. He was bleeding profusely now on our expensive carpet. As they approached the broom closet, they avoided deftly the more expensive orientals and threw him in. Angelina's putter had been taken from my next door neighbor, Henry Warshowski – who occasionally practiced putting in his office. The putter was now bloody and bent. Henry was rather proud that his putter had been put to such good use and explained that "it was just his old White Odyssey. No harm." Angelia, all five feet and 105 pounds, was flexing her biceps to the cheers of the onlookers. I however was feeling rushes of adrenalin and was afraid I might throw up in front of everyone. I sat and put my head between my knees while gingerly feeling my split lip and taking some deep breaths. My hands were shaking so crossed them under my chest.

The cops and an EMT squad came up fairly soon and examined Vargas. It seemed Angelina had hit him pretty hard. The EMT people wheeled Vargas out and were taking him to a local hospital where he would be under police guard. As the cops asked around, it seemed Vargas and Scuzz had come in together. The receptionist said she saw Scuzz talking in a low voice to Vargas who then left in my direction. All this was on our closed circuit system. When the noise erupted, Scuzz had taken off. An APB was put out for Scuzz, especially at the airport for planes to Miami.

Slowly, calm returned to the office. I set my desk chair upright, and called back the distraught client and calmed her down. Then I sat back and took some more deep breaths to assess what had just happened. Angelina, now the hero of the day, stuck her head in, "So who was she?"

"I gave her a puzzled look, "She?"

"I know what's going on, you hound. You're doing some ballagulla's squeeze."

"No… No…" I stammered.

"Oh, I know the type, you hound. Don't mess with their women. I could have told you that."

I tried a sheepish grin, but Angelina had the hunting instincts of a wolf. She knew vaguely about Jean, and heard descriptions of Alicia Allende. She was also slightly proud of the fact that her boss was a bit of "a hound." She was also feeling very proud of her rescue with the bent putter blood, which the office would later take to be mounted on a plaque over her desk.

I went out of the office and called Jean on her new cell number and described the scene. She said she would send Angelina a basket of fruit. I could only wonder what she might send me and how it would be wrapped. When I asked about my reward, she told me I probably deserved it from past jealous boyfriends. At least, Scuzz didn't know where she was, nor apparently did Honey.

I was still feeling the adrenalin rush so I couldn't concentrate on doing more work. I just leaned back and looked out the window. Why was Scuzz so upset? Was it just Jean or was there more to it?

Scuzz in the Garage

My life was alternating now between moments of high intensity and calm – boring paperwork, long hand holding phone calls with clients, firm administrative meetings. Jean was still safely in Horton's cabin in the Poconos. A few buyers came by with agents, but it was the off season and there were few buyers. There was now a large escrow account in our firm from Horton's insurance payment without the double indemnity portion. We still had no idea where the original Will was, so it still looked like Honey as the only relative was the heir. The homicide investigation was quiet.

As in the Newberry matter, I was very concerned that the evidence might be growing cold or was being covered up. The feds had still not let me know if they were taking over the whistleblower suit.

I thought much about Jean. I had not been a particularly good husband before and was carrying some guilt about that. Could I handle a long term relationship or even the M word? She was undoubtedly gorgeous, a genuine head turner, and she definitely liked me. We spoke every day now. She was happy leading a quiet life in the Poconos. She had been accepted at Drexel and Temple for architecture studies leading to a degree in interior design. I guess she intended to be in Philadelphia for a while at least.

Vargas was out of the hospital and in the infirmary wing at the local prison – Holmesburg. His preliminary hearing about his assault on me had been postponed several times, but his bail was set at $500,000 so he wasn't going anywhere. Some associates of Scuzz had had a few meetings with him and he had a lawyer. Scuzz was still on the loose, but considered an accomplice of Vargas for the assault. Jean had not wanted to press separate changes for her injuries, but I was definitely expecting to see a full criminal trial for Vargas, and hopefully Scuzz.

So things were quiet for a while. I walked home and entered the building through the rear entrance through the parking garage and went to the basement elevators. In the dim light, I saw a figure standing just out of the reach of the overhead lights.

"Stern," I heard and turned. Out of the shadows, I could see a bulky Scuzz coming toward me. I didn't know if he had a gun or a knife so I faced him. I at least was curious about why he had Vargas attack me. He was already wanted as an accomplice for the Vargas attack. What did he want? It didn't take long to find out.

"Where is she?"

"Is that you, Scuzz? Who is she?"

"Don't play dumb, you punk, you know who I mean, Jean!"

"Why do you want her? I hear you beat her up and she ran away." "I have to find her. What has she told you? I have to know. I have to know now. And I'm going to find out." With that, he began pushing me on the shoulders and backing me up.

"Look, you're already wanted for Vargas' attack and this won't help." More violent shoves on the shoulders. His face was in my face now. Scuzz was a heavy set guy about middle age with a bit of a gut. He may have been a tough guy when he was younger, but now he was old and fat. Maybe one day, he had been someone's muscle. Maybe he thought he was intimidating me. I had not been in a fight since fourth grade. I mean I had played sports, football, baseball and I went to the gym regularly but I was brought up in the suburbs and knew nothing of street fights.

"Look Scuzz. I met her once. Had a date for dinner, that was it. She didn't tell me anything then or since. I know from Honey that you beat her up. She ran. That's all I know."

He was now grabbing me by the lapels of my jacket. "Don't give me that. I know she was interested in you. You'd be the one she'd run to. You're a lawyer, you can support her, and she wants to get married and settle down."

"She said all that."

"Yeah. Now where is she and what has she told you?"

"I'd like to help you out just to get rid of you. We had one date for dinner. We discussed personal things. She said she was a hostess for the whales at the casino. She said she was not sleeping with them, only entertaining them while they gambled. That was about it."

More pushing and shoving. I was no longer amused. He then reached back with a fist and seemed to want to hit me in the stomach. Suddenly, I saw red. I remembered my fight in the playground in fourth grade. I was the small kid dressed in nice clothes and the bully from the poor neighborhood was in my face. Same fear factor, same adrenalin pumped in. I blocked his punch with my left hand and swung at him with my right, catching him above the eye and drawing some blood. When I saw the blood, I lost it. I started swinging wildly both fists at whatever I saw, mostly the head, a few to the ribs. Then one I intended as an uppercut, was blocked and landed in a very soft gut. He let out an "ooph" and bent over. He backed up and charged at me like a bull, bent over head first. I do not know what possessed me, but I remembered a move I saw on Mixed Martial Arts. I put my hands on the back of his head and brought my knee up into his face. I think I got him squarely in the nose because he fell back and staggered against the wall. My adrenalin was now pumping and I rained blow after blow at his head. Blood was coming out of his nose, his eyebrows and almost everywhere. He fell to the ground. I jumped with a knee on his back, and kept him facing the ground while I hit him with both fists in the head – the rear of the head, and the face. By now he was lying still. I got off him and rolled him over. He had a gun holster at his hip. I grabbed the gun. He started to look up at me and groaned.

"So you like to beat up women, you coward!"

I was hot and out of control. I kicked him a few times in the balls and the ribs. "So tell me, do you like to beat up women?"

I got a few groans. "What do you think Jean told me?" More groans. A few more kicks to the balls. "What do you want Jean for?" More groans. A few kicks to the ribs. I wasn't proud of the extra damage, but to be honest, it did feel good.

I rolled him over and took off his belt. I bound him with it by the wrists and ankles, and called 911 anonymously.

"I got a hospital case. Basement of One Franklin House." I gave him a few more kicks. My nice suit jacket was a mess and now I had blood on the cuffs of my pants. I would phone the police later and tell them they could arrest Scuzz at the hospital.

I hid inside my car and watched out the window until the police and the ambulance showed up. In Center City, they were pretty diligent. Scuzz was pushed on a gurney to the ambulance within 15 minutes. I called Jean and told her Scuzz had attacked me and wanted to know where she was and what she hold told me.

I was curious about why he was so curious. What did Jean know that Scuzz was so interested in protecting? Why had he beat her up? Of course, some men just beat women up who give them a hard time. But somehow there was more to it than that. I left out the part about our fight, but told her Scuzz was in police custody. I could feel her starting to be nervous and beginning to cry on the phone. "I can't tell you yet."

"What can't you tell me?"

"It's something bad. I can't tell you yet." By now she was sobbing. What was this mystery? She was in no mood to be cross-examined so I let it ride for another day.

What did Jean know?

Conference with New Jersey Congressman

I hadn't heard anything about the New Jersey Commission matter with this Newberry guy. I had a whistleblower complaint prepared for some time now, and had been tinkering with it off and on to make it better and tighter with the mound of evidence I had been given. Normally when an attorney drafts a complaint, he wants to use the "bare bones" approach – just enough information to notify opposing counsel what the case is about and the issues involved. The rest is supplied through a lengthy (and expensive) process of discovery using sworn depositions under oath, formal requests for documents, and long lists of written and finely tuned questions called Interrogatories. Woe to the litigant who either conceals or falsifies responses to the discovery process. Federal judges who supervise these pre-trial activities are very cranky and expect prompt and complete cooperation between the parties to the lawsuit. The penalties for non-compliance can be devastating.

I intentionally did not take the "bare bones" approach and spelled out in detail all the facts, some relevant, some not. I wanted the press to have a full picture of what this case was about so they could report it accurately and hammer the Newberry people in the press before their lawyers and other politicians could put a spin on it. We lawyers have an unusual privilege. Matters before the court can usually not be the subject of a libel action. Unless we are improperly making intentionally false statements, and have no basis for believing what we say is worthy of a lawsuit, and is not done for some other nefarious purpose, we can't be sued. This complaint was my best chance to bring the entire matter out in the public. I laid everything out as clearly as possible. But I had to wait for the feds to tell me whether they would take on the case or not. And I waited.

Then, I got a call from a New Jersey congressman, Neil Flaherty – could I meet with some "government officials" in his office in Newark to discuss the case. This was a total surprise. As we know, there are several branches of government in our country – Executive (the President et al.), the Legislative (Congress, House and Senate) and the Judiciary (the Courts). They are intentionally separate and guard their prerogatives closely. The Justice Department is under the Executive rubric and they would decide the fate of the prosecution of this Newberry matter, not Congress. So why was the congressman calling me about the case. How had he even heard of it? I smelled a rat. A big stinky rat. I was even more alarmed to hear that they wished my still as yet undisclosed client to attend the meeting. Not only that. They wanted me to scurry up to Newark for this meeting, not in my office, I could feel something was up. Rather than refuse such a meeting, I like any good lawyer is always willing to listen. So I trundled up to Newark for the meeting, but with a bit of an attitude.

Now Newark is a perfect model of poor urban planning – the old center of the city has moved to a ring of businesses and suburbs around the urban area, leaving a doughnut hole in the center of old federal, and state offices, and little else. This doughnut hole design plagues most of our eastern cities and is a symptom of inept city politicians. So I got off the turnpike and drove into the center of Newark which was now a giant parking lot with old 1930s office buildings housing the courts and federal offices. I went into the designated office building and down the lonely marble-lined corridor to Congressman Flaherty's office. I was not going to reveal my clients name at this stage at any cost, but stashed her at home just in case she was needed. They were not getting her identity so cheaply.

I was escorted into a large conference room where suits had assembled and were amiably chatting over coffee and several boxes of doughnuts. Some low level lawyer from Justice – a young nervous female in a Hillary pants suit with no makeup and a frumpy hairdo and a serious expression introduced herself as Harriet Miller and told me she was assigned to this matter. I half expected she was wearing orthodontic braces – she was so young and nervous. This was a big important case. Why had some fledgling been given the matter? She introduced Congressman Flaherty and a stout serious fellow in his – I'd guess – 50s as Joseph O'Brien – Mr. Newberry's lawyer. What the hell was Newberry's lawyer doing here? I hadn't even brought the case yet. Only Justice outside of my office had been notified. Yet here was a congressman and a Newberry lawyer who now apparently were up to speed on the lengthy suit and memo I had sent to Justice over a month ago. But a good lawyer listens. Listens, stalls and gathers any helpful facts.

Flaherty was an older fellow, plump and with a full head of white hair and a big smile. He had represented a carefully gerrymandered district which incorporated enough white working class ethnic suburbs and city precincts to smother out any upstart vote from the black neighborhoods in his district. He produced regular comfortable election percentages, yet managed to collect large campaign donations which he shared with fellow politicians running for office and mostly family and friends who nominally worked on his campaigns. A career politician who got by, safely toeing the party mark. As expected, he said nothing and was simply lending the appearance of power his office extended.

Joseph O'Brien cleared his throat and started. "Mr. Stern, good of you to come." He then started the usual game of who he or his firm knew of me and my firm. Then, to show he had researched me online and elsewhere, he began to tell me about all the things we had in common: Friends from college, golfing partners, neighborhood friends. Although I had absolutely no interest in traveling an hour and a half in the morning to meet these people or learning about our acquaintances in common, I had to listen and be amicable. Lawyers, good lawyers, do not trash talk unless they really mean it and are sure of victory. Lawsuits can turn on a dime – one little fact – even if relevant, can upset the best laid plans and you might need to settle the case to save your fees, your reputation or even your ass. We always had to maintain the veneer of amicability. So I listened and chatted. We are the ultimate in passive-aggressive.

At some point, O'Brien began to shuffle some papers on the table in front of him. I vaguely could make out our letterhead on our office stationary. A good lawyer also can read upside down anything in front of someone and put it to good use. So I interrupted. "Joe (we were by now "Joe" and "Pete") is that my letter to Justice on the Newberry matter?" Yes, it sure as hell was. And what was he doing with a confidential Justice document on a supposedly confidential whistleblower matter by my client. It was now clear Newberry had some major grease. Justice had compromised my matter while Ms. Hillary Pantsuit and her boss sat on it and stewed about what to do with this political hot potato. I had not expected this. Hillary Pantsuit and her boss were Democrats and supposedly in a liberal Justice Department. Flaherty was an old line Republican and so was Newberry. How did this document bridge the gap? Was it that all politicians are all in a club that protect each other from scandal? Was this the old politicians' club? Yes, it must be. O'Brien reddened that I had recognized his possession of my submission to Justice to notify them of the whole whistleblower suit. He should not have had it. Hillary Pantsuit or her boss should not have given it to him. Yet he had it. And I knew it. The pleasantries were now mercifully over. Down to business.

"Why yes, Peter, (no longer "Pete," somehow I was now "Peter") we had heard your complaint was in the works and wanted to talk to you about it."

I could not help expressing a little irritation at the delay I felt from Justice in responding. So I let a not so subtle shot at Justice creep out. "Well, you're way ahead of Justice. Haven't heard from them in weeks." Hillary Pantsuit deadpanned. Maybe she didn't even appreciate my gibe.

O'Brien shifted in his seat and frowned. "Perhaps we should discuss it first."

"What's there to discuss?" I knew damn well, but wanted him to say it.

"As you can imagine Mr. Newberry is upset about these allegations. It would be devastating if they were made public. You have laid out many of these accusations and made him and his friends look particularly bad."

"If these things are true, yes I can certainly see that. And if they are true, should they suffer accordingly."

"If true, yes. But if not, the damage to them would be irreparable."

"Quite so. But I can have confidence that what I have put in the complaint is factual. Don't I have an ethical duty as a lawyer to pursue it?" We were just fencing a bit now. I had to stall and wait for him to make the first offer of settlement. We were verging on the edge of illegality at worst and unethical behavior at best. O'Brien was clearly here to offer me something to settle this entire matter against all of Newberry's people – essentially all criminal activities and my client and I would get something for it. But the crimes were not against us, but against the people of New Jersey and Pennsylvania. So in effect we were being bribed to walk away from a criminal complaint in which we were essentially blackmailing the Newberry crowd. Ugly! Ugly! Ugly! All to preserve a corrupt set of politicians. And with the help of an elected congressman so he could help a fellow crony. The matter also had to be settled before it hit the courthouse or the press would get hold of it and the Newberry goose would be cooked. Now was the best time to settle the case from the Newberry perspective. I could squeeze some serious money out of the wealthy Newberry coffers for agreeing to cover up the whole affair. I would feel lousy about the cover up, but I represented a client. It was not my decision. Ernestine had the final word, not me. I was neither her priest, nor shrink. I was her lawyer. A distinction, I must honor.

I could feel a layer of grime covering me, but I had to say the words. "What do you have in mind, Joe?" I knew I had him by the short hairs now, but he would feel me out with a low ball offer to test my confidence. But I had to add, "As you know, I had to resign from the Commission to take this case, because of the possible conflict of interest."

Somehow, I felt I was in a twilight zone where all the people in the room were quietly selling their souls to the devil. Some sleazy politician had been ripping off the people of Pennsylvania and New Jersey for years and he had sent his lawyer, a congressman and an assistant U.S.

attorney to plead his case to me. The offer was even more stunning.

"Pete, we can offer your client $500,000, and put you back on the Commission if we can get this thing to go away." I was aghast. Of course, I had to present this offer to my client, but it was ridiculous. I had to speak up.

"Joe, frankly, I find this low ball offer insulting, but will of course, present it to my client. But I certainly won't recommend it."

"What would you recommend?"

"For starters, I would want the entire Newberry group to repay the money they have taken over the last five years as determined by an independent audit by a reputable accounting firm. I would want those responsible to resign their positions and plead guilty to the appropriate crimes and be sentenced under the Federal Sentencing Guidelines."

"But, Peter, (again "Peter") that's what you get if you win everything after a trial."

"I would agree."

"But you haven't won yet."

"And the press hasn't heard the complaint I would file yet. Nor have your clients, I don't know who all you represent, spent the hundreds of thousands in legal fees defending it."

"Wouldn't you want your seat back on the Commission?"

"If I win the lawsuit, my office reception area would be lined wall-to-wall with whistleblowers wanting to bring suit. Besides doesn't this meeting even strike you as a little illegal?"

"Well, Peter (still "Peter") call your client. Let's see what we can do." I went into the parking lot to speak to Ernestine on my cell. She was overjoyed to hear the sum of $500,000 bandied about, but I had to explain how much more the case was worth. Many people with the possibility of big legal recoveries leap at the first offer; they are not used to having large sums of money, often squander it quickly or attract a lot of hangers-on. I had to hold her back; this possible recovery could be in the seven figure range and would be worthy of professional management. I also reminded her of the zeal with which she pursued the case original when she really did not expect a financial return. I persuaded her to reject the offer and wait a bit longer. This was an excellent chance to get a better offer just before the news hit the media. A quiet settlement would be worth much to the Newberry people. I rejected it.

"Well, Peter, what do you want?"

"I think I have a good case, I want a lot more. Plus, my client wants some justice – to clean up the Commission."

"Does he want money?" Aha "he." They didn't know who my client was.

"Of course, that too, but my client expects justice."

Taking the moral high ground and getting preachy in negotiations is a nice tactic. In reality, a lawyer is bound to a different set of standards. As a fiduciary or trusted agent of a client, he is bound by a Code of Ethics enforced by the appropriate bar association to act strictly and only in the best interests of his client. If his client tells him something he can never reveal it without the client's permission. If he knows a client has committed a crime, he must still require the prosecutor to prove it. The people in this room represented clients and had to get the best result possible for them even if it meant covering up a crime. My preaching was simply a way of harassing them personally. In a legal context, I knew I was acting irrationally by pointing out their lack of morals. On the other hand, I was subtly pointing out that if I revealed their efforts to "bribe" any client to give up her whistleblower claim, I was threatening them in a political arena – suggesting they all were in a league with crooks and the public might find out. When fighting someone rational, you can expect them to play by the rules and expect their tactics to be predictable. I was now becoming irrational and unpredictable. This would prove worrisome for their clients.

I personally felt the Newberry faction deserved criminal convictions, and a full restitution of what they managed to squeeze out of a government agency. What would I take? Whatever I could get them to offer. And time was on my side. If I filed my Complaint in a public courthouse, it would be in the hands of the media within 24 hours. Then, any effort to settle the case would expose it to public scrutiny. So I said, "Look, I have already granted the feds a month's extension to determine whether the will take up this matter. I can't wait any longer. My evidence might grow stale. I have to file in two days."

"Whoa! Peter what's the hurry?"

"Like I said evidence may have a way if disappearing. So 48 hours it is."

"We don't know what you want."

I was about to say "justice," but to a group of lawyers that would be over the edge. So I said, "Your offer was too low to provoke a counter, so if you have nothing more to say I'll have to leave."

"Wait, wait. Let us call the client. Can you, say, take a walk around the parking lot and come back?"

"That I can do." So I walked. I brought my client up to date. I called the office to see if anything important was going on. I called Jean. She was still upset about telling me something. I checked in on Scuzz and Vargas in the hospitals. They had been given bedside bail hearings and were being held on $500,000 bail each. They were also both sore, but recovering. Soon, my cell rang.

"Peter, come back." A good lawyer is always willing to listen, so I went back, and seated myself at the table.

"Peter, how bad do you need guilty pleas from everyone?"

"Pretty bad. At least the major people, I'd leave the minor ones in the discretion of the FBI and the U.S. Attorney."

"Does his wife have to plead guilty?"

"I would say yes, but perhaps with a recommendation for probation – no jail time."

"So, how about $3,000,000 in restitution and your seat back on the Commission."

"A bit light, Joe. This has been going on for five years. I calculate a possible $10 mill."

"OK, guilty plea for Mr., guilty pleas for everyone else with a recommendation for probation, $5 million plus your seat back."

"I'll ask my client." She would have settled for a lot less. She was not concerned about losing her job and being in the newspapers. Here, she could keep about $1 million and not lose her friends at work. Of course, we would have to funnel the funds through my firm's escrow account. I would then make sure she had a reliable financial advisor. Our firm sent a lot of this financial planning to a trust officer at Franklin Bank & Trust. I felt I had done a good job. My fee would be very decent. Of course, the whole deal would be approved by a federal judge who had absolute discretion to accept or reject any part of it. Usually, judges like to see both or all sides to a suit agree so they rarely upset a negotiated settlement. There is a way these deals are done discretely. Instead of having a full blown grand jury review the testimony and issue an indictment, the U.S. Attorney issues an "Information" and sets up a quiet hearing before a judge. This would avoid a lot of press hoohah and embarrassment to the parties. Of course, the media always has a reporter camped out at the federal courthouse and if he or she gets wind of something, it does get into the media.

I don't know why but the deal didn't set right with me. Somehow, it bothered me that a congressman got involved helping a crooked crony, and that the feds sent my Complaint and memo over to the crooked party before the suit had even been filed. I suppose the feds would say they were doing some investigation of my claims before jumping on board. I really didn't like the fact that they were participating in a negotiation to lessen the impact on a thoroughly corrupt politician. I had to know what the connection was there. Especially I did not like the fact that they sent Hillary Pantsuit over instead of someone in charge, someone who actually knew what they were doing, someone with the true mission of the Justice Department to do justice rather than someone who would give the deal the okey-dokey. Yes, it bothered me. I mean the deal itself was not bad, perhaps a bit light on the money and the underlings got off with probation – basically a federal slap on the wrist, but they never had to be exposed to the public shame they deserved. That quiet deal saved them that, but it was not something I had expressly agreed to.

I wrestled with the thought that full justice would not be done. I know a few reporters, some I rated highly for integrity and some I played softball with. Not the metaphorical softball, real softball – a Sunday morning pickup game. So I called a guy who covered state government and was a decent outfielder and told him to expect an Email about the mass Newberry guilty pleas before a federal judge. I went to a public computer center and Emailed him Harry Horton's file. A totally anonymous transaction. My buddy must have vetted it all very nicely to verify the facts in the file because a major story appeared in the *Philadelphia Inquirer* before the guilty plea hearing. It raised quite a stink. It left me and my client out of the deal and gave full credit to Hillary Pantsuit who turned out to be some judge's daughter. But the Newberry clan got their due. God was in his heaven and all was right with the world.

Alicia Seeks What's Due

I could only imagine the stir in our office as Alicia came to the reception area. She as always was a statuesque figure – six feet in heels dressed in shimmering silver – silver hair, shimmering silk blouse, smooth silk skirt, mini skirt, and a devastating look with high cheek bones and piercing blue eyes staring out of slits. She was directed back to my office and met by Angelina. With a smirk on her face, Angelina poked her head in my door and suppressing a giggle she said, "Miss Allende is here."

With a killer smile, Alicia strutted into my office and unbidden, folded into a chair and elegantly crossed one knee over the other – revealing elegant knees. "So, Peter, you did well with the Newberry thing. I knew I had the right man for the job." Alicia was a consummate politician. First, she had excellent contacts who fed her inside dope on everyone important or even mildly important and she stashed it away carefully. The whole Newbery deal had not made the papers yet and, until then, was supposed to be confidential.

But Alicia knew. I also knew that Alicia would not be slow to call in her favors granted. I had gotten a big favor. She did not even know how to tell me, so I volunteered. "Alicia, I am very grateful. Everything you said was true."

"Peter, you played your cards well." OK, enough of this mutual back scratching.

"Alicia, I would like to help you on Harry's estate."

"Good! So what about forging the real Will and presenting it as the real one." She had wanted this before. The idea was a bad one, but had its merits from a biblical point of view. She would get what was intended she should receive, despite evil actions which might have prevented it.

"OK, let me tell you about the dangers. First, forgery is difficult and can be discovered by good experts. I mean the computer type face has to match exactly. The signatures of all parties have to be beyond reproach. A Will has four signatures – the decedent, two witnesses and the notary. Plus the notary seal has to be identical. Then, let's suppose all this passes and then the original original shows up."

"But, Peter, we're talking a couple million dollars."

"True, but Alicia, you are a big target. Some dirt on you will be all over the papers and TV."

"Look, Peter, I helped you big time. I need help now."

"I got it. But I'm working on a few ideas. If the person who may have stolen the Will, gets into trouble maybe we have some leverage."

"You mean Honey, of course. That tramp." She hadn't talked to Honey in 20 years. "She couldn't even come up for her mother's funeral for Christ sake."

"Let's suppose she murdered Harry. She couldn't inherit under Pennsylvania law. We call it the Slayer's Act."

"I've heard of that. If she can't claim the estate, then it's me against the State of Pennsylvania with a copy of the Will and lots of testimony on his intent. Is that it?"

"Yes, exactly. Whoever you were talking to got it right."

"Are you kidding, the bureaucrat who runs the escheat department works for a good friend."

"A good friend."

"Yes. Peter, a good friend." I knew not to ask further.

"So basically if Honey killed Harry and stole the Will and she gets convicted, it's a much different case."

"Got it. She unraveled those elegant knees and rose to her full height. We shook hands. I had set something in motion. I didn't know what. Alicia was a very shrewd operator and had friends.

Two days later, I found out: Hackett from the Attorney General's Office had arrested Honey on murder charges.

Not much after that I got a call from Honey. "Peter, can we talk?" "Honey, I don't think I can be your lawyer, so if you say something to me, I may have to testify."

"Peter, I'm gonna make bail in a couple of hours and I want to talk to you. I didn't do this. Please, meet me at Harry's apartment." She had been staying at Harry's apartment since she got back from the hospital for her kidney problems. As long as she claimed innocence and wasn't going to incriminate herself, I could listen. A good lawyer always listens. So I said we'd meet.

Honey's Preliminary Hearing

Honey's preliminary hearing was scheduled promptly after her arrest. A preliminary hearing is just that – preliminary. The prosecutor just presents enough facts to prove that it is more likely than not that the defendant committed the crime charged. The reasonable doubt standard is for the final trial. All the prosecutor has to prove is a prima facie case and the defense does not get to do much. Of course they can cross-examine the witnesses but only to a limited extent and usually they can't present evidence in defense. A good defense lawyer will try to get as much information as he can about the case against his client and the prosecutor tries to conceal as much as he can.

So the Assistant Attorney General and Hackett had the burden of putting on just enough to convince the judge to hold the defendant for a final trial. I knew Hackett was just that – a hack, and a lazy one. Someone had put a bug up his ass to get Honey on trial and I had a few doubts that Alicia wanted Honey declared a murderer so she couldn't inherit Harry's estate. So Hackett got called in and told to arrest and prosecute.

I went to the hearing at the county seat in the Poconos. I felt I had traveled back in time at least 100 years. The courthouse was built in the 1880s and it showed. It was a large brownstone edifice in pseudo-

Roman style with a few brown columns at the entrance. The walls were covered to shoulder height in multicolored ceramic tile with ornate molding at the top. The floor was green and red – worn – well-worn linoleum from at least the thirties, and immense chandeliers hung from the high ceiling to illuminate dimly the hallways. The courtroom had identical tile walls and ornate molding, and the same dim chandeliers. The ceiling was at least 25 feet above. The judge's bench was an ornate carved affair about 10 feet high with a witness box to the left. The jury box was also to the left and just as ornate. The whole ambience was an overwhelming weighty presence as if the last days of judgment were about to take place. It was meant to impress the masses with the enormous power of the law.

Because this preliminary hearing was bound to attract publicity and reports, the judge of the county decided to take over the hearing replacing the district justice who heard mostly less important matters. The district justice was a local guy with no law degree, elected every four years. A mistake by this guy would be blown up in the papers and on TV. So the judge had to take over, and, besides, he would be a big deal in the county ever after.

It was a marvelous chance for the judge to preen in front of the camera and get his name in the papers. Most judges in the larger cities sit fulltime and handle large cases routinely. In this podunk, the judge sat about three quarters of the time and took off for deer season, and most of the summer to hunt and fish. To show his power, the judge arrived a half hour late although it was the most important event in the county in the last 10 years.

Honey and a Philadelphia attorney sat at counsel's table and fidgeted. A few private detectives sat behind. Hackett sat at his table with a few detectives next to the empty jury box.

The court crier intoned, "All rise, the Honorable Tiller presiding. The court is declared open." In strode a miniscule tired looking fellow in a judicial robe who mounted the bench and for good measure pounded the gavel.

"What do we have today, Mr. Perkins?" he said to the court crier, as if he didn't know. He must have been agitating for at least a week waiting for this case and knew damn well what was on the docket.

"The matter of Commonwealth v. Horton, sir – a preliminary hearing."

"Very well, Mr. Prosecutor identify yourself for the record."

"Assistant Attorney General Hackett, Your Honor."

"And you, sir."

"Victor Imperatore, Your Honor, for the defense." The court reporter was already clicking away. Imperatore was a well-seasoned Philadelphia lawyer – not particularly bright, but connected. He represented drug gangs and lower level mob figures. It showed me Honey was connected. I would guess Scuzz or the casino was paying. I sat in the back and took notes.

The first witness was the officer who was called to the scene. He described Harry lying on his back on his deck and in front of a charcoal grill, burnt from about his knees to his chest. There was a can of charcoal lighter fluid to Harry's right, a steak on a shelf of the grill. Then, the coroner described the burn wound extensively and explained that the corpse was burnt through to his back. There was charcoal lighter fluid on the corpse's torso. On the decedent's skull in the rear was a large bruise with some dried blood. The bruise was about three inches wide and from a blunt instrument. At this point, about 150 black and white photos were identified, and moved into evidence. He explained that as a result of my request, blood samples were taken. While it was inconclusive to be absolutely sure, there might have been some traces of Diprivan – a drug often used to cause a patient to relax prior to surgery. This is the first I heard of this drug although I had asked for and, I might add, paid for the blood tests. At the suggestion of the attorney for the decedent, an examination of the body disclosed two minute pin pricks – consistent with an injection – at the inside of the decedent's elbow.

Imperatore cross-examined the witnesses and established that the scene and the corpse could have been consistent with the decedent accidentally causing a large flame with the lighter fluid which caused him to fall back and hit his head on the bench immediately behind him and become conscious while the lighter fluid spilled on his torso and was ignited. The officer and the coroner had to concede that, yes, it was quite possible to explain the scene in that manner, but the possible traces of Diprivan in the blood test suggested he might have been drugged before he was knocked on the head before he burned.

Hackett on redirect examination brought out the fact that the decedent's shoes were expensive highly polished Italian loafers, and had no scratch marks on the heals, and no dirt or mud on the soles. This lead him to suggest Harry had not been walking in the muddy terrain in the Poconos near his cabin and had been carried to the site.

One thing I had not heard before was the presence of Diprivan in Harry's blood. As the case was moving on, I Googled it and found that it was a drug administered to patients before operation to cause them to relax. It wasn't really a total anesthetic to knock them out. It raised a number of issues in my mind. If Honey's henchman had stolen Harry's kidney for Honey, would Harry have felt the kidney being removed or maybe awakened from the pain. Or had some further agent been used to be sure he was out. Could that have been the blow to the back of his head? The coroner never did determine actual cause of death. Could he have died from the blow? Questions raised but not answered.

So far, as I jotted down my notes, I still had no answers and could not really pin Harry's death on anyone or rule out an accident.

Then Hackett lumbered inartfully on to the next phase. Imperatore attacked Hackett's many blunders on legal grounds trying to introduce evidence. With a kind and often illegal help from Judge Tiller, the next points of evidence managed to get on the record. Honey had a diseased kidney for many years and had been on dialysis. She was at the point where she needed a transplant. She got a transplant in Cuba about the time that Harry died. She was shown on video boarding a plane in Miami to Havana and returning a week later. She later was admitted to a hospital in Philadelphia for complications from the possible rejection of the new kidney. After stumbling through the evidentiary rules to let in all the medical evidence Hackett staggered on to Harry's estate. He managed to prove that Honey claimed in papers filed with the estate proceeding in Philadelphia that she was Harry's sole intestate heir and that there was as yet no Will found saying otherwise. So she would be the only one to inherit Harry's estate estimated at $3 million.

Imperatore managed to bring out on cross-examination that Honey was not anywhere near Philadelphia when Harry died. But he had also done his homework on kidney transplants. While the coroner proved that Harry's blood type was compatible with Honey's for a transplant, he admitted that blood types were inconclusive, and the mere similarity of DNA would not permit a successful transplant. A tissue match was necessary, and there had been no tissue match to anyone's knowledge. So the large elephant in the room was whether Harry's tissue matched Honey's. This would have required a biopsy of Harry and none seemed to have been done. Perhaps in Cuba, someone may have compared the two tissue samples, but those records were inaccessible. Hackett had not done his homework and did not realize this hole was in his case. At this point, Judge Tiller called a recess until the next day. As everyone walked out of the courthouse, there was a general hubbub. Everyone was speculating about what they had heard. There was circumstantial evidence, but nothing conclusive. Reporters and curious people of all sorts began to dial anyone they knew who might comment on the medical evidence. I of course did the same. Yes, a tissue match was absolutely necessary, yes the tissue from a sibling might match but not for sure. Often people with little genetically in common, matched. The guy I called was one of my golf buddies, a retired gynecologist, Howard Rosenblatt. He was amazed to hear how little research the lawyers had done on kidney transplants, especially in such a big case. Anyone performing a kidney transplant without a positive tissue match would be committing malpractice. Any decent doctor would know this. But then Howard said something startling, "You know, the diseased kidney is never removed the new one is simply put in the body next to it."

"Whoa, the old kidney and the new kidney are sitting there side by side?"

"That's how it's done."

"So we could do a tissue match and get a DNA sample with two biopsies of the lady's kidneys."

"I don't see why not." I was dumbfounded that Hackett had stumbled into this arrest of Honey without asking these questions of an expert witness. I felt ashamed myself that they had not occurred to me earlier, but then it wasn't my case.

The next morning, Judge Tiller arrived on time for court and seemed anxious. He must have gone online to research kidney transplants. It would have been improper for him to consult an expert outside of the courtroom, but he could always consult outside research on his own. The crier opened court, and the judge addressed Hackett.

"Mr. Hackett, is it your contention that Harry Horton was killed and his kidney removed and placed in the defendant, his sister, Ms. Horton?"

"Yes, Your Honor."

"Is it true that you have no evidence to present of a tissue match between donor and donee?"

"Yes, Your Honor. But they are siblings and the blood test is compatible."

"Isn't it possible that even so the tissue might not match and it could cause Ms. Horton's death?"

"I don't know that, Your Honor." At this point, Imperatore bolted from his seat and addressed the court.

"Hold on just a second, Mr. Imperatore, hold on. Let me finish here." Imperatore sat and began to fidget. "Now, Mr. Hackett, do I understand that the diseased kidney and the new kidney are both inside Ms. Horton?"

"I don't know that, Your Honor."

"I see. Well, I hereby authorize a search warrant for Ms. Horton's kidneys to conduct a biopsy and tissue match and further to take DNA tests of the new and the old kidney if both exist in her abdomen."

"But Your Honor." Both attorneys blurted. A DNA match which showed the new kidney came from someone other than Harry Horton would destroy a key element of Hackett's case, while a strong DNA profile would show she was the recipient of body parts stolen from a murder victim. A risk for each attorney. Hackett could not object, he had raised the issue and the judge could always seek out evidence independently. Imperatore had ample grounds for his objection. Such an invasion of his client could be medically dangerous, and might be an unconstitutional search. There were ample cases in which the courts permitted taking blood samples or other tissue from defendants, so that was not a strong issue. Imperatore had no idea whether the biopsy might be dangerous, but he objected out of habit. Why risk absolute proof of his client possessing a stolen kidney. Imperatore could not let damaging evidence in without a fight. A lawyer never knows if a client has told him the full story so he attacks the case from all angles even though the evidence might be favorable. Of course, he filed an appeal – an emergency appeal to prevent this incursion into his client.

And also, the preliminary hearing quietly dissolved. Judge Tiller suspended the hearing until this issue could be decided. Honey could be seen arguing with her attorney to no avail. Hackett packed up several suitcases of papers and he and his minions filed glumly out of court. The media wandered out of court shaking their heads. No resolution was a resolution no one wanted. More delay. As they were leaving, Honey signaled me to give her a call. What could she want?

Honey Talk

I had tried to avoid Honey before. I could feel a conflict of interest waiting to happen. I mean she had somehow fixed me up with Jean for some reason, probably a bribe to get me to be more sympathetic to her claim to Harry's estate. Clearly, the Will was missing, the Will my office had prepared for Harry and still had a copy of in our files. If we might be a bit less diligent in our search for the original, she would inherit a handsome sum – one she probably did not deserve since she hadn't had contact with Harry for over 20 years. Plus, I suspected her of murdering Harry for his kidney. I mean it smelled of murder somehow. She had been lucky so far. The Will was missing, the local police thought the death was accidental, and Hackett – an incompetent had been assigned to the murder case. What could I do in this mess, but create another complication. Lawsuits do not need complications and I could be one. Besides, Alicia must be behind Hackett's latest push, and she was a force to be reckoned with. She would not like me talking to Honey.

But Honey had been insistent. A good lawyer listens. So I would listen. She was still recuperating from the complications after her kidney surgery and staying in Harry's condo, a few blocks from my office.

She let me in to the apartment and looked extremely healthy to me. She was wrapped in some kind of shimmery gold robe-like thing with her ample cleavage on display. Her hair was recently done and her makeup – a bit too much but fresh in amber tones. I was being set up somehow and felt like Adam being invited to sample the forbidden fruit, not to mix mythic citations, but a golden apple. She had a freshly made pitcher of mimosas on the coffee table - someone had told her it was my drink of choice. Not true but not far from true. She was definitely an accomplished hostess from her many years entertaining whales at the casino and I was being entertained. We sat, she poured, I sipped. Her ample cleavage on glorious display as she poured. Men do know these things, don't they?

"So, Honey, I saw the preliminary hearing and see that it is a bit of a mess."

"My lawyer thought so too, but he won't listen to me. Men don't listen, they think we're stupid."

"So I hear."

"I can feel you listen."

"OK, I'm listening."

"Look, Peter, I've been working for the casino for years now. Scuzz and I used to be an item. Of course, he was always cheating on me. When I'd complain, he whacked me around. So I shut up. It wasn't an easy time. But I'm not dumb. I kept my eyes and ears open. I know a few things, ok."

"On Scuzz?"

"On them all. I heard about you and this whistleblower. Good job. I mean you know how to handle the informers. I was sorry to hear Vargas and Scuzz went after you, but it looks like you came out ahead."

"That was luck. I could have been hurt."

"Yeah, I guess. But look, I know things. So does Jean. They can't let that out. That's why they have to get to Jean and quiet her down. Me, they can quiet down without much."

"How do you mean?"

"Once, I was a top girl in the system. I mean I brought in the whales and kept them happy. A little too happy for my own good. I drank, I did dust, and worst of all I gambled. They, the house, are very happy to have you in big to them. Then they control you, but I didn't see it coming. I should have, but I didn't. I thought Scuzz would always protect me. Instead he owned me. He fed me booze and coke, he got me further in debt, and sometimes he beat me up. But I thought everything would be alright. So I became the mother superior for the girls in the casino, as I got a bit older and Scuzz played around a lot more."

"I get the picture."

"So it begins to dawn on me that I have to protect myself so I collect information, names and stuff, overhear conversation, a little pillow talk, catch some bragging from the whales after a few drinks."

"I see." A good lawyer occasionally gets rewarded for listening.

"So Scuzz kind of still has a thing for me and I have something on him. But he and the house are holding some notes of mine. I'm getting a little older, so I got to protect myself. So we each got something on each other. Anyway, my kidney starts to go. I hide it for a while. I get sick and miss work. Scuzz finds out. Now, he's still got a thing for me, and I owe the house big time. So he arranges for a kidney transplant in Cuba. I'm game. So I say ok. So I get on the plane, go to this Cuba hospital in a nice resort in Cienfuegos and get it done. I recupe in the sun for a week and feel pretty good while the scar heals. I have to say those Cuban docs are good, very professional and the hospital was first class. I get it that they do a lot of mob work, and lots of secret foreign bigwigs who don't want knowledge of their health problems to get out. They also do boobs, face lifts, tummy tucks, and liver transplants – all cheap and confidential. But bottom line: that's all I know about that. So I came home, and boop! Harry dies. Scuzz hears about this and sees a way to get me to pay off the casino out of his inheritance. He does some research on the whole thing and figures I'm the sole heir. He promises to wipe out my debt and give me half of the estate, so I go along. It was his idea to send you Jean to soften you up on the missing Will. I liked the idea, too. So I bring up Jean. Unfortunately, you like her a little too much for Scuzz' likes and she likes you. Scuzz is not happy."

"But why send Vargas to threaten me?"

"She may know stuff too, and he likes her. She has taken my place as one of his favorites. That's why I sent her to you. To get in a zinger on Scuzz. He doesn't like his girls to get involved. She looked kind of involved. And he was pissed at me. He had some words with her."

"Yeah, some words. He beat her up."

"So I hear. I'm sorry about that. Anyway, she takes off. She's not like me. She didn't get into the system. She's kind of a hippy chick, doesn't appreciate big money, fancy clothes, jewels, you know. She doesn't gamble, doesn't drink too much, and was going to school. She wasn't a floozy, but she was a big earner. The men liked her and she played them. When Scuzz hit her, she must have decided she didn't like the life. So she split."

"Does anyone know where she split?"

"Haven't heard, but they figured you. She liked you and you could protect her, being a lawyer and all. So they figure she ran to you 'cause you had some money and connections. So they tried to squeeze you to scare her and find her whereabouts".

"But what would she know?"

"If she knows half of what I know, she knows a lot."

"What does she know?"

"I can't get into that now. Not without a deal. That's my ace in the hole and I need a big enough pal to play it."

"Uh-huh. So you got stuff on Scuzz and the gang?"

"Big time."

"And he has stuff on you?"

"Well, he holds my notes. And he has stuff on me."

"Does he have anything on Jean?"

"Not that I know of. She's a good girl. You should think about that."

"OK, OK, mother superior, you've done enough already. But, look, what did you call me over for?"

"It's all bogus, this murder rap."

"So you say. But there's a lot of smoke. I mean you get a kidney at the same time Harry gets burned up in the spot where his kidney would be. You must have the same DNA, and your blood type matches.

If they find his kidney inside you, you're cooked."

"It's not his kidney."

"Are you sure? I mean your lawyer will put up a helluva fight to prevent them doing a biopsy of your kidney."

"Let them biopsy all they want, there won't be a DNA match."

"How are you so sure?"

"I'm pretty sure his father wasn't mine. I found out momma was a rolling stone, if you know what I mean."

"OK, I get that, but you're mom's DNA would be in Harry's kidney." "I checked on that. Very low probability."

"You checked?"

"Well, the lawyer checked, but he doesn't want to take the risk that we both had the same fathers which brings the DNA match up from 50% to 99%."

"That's a bad gamble. I would have done the same as he. It could have been your father's DNA, why take the chance?"

"I also know I got another kidney from someone else."

"How do you know that?"

"The Cuban doc told me."

"So you were lucky enough to get a Cuban match that fast."

"Look, Mr. Stern, you don't know what goes on in Cuba and I'm not going to explain it. But that's not Harry's kidney in me. Take my word for it. My lawyer doesn't listen, but I'd be happy to have them biopsy my kidney."

"OK, OK, I guess I don't want to know any more. So when Imperatore loses his appeal and they do your biopsy, you could walk."

"Absolutely."

"Why tell me then?"

"My lawyer says they can still try the murder case against me in probate court when they try to claim I can't inherit because I murdered Harry."

"He's right about that."

"He says the standard of proof is different, not beyond a reasonable doubt but by a preponderance of the evidence."

"That's true."

"So I could still lose. Even without Harry's kidney inside me."

"That's possible."

"So I figure this way. If Harry's death was an accident, the estate gets double the insurance payment."

"So if I agree to split the estate with whoever is named in a copy of the Will, no one will try to prove I killed Harry, right?"

"Well, yes and no. The insurance company might, but not the heirs you settle with."

"But then it's me and the other heirs against some old insurance company, and not me against the heirs."

"That's right. It's a different case, and it's a jury trial instead of a judge deciding the case alone."

"OK, that's what Imperatore tells me. I checked it out with Scuzz' lawyers as well. I wanted to hear it from you. If I agree to split the estate, do you care?"

"I'd have to think about that, but usually a settlement is better than a trial for everyone."

"OK." By now, the pitcher of mimosas was about empty and I hadn't had much of it, but Honey managed to keep pouring and exposing her ample bosom. Was I being offered possibly a further inducement to encourage a settlement? Maybe. But I had a thought of Jean. Somewhere, somehow, my reptilian brain was being overridden by, what, something. I passed on the possibly proffered opportunity. I was sure Honey would have been great in the sack, but no, I decided no.

Honey seemed to have accomplished what she wanted. We discussed Jean a bit more, and how nice a girl she was and how unhappy I was single. I really wasn't. But Honey was sure I was. All women think a single guy must be miserable. On that note, I shook hands, let the record show, shook hands, and I left the condo with much to think about.

Honey Biopsy

With the issue of Honey's possible theft of Harry's kidney up in the air at the preliminary hearing it was eminently clear that an issue could be resolved by a biopsy of Honey's new kidney. As lawyers do, Honey's lawyer saw the opportunity to be obstructive about something and objected vehemently to any such invasion of his client's body. The prosecutor submitted a search warrant to Judge Tillis which he signed. The defense filed an immediate appeal to the Superior Court, the intermediate court between the trial level and the Supreme Court of Pennsylvania. Since the appeal requested an expedited hearing because the lower court preliminary hearing was suspended until this issue could be resolved, the Superior Court scheduled arguments on the appeal within 10 days. Although recognizing the emergency nature of the appeal and, despite being under the glare of the press covering the trial, the Superior Court did what appellate courts do, they punted. Yes, they sent the entire matter back to Judge Tillis to hold a hearing to determine whether a biopsy posed a threat to Honey's health. Judge Tillis scheduled a hearing within 10 days, to hear expert medical testimony on the issue. Once again, an assembly of media people, curiosity seekers, and many others, crowded into Judge Tillis' ornate nineteenth century courtroom to hear yet another stage in the murder case. The prosecutors as expected said the procedure was safe and without risk. Defense lawyers, amply funded by unknown backers of Honey, came in with a few meagre case studies of operative misadventures not of kidney biopsies but biopsies in general. Judge Tillis ruled almost immediately that the biopsy could proceed with a doctor of Honey's choice with the tissue to be examined by a representative from each side of the case. The procedure to take place within one week.

The biopsy was completed promptly without mishap on both the original kidney and the new kidney. The tissue match was found to be reasonably close for a transplant, but the DNA results were slow to come. A hearing was scheduled for the DNA results to be announced in open court. Once again, an assemblage of the usual onlookers showed up. Judge Tiller demanded order, the prosecutor called the DNA expert to the stand and qualified him as an expert from the University of Pennsylvania Hospital. Dr. Bertelheim, a nervous, timid, woman in her mid-fifties took the stand and the prosecutor intoned.

"Ms. Bertelheim, what were the results of your examination of tissue from Ms. Horton's kidney and Ms. Horton's new kidney?"

"To simplify, there is no match of the sort you would expect from siblings." She then began to go on to explain the complicated science of genetic samplings, female and male chromosomes, selected genome matching sites, percentage of matching probability and so on for about an hour. Her initial statement drew gasps from those who were sure Honey was guilty. A general hubbub rose in the court and slowly subsided as Dr. Bertelheim filled in the scientific background to explain her findings. So Harry's kidney was not inside Honey. That much was clear. The prosecution, Mr. Hackett, realizing what a gigantic blunder he had made arresting Honey without a full investigation, was fidgeting, all during the expert testimony. At this point desperation set in. He was going to ask some "Hail Mary" questions.

"Dr. Bertelheim, could this DNA comparison be explained by Ms. Horton having a different father from Mr. Horton?"

"Of course, we checked that possibility through the usual matching points and found no correlation between the DNA which might be attributed to a common female – i.e. a mother." Once again, a lengthy scientific explanation went on for a half hour as she explained the types of genes' sites which might alone show female characteristics. Hackett still slumping asked one more.

"Can you characterize whom the male donor might have been?"

"Generally yes. We believe the male to have been a combination of Hispanic and African genes." A major hubbub again arose. Startling evidence. She had gotten a donor kidney and probably from a Cuban male. Honey beamed, she had known all along, but hadn't told anyone. She seemed to have enjoyed the show and the spectacular downfall of Hackett. Why hadn't she simply told her lawyers and presented evidence herself. Maybe she wasn't sure. Anyway, the tab for the lawyers was on Scuzz and she was enjoying the attention.

Although Hackett made some last ditch arguments to try to preserve the case, they fell on deaf ears. As the defense lawyers rose to counter the arguments, Judge Tillis waved them down. "Gentlemen, I found the evidence of the possible involvement of Ms. Horton in the death of Mr. Horton to be inadequate to hold this matter for trial. Dismissed!" Of course, Ms. Horton hugged all of her fleet of defense counsel, beamed at me and stared down the press as she walked out of court.

It was not a complete exoneration of Honey. I mean she still could have had Harry's kidney stolen from his dying body and exchanged it in Cuba once it was discovered that there was an inadequate tissue match. But those records were hidden behind an impenetrable diplomatic barrier and would remain firmly within Cuban medical archives. Certainly, Harry's death remained suspicious, but to link Honey's desire for his kidney as a motive would have to be left unproven. The consequences for Honey were great. The insurance carrier might now be stuck with a finding that Harry's death was an accident. Honey might still receive her intestate right to the estate since it could not be proven she was the murderer. So a double insurance policy and a clear path to an inheritance. I hate to add that she also had a serviceable new kidney. Things were definitely looking up for Honey.

Honey Moves for Intestate Distribution

After successfully prevailing at the preliminary hearing on the murder charge against her, Honey was emboldened to seek a distribution of Harry's estate. Without a Will in evidence Honey would claim to be the sole intestate heir. At this, she risked a non-jury trial again on two points: whether my firm's copy of the Will was a valid substitute for the original and whether she had murdered Harry. Yes. The mere dismissal of the charges at the preliminary hearing was not the final word. First, Honey would always be re-arrested if more evidence surfaced in the criminal trial, but also, the issue of her right to inherit if she murdered him could again be raised in a non-jury proceeding. If the judge determined that it was "more likely than not" that she had Harry murdered, she would be barred under the Slayer's Act in Pennsylvania from benefitting from the estate. This trial would be different. The standard for finding murder was not beyond a reasonable doubt, but more likely than not. And this time she would not be entitled to a jury, but only a judge would decide on the facts.

My firm, of course, was served with the papers to set the matter down for a hearing. Since we wrote the Will of which only a copy could be found, we could not represent as lawyers any side in the case since we would be witnesses. So we advised Alicia to get a lawyer, subpoena our firm and try to get the court to accept a copy of the Will – a long shot at best. Her best shot had to be to prove the murder case. Alicia was no fool and went out to get the best lawyer for the job – one who knew the trial judge.

The probate court where Wills and other issues like that are decided is a small closed fraternity. The judges are usually former estates lawyers and as a result are old fuddy-duddies. They know the law, are very pedantic about it and insist on good manners, proper dress and social connections – either old line society or well to-do Jewish, Italians or Irish. Alicia got herself one of these – Bennington Brabont. His suit was at least 20 years old, out-of-style, flood pants, and he wore a bow tie and a button down blue Oxford shirt. He affected a British accent. Parts of his family went back to the early Quakers, but his family money came from coal miners where Irish workers fresh off the boat labored to exhaustion in unsafe unhealthy mines and frequently died in mining disasters, but now he claimed to be a patrician and ennobled.

Honey's lawyer probably paid for by Scuzz was a loud mouth, obnoxious personal injury lawyer from South Philly. He wore tailor made – wide lapelled double breasted suits designed to conceal his considerable girth. He was no slouch, but was unblooded in the probate courts and had no claim to nobility.

Judge Peabody, an elderly senior judge, previously from a stuffy big firm, called for a pretrial conference. An ordinary exercise to educate himself about the case and get some of the issues defined. He absorbed each sides' presentation and then demanded a full blown pretrial memorandum. These heavyweight documents had each side define the issues, cite legal authority, name the witnesses, and summarize what they were expected to say on the stand. An onerous task for each side. After he reviewed each of these presentations, he called for another pre-trial conference and asked all parties to be present. This was a sure sign he wished to have the sides agree to settle the case. At the appointed time, all sides appeared. Honey, her lawyer, Alicia, hers as well and Roger Humphries from my firm who had drawn the Will for Harry. Jean began to beg me to have her attend, for some reason she wished to see me in action. I tried to explain that I had little to do except represent our firm's small interest in the outcome. I was also concerned that Scuzz might also show up and might try to threaten her in some way. But Jean was not to be deterred, so I relented: she could attend, but had to be quiet. I have to admit that I was more than a little embarrassed by her presence. First, she was knockout beautiful, but she had been a sort of gift from Honey. Scuzz had beaten her up, and she had some secret information on Scuzz. She was sure to stir up feelings. As such, she might be deemed to have compromised my integrity. Also, I wanted to avoid a scene between her and Scuzz.

The judge's chambers included a large conference room. Philadelphia's City Hall was an unusual mixture. Built at about the turn of the century, it was a mixture of ornate styles amply funded at the time by the corrupt Republican administrations. It was called "The Second Empire" style and was festooned with concrete, 250 sculptures by Alexander Calder of Indians, cattle, and other symbols and topped by a bronze statue of William Penn holding a scroll which presumably was his charter from the English crown for the Pennsylvania colony. From a certain angle, however, it looked like Billy Penn was holding his penis erect facing North Philly. The interior of City Hall was however seedy. Long worn out linoleum – chipped and scarred is on each floor, yet ornate gilded moldings adorned most of the ceilings throughout. We found Judge Peabody's chambers and began to file in. Sure enough, Scuzz did appear and sported a large bandage across his nose over which he glared at me and Jean as he sat by Honey's side. I nodded politely in his direction while poorly suppressing a smirk. Next to me sat Roger Humphries, the estates lawyer from our firm who had drawn the Will for Honey. He was prepared to testify about his many discussions with Harry in which he expressed clearly his intent not to leave his estate to Honey, but to leave the bulk of it to his longtime friend, Alicia Allende whom he referred to by both her assumed name and her given name, Mary Ann Malinowski in case there was any doubt as to whom he intended. Poor Roger, was himself an old fuddy-duddy and unaccustomed to violent confrontation and looked aghast at Scuzz' malevolent glare at me. He was also scandalized by my having brought Jean to the conference. Things of this sort were rarely tolerated in probate court.

The judge at last appeared mercifully at last to relieve the silent but palpable tension in the air as the parties now stared off in different directions avoiding eye contact.

"Gentlemen and ladies, I have called you here to attempt to

resolve this matter. I have read your respective presentations and find that there may be ample weight on either side for a verdict in favor of either party. On the one hand, it may be that I must find, as a civil matter, that Ms. Horton caused the death of Mr. Horton which may be a great public embarrassment to her. I might also find that I must ignore the decedent's very wishes expressed in a Will drawn by a reputable law firm and practitioner. Since there is a substantial amount of money involved, it might be best to resolve the matter by compromise since the winner of the trial would receive all and the loser none. Accordingly, I will ask your lawyers to make presentations in an attempt to persuade you of the strength of their cases to show you the prospect that either might prevail. To avoid prejudicing myself, I will retire from this session and allow you all to attempt to persuade your opponents of the risk they face by going to trial." With that the judge, his clerk, his courtroom deputy and his secretary rose and left. The room was silent for an awkward several minutes.

At last, Horace Bonifiglio, Honey's lawyer got up and began to harangue. He bellowed, "Look, Ms. Allende, you got no case. You got no Will. Under PA law you gotta have the original. We all know that. And they couldn't prove a murder case against Honey. She didn't have Harry's kidney. Period. End of story. We win. You got that."

Bennington Brabant, a silver haired, tall and distinguished looking man, and Alicia's lawyer, took a few minutes, assembling his papers and clearing his throat. "Horace, if I may call you that. There is ample precedent for this court to decide that a copy of a Will may be admitted to probate if his wishes are strongly expressed." With that, he began to recite the names of the cases and handed copies across the table, as if Bonifiglio couldn't possibly have known how to do actual research. It is fair to say that Bonifiglio's clerk did collect them carefully into a file. "It is also possible to prove an intentional homicide in probate court by circumstantial evidence." Again more copies of appellate decisions were slid across the table and collected by the clerk. "And circumstantial evidence we have in abundance." He began to recite the suspicious nature of Harry's death and the very fortuitous timing of the burning of the area of Harry's kidney and the implanting of a new kidney within Honey as well as the presence of Diprivan in Harry's system.

Bonifiglio rose and blushed. "Look, Honey was nowhere near Harry at the time of death. She was on her way to Cuba."

"Ah, but we have pictures of Mr. Vargas boarding the same plane with a cooler, perhaps containing a refrigerated familial kidney."

"But the kidneys don't match."

"Maybe one kidney was traded for one that did."

And so, the recitation of evidence went on.

Although keeping my mouth shut was a virtue in most occasions, I felt myself standing almost involuntarily.

"Whoa, whoa. Let's think reasonably here. If they prove a murder case, Honey of course gets nothing, but the estate loses half the insurance money. So Ms. Allende gets only half of the estate. If we settle, there is still the possibility that the estate gets the double indemnity amount and won't be able to rely on a finding that there was a murder. So it seems obvious that we settle with each side getting half of the full double indemnity amount."

Both lawyers folded their arms and looked at me as if I had sprouted horns. I hadn't gotten through to them. So we sat for a few hours debating the minutiae of the evidence to no avail. At lunchtime, the judge and his entourage excused us for the day and told us to return tomorrow morning "with a fresh attitude." We left. On the way out, Scuzz walked beside Jean and whispered something to her. She turned angrily and whispered back in an angry tone. He nodded and walked off. I walked back to the office with Jean and Roger.

I asked Jean what Scuzz had said. She put her hand to her face and said, "Not now, Peter. Not yet."

Post Settlement Conference

We trundled back to the office after the unproductive settlement conference. Jean and I walked down the corridor past Angelina to my office. She was about to ask how it went when her eyes were drawn to Jean like a laser. "Uh-huh," she said, then, "Ah-hah! Now I see." She was obviously impressed with Jean. Of course as my personal she-wolf protector, she would demand a full explanation and background check and give me a complete unsolicited review of my new squeeze, but she did manage to get out, "So how did it go?" I went through the particulars with her nodding. "So no progress?"

"None, really. A lot of bluster, no substance." As we stood in my doorway, a number of the lawyers and staff walked by. Soon it became a gander fest as about the entire office walked by to get a look at Jean, who stood by modestly appearing to be unaware of the attention sitting in front of my desk. Lawyers chose this moment to raise issues or questions with me that were months old and now irrelevant. Of course, the irrepressible Angelina could not withhold a chuckle. Eventually, even Roger Humphries walked by to see what the commotion was about.

"Oh by the way, Peter, I have been collecting all of Horton's mail sent from the real estate manager in the Poconos."

"Really, Roger, how much is there?"

"Oh, boxes full. The mail had been collecting on Horton's mail box at the management center and the manager had been saving it. He called me some time ago and asked if he should send it here. So

I have it stacked in a closet. Do you want to look at it?" Of course, I wanted to look at it. At this point, things were not going well and I would grasp at any straw. But it had been irresponsible for Roger not to tell me earlier. Of course, it probably should have crossed my mind to ask. Now, we had some time as I got the hand truck out of the mailroom and brought the boxes to the small conference room to sort through. I borrowed a few spare paralegals to help Angelina and me to sort through the stacks. Jean volunteered to help as well.

My instructions were to put all the obvious junk mail and advertisements in one box to be thrown out, the rest were to be put in the center of the conference table. Maybe something would turn up. Soon a small pile of questionable mail began to accumulate in the middle and several boxes were now filled with junk mail. I began to sort through the pile of possible of interest. Even that was junk mail for the most part, masquerading as real mail. But that went as well. There were some bills – a few utility bills, a few delinquency notices, newsletters from the gated community, and then some from a local bank with monthly statements from a checking account. Apparently, Harry kept a small local account, but it was dwindling each month as a $5 maintenance fee was charged. There was only $82 left in the account now. But there was one curious charge on the account – "Deposit box, annual fee. $40.00." Apparently Harry was keeping a safe deposit box at a local bank in the Poconos. When the impact of this information hit me, I exploded out of the chair. We had to go to the safe deposit box immediately. Maybe, the Will was there. Without any explanation to those sorting the mail, I bolted out of the room and sprinted to Roger's office. I would need the document appointing our firm as administrators for the Horton Estate. Fortunately, we had both my name and Roger's on the certificate so I could get access to the safe deposit box alone. I called the bank to see how late they would be open. Alas, they kept banker's hours and closed at 4:00 p.m. and open at 9:00 a.m. the next day. I wasn't sure if I could make it today, but I would try. If I didn't make it I would stop by first thing the next morning. I could stay in Harry's cabin overnight. Jean offered to come with me. So I left the mail sorters at their work and called Alicia about the developments. She hinted that she had been hard at work preparing a forged duplicate Will, but I had to cut her off before she could entangle me in her scheme.

With the Administrators Certificate in hand and some of the file, I ran down to my car with Jean close at hand. I was so wound up I wasn't much of a conversationalist much of the way up the Northeast Extension of the Turnpike and I had to watch my speed. I was going through in my mind the events in this case, examining each step. For some reason, I began to question Jean's presence. I mean why would this absolutely gorgeous natural beauty have an interest in me? I mean I was not chopped liver, but she was an all-time head turner. Then, I realized she had been introduced to me by Honey – a possible murderer, and one who may have stolen the Will. Honey was aligned with Scuzz and so could Jean be. Jean had been beaten up by Scuzz apparently, and came running to me. Was I being set up? Jean seemed sincere enough, but now she was getting as close to the whole Will and kidney business as she could get. Could she be up to something? Should I suspect her? I began to ask. "So, Jean tell me about the relationship between Honey and Scuzz."

"Well, he was her boss in Las Vegas when she was younger. They were an item for quite a while. During that time, she got into booze and pills, and she also gambled and got into debt to the casino. I told you all that."

"But she had something on him."

"Yes, she knew about his skimming and his money laundering, maybe something else. She was also the den mother for the hookers and those of us who entertained whales."

"Did he beat them up too?"

"Yes, that was his style."

"So why didn't they leave?"

"They were making very good money. They were hooked on something he got for them. And, they were used to being abused. Low self-esteem, you know."

"So why did he hurt you?"

"He thought I was like the other girls."

"But you weren't?"

"I wasn't hooked on anything. I saw what it did to my parents and I wasn't going to be like that. Second, I didn't hook. And I was too smart for him. I just went along with the program and didn't get in the way. I made big money for them with the whales. They gave me a great apartment and benefits. I was able to go to college. And I kept to myself."

"So what is he doing for Honey now?"

"I think Honey wants to retire. So I think they made a deal. He gets her a kidney transplant. I know that for sure 'cause she told me that. I think he found out about her brother. So I half-believe they decided to kill him and get his money. She would pay back the casino what she owed and she would retire on the rest."

"I can certainly see that by now. So why did he beat you up?"

"I think I might have said something about what I knew."

"You mean the money-laundering and the skimming."

"No, it had to be something else because he kept asking me what I told you."

"I don't think we talked about anything like that."

"I don't think we did, and I don't think I said anything like that to him."

"But it was something you said to him."

"Yes. I guess."

"Did he know Honey had brought you to Philadelphia to meet me?"

"Oh yes, he kept track of all the girls, but he didn't know about you." He heard it from men who were tailing me in Philadelphia."

"So he thought you might have talked to me because I am a lawyer?"

"Something like that."

"Go over in your mind what he said and you said when you came back home and before he beat you up."

"OK. Where were you? In Philadelphia. Why? Honey set me up with you. Why? To get me to have you help her with her brother's estate."

"Then what?"

"I thought he had come up to Philadelphia to spy on me. We girls were always under surveillance anyway. So he asked me how I knew he had gone to Philadelphia. I told him I had heard he went to Philadelphia before. He wanted to know all about that – being in Philly before. I just remembered a conversation I heard, that was all – he drove to Philly and took I-95."

"So he was in Philly before? When?"

"That's all I remember." In a flash, I was on my cell phone to Hackett. He snarled at me, but listened when I said Scuzz had been in Philadelphia before or about the time of Horton's death. I explained that Scuzz was in cahoots with Honey to split the inheritance and get Harry's kidney. He seemed mildly interested. I explained that we didn't have much time since the Will distribution trial might come up soon. We needed him to check Scuzz and the casino credit cards to see if there were any gas, hotel or credit card purchases at about the time of Harry's death. He began to be interested. Although he resented my intrusion in his case he finally agreed to get them. I began to feel somewhat better about Jean. She had given me some information helpful against Honey and Scuzz, she had shown a desire to help me to help Alicia with the Will.

Of course, the bank with the safe deposit box had just closed as we drove, so we went to Harry's cabin for the night. We picked up some cheesesteaks and beer on the way. The cabin was freezing when we went in – the thermostat had been set at 55° as it took some time to heat up so we built a fire in the fireplace. We spread out the cheesesteaks on the coffee table in front of the fire. I had more questions for Jean.

"Jean, what do you want out of life?"

"A normal life. Just normal. I'm tired of the casino and the late hours and loudmouth men. I want a family, kids, you know, normal." Somehow, I couldn't see this exotic creature going to the supermarket in a sweat suit with two kids and her hair in pigtails. Could she? I guess so. "What do you want, Peter?" Uh-oh a bad question. I had been a bachelor for a few years now since the divorce. It wasn't too bad. I found places to hang out, but it was a bit lonely. I earned a good buck, but had no one to spend it on. My ex-wife made the mistake of divorcing me too early and got very little in property distribution or alimony. I paid child support above the standards required without a fight. Did I need another complication in my life? I explained this to Jean.

"Any feelings for your ex?"

"None. That's over. I'm sorry it didn't work out, but she was such a bitch in the end. It cured me of any regrets. I see my daughter whenever I can, but nothing scheduled."

Jean steered the conversation to her anticipated career in art and architecture. She wanted to be mostly an interior designer. She wanted babies. OK, fair enough. A normal life. Fortunately, she drifted into the types of design courses she would take at Temple the next year. She described with disgust the casino designer images. She wanted to have scale, proportion, a human dimension. She showed me on her tablet some of her work done as an intern. Interesting. She then tore into my apartment. Utilitarian, possibly, attractive, no! She was now warming up and launched into the styles the lawyers in my office wore. I tried to explain that lawyers generally try to look conservative and a bit stodgy. She agreed that we'd certainly achieved that look. Why did we look like college freshman from some Ivy League school from the 1960s? Fair enough. Button down shirts, striped ties, wing tip shoes. It was a uniform. She explained no one who wanted a creative solution to a problem would hire someone who looked like that. I explained about "office casual Friday." She could only chuckle.

"You mean pressed pants, shiny loafers, and plaid button down shirts." "Well, sort of. What did you expect, cutoff jeans, a tank top and sandals?"

"Those are your only choices? "Well, I guess my golf shorts and a collared sport shirt"

"A little better. You are a little too tightly wound. But on you, it looks good."

"Well thanks for that."

The cheesesteaks, once begotten outside the precincts of Philadelphia proper lose their edge: soggy rolls, provolone instead of

Cheez Whiz, and crumbled beef not sliced thin. Not the same. We chatted into the night and went to bed. Could tomorrow bring the surprise we were after?

As I rolled over in bed in the morning, I could smell coffee. Jean was up making breakfast – eggs and toast. "Sorry, Peter, the sausage looked bad." She had already showered and had a towel around her head, and wore a terry bathrobe and flip flops. I ate breakfast, and showered as she dressed. We left early and went to the local bank.

As I had hoped the assistant manager read the Administration Certificate and took us to the safe deposit room. In all estates, the bank officers required to inventory the contents. She was a pleasant local woman, and opened the box and spread the contents out on the table. There was a collection of gold coins, a nice antique watch, deeds to some real estate, and – lo and behold – my firm's envelope containing some bulky papers. It was the Will – dated, notarized – original. I made sure the assistant manager described the Will in detail in her report and made copies. She prepared the required form for the deposit box inventory and notarized it. I was almost trembling. This was a find. A complete turn in the case. I packed all the contents in my brief case, signed the receipt and ran to my car. I called Angelina and told her to tell Roger but to tell him to keep his mouth shut. I went through the new twist in the case. OK, Alicia was now a major heir. There were some charities, some direction for his funeral – now irrelevant. Alicia would have to be told not to do anything stupid like producing a forged "original." Yes, I did call her and swore her to secrecy. Now what about the double indemnity life insurance. Was Harry murdered or was it an accident? A matter of $2 million. Jean seemed pleased for the result. She had not been cheering for Honey apparently. I guess she wanted the truth to come out.

My call with Alicia consisted mainly of squeals. This sophisticated, controlled, political animal was like a little girl at Christmas. What would a few million dollars do to her? Soon we got to the Conshohocken exit and took the expressway into Philadelphia. At the office, put the Will in our office safe after showing Roger. He confirmed that it was the real one.

Now, how to play the next card?

Meeting with Digby

Ms. James as always guarded Digby's door. As our senior partner, he was used to being the mother superior, the den mother, and unofficial shrink for the firm. After years of practicing law of all kinds, he has a reservoir of knowledge and experience about the world which was universally respected. I referred to him as the rabbi and as a devout Anglican, but an educated man, he very much appreciated the compliment. I walked in with Horton's original Will clutched closely.

"So, Peter, you have had a few adventures. Tell me everything." And so I did. He enjoyed the part about Honey having both the good and the bad kidney inside her. It was some kind of obscure metaphor about life. He enjoyed the fact of Alicia giving me Harry's positon on the Commission. He especially appreciated Honey's "gift" to me of Jean – of whom he had already had glowing descriptions in the office gossip. He somehow felt she was Helen of Troy given to noble Paris. "So what will you do now?"

"Good question, Digby. I have been through the alternatives and wondered how to resolve this ethical problem. First, we wrote the Will, so our client is Harry Horton and his estate. Our duty is to see his wishes carried out. We do not represent Honey, Alicia or the heirs.

"Quite right, Peter."

"Now, Alicia gets the vast majority of the estate except for a few small bequests. I could simply bring the Will in to court and have it declared the definitive Will. Except the Estate can claim an insurance policy which is double the amount if Harry's death was accidental. If he was murdered, the estate gets only half. Obviously, this is important to Alicia by about a million dollars."

"Well, was he murdered?"

"In brief, yes. I think so." I described all the evidence so far against Honey. Digby was impressed that it was a good circumstantial case, but not one that would support a criminal conviction beyond a reasonable doubt. I told him about Scuzz possibly now having been in Philadelphia during the time of Harry's death. I described the conversation between Jean and Scuzz and Scuzz' threats. As usual Digby listened carefully, interspersing questions.

"So what do you think, Peter?"

"I have a few possibilities. One, I can do nothing and simply let the estate be distributed. Since the issue of accidental death versus murder is still up in the air, Alicia could insist on full payment of the double indemnity while the insurance carrier would have the burden of proving a murder. Two, I could insist on a further investigation of the murder, disappoint Alicia and perhaps never succeed in a full proof of the murder. Alicia has been very good to me, she got me appointed to the Commission and handed me Harry Horton's file on the whole Newberry deal. I must owe her something. On the other hand, Honey introduced me to Jean. I may have an ethical or moral dilemma here. I have gifts from two different women."

"Do you think Harry was murdered for his estate or his kidney?"

"I think so, yes... both."

"So if you succeed in proving Honey or her people murdered Harry, Ms. Allende loses half of the estate or $1 million. But if you do nothing and murder is not proven, she gets double. On the one hand, she will be disappointed in you, and on the other, she will think you are grateful to her for her giving you a spot on the Commission.

"You owe a legal duty to the Estate to ensure that its value is as high as it can be. On the other hand, you should not foster the commission of a crime by allowing the perpetrator to profit from it."

"True again."

"Interesting. Why not speak to Ms. Allende about this? Maybe, she has an opinion. If she agrees to pursue the murder investigation despite its cost to her, I suggest you sue Scuzz and the casino for attacking you and Jean and pursue the theory that the attacks were done to cover up the murder. You could take the depositions under oath of Scuzz and the Vargas character and see what you get. You might get the insurance company to kick in some of the legal fees since it might benefit them."

We discussed the details of Digby's advice a bit more, and I left our meeting in awe of Digby's clear headedness and his ability to break down the issues. After all, that is what a lawyer does. See the issues in isolated form and reach practical conclusions. So I went back to the office and called Alicia.

Talk With Alicia

I wanted to talk with Alicia face-to-face and explain the entire picture. She was not only smart, but savvy as well. She had an excellent grasp of politics and people. On the other hand, we were talking about $1 million of her money. She could easily tell me to stand aside and do nothing. Fair enough, that was her prerogative – it was her money and while she was not the client per se, she could claim that I was interfering with collecting the full value of the estate. She agreed to come to my office where we could discuss this problem in private and at length.

Once again, the office as abuzz as a tall striking woman with platinum silver hair, in a shimmering silver suit with an incredibly short skirt was led down the hall to my office. When the door closed, the buzz went several notes higher.

"Peter, I am most grateful for your retrieving the original Will. What is the problem now?"

"Alicia, once again, I am most grateful for my spot on the Commission and the Newberry file. I have a kind of mixed feeling about the whole murder issue. I felt I had to discuss it with you. While you are not the client of our firm per se, you do have a right to complain if the value of the estate is diminished if I participate in the murder investigation. You recall that, if we had no original Will, proof of a murder would invalidate Honey's claim to the estate. Now with the Will in hand, proof of murder would cause you to lose $1 million."

"I see. Interesting problem. You would have to reverse course."

"You got it."

"Now this Honey, I've seen her in action. She's a shrewd one. Do you think she got the casino people to do it?"

"I do."

"But the murder charges were dropped. They couldn't prove it because her new kidney did not match the DNA of her old kidney."

"That's right but it is not double jeopardy. They can also re-arrest her and try to prove murder once again."

"Suppose, they traded Mr. Horton's kidney in Cuba for one that did match."

"Exactly what I think happened."

"So why would the casino people want to help her?"

"First, she owed them lots of money which she would repay out of her inheritance. Second, she was an old girl friend of this guy Scuzz and she wanted to retire, have a new kidney and have enough money to live on."

"I see. Now if she gets nothing, she has her kidney problem solved, but no money and is indebted to the casino for life."

"So she desperately needs money or she lives out her years in poverty, she has no disability to claim, and she only has a few years of her looks left to work for the casino."

"So far so good."

"If I tell you to back off the murder investigation or it is never sufficiently proven, I get an extra $1 million."

"True again."

"On what you have now, you can't get a murder trial much less a conviction."

"True."

"Hmm. Is it possible the casino people did the murder without this Honey's knowledge or compliance?"

"I doubt it."

"As you know, Harry was a very close friend of mine and he left me a lot of money. Something tells me if he was murdered I would like to see them caught and punished."

"In that case, Alicia, one suggestion we had was to pursue a suit against this guy Scuzzo and his muscle Vargas for trying to cover up the murder by attacking this lady Jean and me. I could cross examine him on all the murder issues during a deposition under oath."

"Yeah, I heard about that. Your secretary put one in the hospital with a putter to the back of his head. I must congratulate her on the way out. What does she weight about 100 pounds?"

"Yeah, give or take."

"What happens if you win the suit?"

"The court awards money damages."

"To you and to this lady Jean."

"Could be, but a difficult case."

"But if you prove a cover-up for a murder, do you not prove that they were in on the murder?"

"Possibly."

"Who pays for the lawsuits?"

"I can get the insurance carrier to chip in. I mean they would save a payout of $1 million."

OK, it's simpler than I thought. You sue, if you win I get the proceeds after legal fees. If you lose, I get another $1 million. Just chalk it up to my wanting to know if Harry was murdered and by whom."

"Wow, Alicia, that's brilliant. I really want to find out myself."

"I knew you did, Peter. Even though Honey gave you her best girl."

"How did you hear about that?"

"Peter, please! I've got friends." She certainly did.

"My best to Jean. I hope it works out." I had to blush, did everyone know? Alicia was the most savvy I knew."

We shook on the deal. I was free to go after Honey, Scuzz and Vargas. I called the insurance company, they were ready to go, full legal fees. Of course, I could not use our law firm. Too many conflicts.

I called my buddy, Howard Spearman. He was a brilliant trial lawyer. We would meet and I would turn over my file.

Talk With Jean

It was seeping through my consciousness that Honey had not really denied causing the death of her brother Harry and removing his kidney to be placed in her body. She hinted that perhaps Harry's father was not hers and the DNA would not be similar. She also seemed to know the new kidney would not match Harry's DNA. She didn't say how she knew this, but seemed to insist that her lawyer not oppose the Attorney General's motion to take a biopsy. Of course, if the new kidney's DNA was a match to Harry's, it would be very incriminating. She would have been caught red-handed or should I say what – red something or other. On the other hand – to strain a metaphor - if it didn't match, there might be a huge gap to fill to avoid raising reasonable doubt.

I walked home from Harry's condo where Honey was staying and was met outside my own condo building by a somewhat frumpy lady in a wrinkled trench coat and a bucket hat.

"Hello, handsome," the lady said. I looked up. The lady was carrying a bag of groceries. I nodded hello and kept walking. The lady fell into step with me. "What's a girl to do to get a date in this town?" I looked up. The lady had removed her sunglasses and Jean's brilliant blue eyes were sparkling at me.

"Jean. What…?" I wasn't sure what to say. Jean was supposed to be hiding out in the Poconos. Some bad people were after her, and, not too incidentally, me. I meant to ask her why she was here and didn't she know it was dangerous.

"Peter, I got bored and lonely up in the mountains. So I came down. I'll make dinner. Is that okay?"

"Of course, come on in."

As we rode the elevator, she said she'd heard about Vargas' and Scuzz' attacks on me. She said she was sorry she had caused all this trouble.

"Jean, I have to know some things."

"Yes, yes, I know. I'll tell you the whole story. Over dinner." When we went into my apartment, she went to the kitchen and began preparing dinner. "Peter, I got a bottle of wine open, it's on the sidebar. Pour me one."

Yes there was a new bottle – open and breathing – of red – a pinot noir. I poured two glasses and came into the kitchen.

She was making a tomato sauce and stirring things into it, and rolling some meatballs – the real kind with ground beef and pork, parmesan, garlic and other things.

"So you didn't buy some bottle of sauce and some frozen meatballs."
"Peter, please. I used to cook my family meals since I was 12 and my mother was Italian. I do things the right way."

I'm impressed. Who taught you?"

"When my folks were wasted, I'd call up my neighbors, or my teacher at school. After a while, I watched the cooking shows on TV. I like to cook." She was slicing up a salad now. Soon, dinner was served. "I don't like cooking for just me."

"Jean, this is delicious. I mean really good."

"Oh, spaghetti and meatballs are easy. I really like a better challenge, but I didn't know what you had in your kitchen."

"OK, now, Jean. I've got a ton of questions. I mean that's what lawyers do, we ask questions."

"Fire away."

"Alright, I only know you are Jean. What is your real name?"

"Oh! I was afraid you'd ask that. I'm Jean Schmedlap."

I started to smile. She might be putting me on. But she had an earnest face and seemed embarrassed. "I've been stuck with that name for years. Even in middle school and high school. I would be teased.

Yes. I am Jean Marie Schmedlap. I have to get rid of that last name. I'm not too fond of my parents so I don't have to keep their name. At least they didn't hyphenate. That's why I'm not on Facebook, or LinkedIn or the other websites. I go by the name Jean Jewel. I have to get rid of that name too. That's my casino name."

I kept my mouth shut about the obvious implications of the M word, but I had been thinking about it. I hadn't been a good husband before, too many nights at work. My divorce had been amicable enough. I felt guilty my ex hadn't gotten the relationship she wanted. I was more than a little gun-shy about remarriage or should I have said the re-M word. I avoided suggesting how she should change her name. If I suggested a legal name change, I knew that was trouble. So I kept my mouth shut. That's another thing lawyers learn to do.

"OK, next question. Both Vargas and Scuzz were very eager to find out where you were hiding. They seemed to want to intimidate you because of something you know."

"I kept my eyes and ears open while I worked at the casino. I know lots of things. I always knew I'd have to protect myself so I kept a diary and wrote things down."

"So what did they do? Prostitution, tax fraud, skimming casino profits?"

"No. That's closely watched by the Casino Commission." Basically, money laundering."

"How did that work?"

"As you know Honey, the other girls and I entertained the whales. The whales had hot money. They were upper level government people from third world countries or Russia with a stash of corruption money bribes, siphoning deals off of exports or imports, more than a few Russians, lots of Latin Americans, lots of Africans. Sometimes a few American gangsters, or con men. We brought them in, and then Scuzz and his guys would figure out a way to put the foreign currency into safe American investments or other things. Our fee was usually 30%

depending on how risky everything was. These whales would come in with wads of cash stuffed everywhere – most often in golf bags. They'd get gold coins, jewels, artwork, antiques – sometimes they'd take it home, sometimes they'd put it in a safe deposit box. Bigger money would go into real estate, oil wells, etc. – all as limited partnership interests in offshore companies. Mostly we would buy expensive condos in the U.S. from developers. Just look around Florida and see how many condos are in foreign names or obscure LLCs. That's laundered money. We had lawyers in Miami and offshore do the paperwork. We took their dirty money and made it into clean investments – untraceable. When these guys had to flee their country they had a nice stash on the outside."

"How do you learn all this?"

"These whales aren't very bright. Usually they are just military men, or crony thugs of the boss of the country or the mob. So they talk. They like to brag if you will listen. Most of the girls were too stupid to be interested. I listened and egged them on.

"They were happy to blab to a pretty girl. They didn't think women were bright enough to understand. So they dropped names, they left behind correspondence. Best of all, they had pockets full of cash, so they tipped well. I did very well, but I also knew this information was valuable. Honey always did too. She was no dummy. We each had a lot of good stuff on a lot of whales and the casino as well. As long as we looked pretty and played dumb, we heard a lot. I put mine away carefully every night. Names, times, dates, places, amounts, you name it I recorded it in my diary. I put it in a computer file and locked it away. I knew it would be valuable for my protection. You understand I never really liked the life. I'm not a fancy girl – fancy clothes, shoes, jewels, makeup, cars – they don't mean much to me. But I was picked off the UNLV campus and, kind of by accident, I was a success in the business. Honey taught me and protected me. I made lots of money and got lots of tips. They gave me a nice condo. Then they moved me to Miami. All I had to do was dress up, be polite and flirt with the whales. I got a percentage of what they spent, what they played. I was never supposed to know about the money laundering, but the whales loved to brag and show me how big and important they were. I was their arm-candy and they loved the attention."

"So why did you leave? What happened with Scuzz?"

"For a while he was after me big time. I know better than that. So I put up with his harassment and grabbing. If he got to be too much, I just went blah around him, and told him to find the other girls. He got mad and used to hit me, but he realized that I was not that interested. What really pissed him off was when Honey sent me to you to get you on her side in the Will contest. He knew he could compete with the loud mouth whales, but a smart lawyer, he knew would be trouble. Besides you weren't in Miami. He had me followed while I was with you, and he heard about the second date. The trip to the Art Museum. He knew I was a hippie chick who liked culture, and he knew I would like that date. So when I got back, he was really angry, but he knew the whole thing was pretty innocent. He didn't believe Honey's explanation or mine. So he beat me up. That embarrassed and humiliated me. I know my time with the casino was up. I told him I wanted to leave and he threatened me. I made the mistake of threatening him back… with my knowledge of the money laundering and skimming. He didn't like that. He's a bully and he expects to intimidate people. When I was not intimidated he couldn't take it. When I ran off to Philadelphia, he knew I was a big problem. I don't know how he figured I ran to Philadelphia, but he must have figured you could protect me. So I guess I got you into this mess. I'm sorry, I owe you."

"Wow, I can see how scared you must have been."

"Well, some of the girls just take it and live the high life. It wasn't for me. Besides, I don't just give up and get intimidated."

"So what do you do now?"

"I got accepted at Temple in art and architecture, I need three semesters to graduate. So I have to live in Philadelphia. So where do I stay?"

"Temple's on Broad Street, so you can stay anywhere near the subway. So that's Center City, South Philly, lots of nice places." I was avoiding the obvious. I'm such a coward.

"How about us?" Uh-oh! Why do women do this? I don't feel comfortable expressing my feelings. This bombshell rocked me some.

She could tell. She was smirking. She knew she was giving me a super shock. "Jean, I… I…"

"Well said counselor, do I get the message?"

"No… I… I… Dammit. Yes. I want you to be my girlfriend. Yes. I like you a lot. I want this to continue." How it was her turn to blush. As beautiful and worldly as she was, she too was surprised, not by what I felt, but that I actually said it. I hadn't said the L word, but I was close.

"Yes, I want this to continue." There, I'd said it. "But will Scuzz be after you still?"

"I think if he knows I'm with you now, and that you know what to do with my files. I think he may back off. I'm not sure whether Honey's on my side or his. We have to be careful about her. But I think you should tell her about my files and see if she tells Scuzz."

"Scuzz and Vargas are still recovering from their injuries and are on bail, they can't leave Miami without permission. Of course, they can still do that anyway. But if they're caught in Philadelphia before trial, their bail is revoked and they go to jail until trial and face new criminal charges."

I was not sure why this really beautiful woman was interested in me. I mean I'm not chopped liver, but I'm not a show stopper. I have had this theory about women that very well may get me in trouble. Men see women initially as sex objects, when they get a bit more mature they look for a bit more, but they usually judge women in isolation – as they are with him not as part of a social group. Women seek their mates as part of a social group. Maybe they sense their own physical weakness or their inability to protect themselves, so they are drawn to males who are respected in the community they wish to live in and who will protect them. Could that be what she saw? A successful lawyer who could provide for and protect a family. These thoughts ran through my head as Jean talked and I looked at her perfect features. As she stopped, I came to my senses and re-assumed my lawyer-like mode.

"Jean, this information has great value. First we need to produce a second copy and let Scuzz know if any harm comes to you or, and I do not hesitate to say, me, the second copy goes to the authorities, let's say the FBI or something. Next, Scuzz is already in mild trouble for his fight with me. It would make for a helluva case against him and the casino. A federal case. Big time. I know a thing or two about whistleblowers now, it could mean a very healthy check for you. Why don't you think about that and let me know if you are willing to go that route."

"I know. I've thought about it. I don't want to be in Witness Protection. Could I be protected?"

"That depends on whether it's just Scuzz and the casino, or if it's part of a bigger mob operation. But once your diary is out, there's little reason to harm you. I don't think you'd have to testify and your targets are mainly the whales. They would be persuaded to roll over on the casino and Scuzz as I see it. But I'd have to think this through a bit more. I'd like to talk to a friend of mine at the FBI, off the record and see what he thinks. May I do that?"

"Would he keep this confidential and would he have to know my name for this talk?"

"Yes, he could be trusted to keep it confidential and he wouldn't learn your name unless I was sure of your safety."

"OK, talk to him, see what he thinks."

Things quieted down, we watched an old movie and she spent the night and several more in my apartment.

Suit Against Scuzz and the Casino

I called Howard Spearman and arranged for a meeting to discuss my suit against Scuzz and the casino.

Howard's office was different from ours. It was high style with strong hip designer influences. Modern steel sculptures hung on the walls, abstract paintings, and geometric designs on the thick tufted carpet. The receptionist sat at a chrome and glass desk. She had black lipstick, shiny black short hair and heavy black eye makeup. I thought I had walked into some science fiction set. Money blared out at us. New money. Big dollars. Howard wanted people to know he made big bucks for himself and his clients. Whether he actually made it or not was another matter. Maybe his wealthy in-laws put up the money, or maybe his annoying wife once known as Andy in high school now referred to as Audra. She was one of those women who with little education or brains, but lots of money claims to know all about business, law and politics, but in reality knows embarrassingly little. Now she sat on lots of boards and offered her inane advice. Yet her money commanded people's attention so she persisted.

Howard on the other hand was a bright guy, in law school, a complete nerd, but now dressed by his wife and her consultant wore the latest designer names. His hair was cut into something European, his hands were manicured. Did I detect a small nose job and some fat suctioning? Yes I did. But he was a bright guy. Just what I needed. I explained the case to him – one lawyer to another. He immediately picked up that he would have to try a murder case within a minor assault and battery case. And a murder case that had not passed muster before. He was impressed that this was a high profile case – one that would keep him in the limelight and in constant contact with the press, but one that had a low probability of success. Since he usually worked on a contingency – i.e. a percentage of the money collected, he was not anxious to take it on. But I said the magic words: "hourly basis." He was going to be paid for his time. We negotiated a fair rate considering the publicity and that most of it would be paid by the insurance carrier to whom a finding of murder would save them $1 million. The main point I wanted to have him make that Scuzz and Vargas attacked me to cover up a murder case. On the way, he could make some money, but he had to do what I wanted first. He got the message at $500 per hour.

Paperwork for Suits

After talking to Alicia, I was amazed at her response. I think most people would have taken the second million and run. I certainly can understand her long term relationship with Harry would lead her to seek out his killer, if there was one. But I had to see Alicia as a political animal. While a million dollars was nice she was already well fixed, and committed to being single. Political bargaining chips were the currency she dealt in. She had handed to me Harry's seat on the Commission and his whistleblower file to me for something intangible: My loyalty, a favor to be called in later. Now, she was willing to trade in a million dollars in hard cash, for a stake in the outcome of two iffy lawsuits against Scuzz, Vargas and the casino. But she liked the action of a lawyer dedicated to her poking around among possible nefarious dealings to see if she could get something on someone important – a new bargaining chip to play. Since I didn't think like her, I had not anticipated her reaction, but now I could see it. Alicia was a very sly fox.

With that in mind, I started work on the lawsuits and the whistleblower case Jean might bring against the casino for money-laundering for the whales she had entertained.

I shut the door to my office, and started to outline the cases. The assault case against Scuzz and Vargas were pretty straight forward. Scuzz might have some money, and could afford a decent settlement. Vargas was just a thug and probably had little to offer. No, the case had to be against the casino. This would be a difficult issue to contend that Scuzz and Vargas were trying to cover up a scheme to murder Harry and their money-laundering. Since I did not want to alarm any of the whales, I had to leave their actual names out of the complaint. It was my intention to keep a close eye of the men on the list and subpoena them when they returned to Miami. I had hoped this would scare the casino people as they saw their customers slowly compromised by the deposition they would be forced to attend. Certainly it would be embarrassing to the whales since they were being accused of hiding corrupt money in the U.S. or offshore. Certainly, it jeopardized the business that Scuzz and the casino were doing. Of course, Spearman would be the one bringing the suits on behalf of Jean and me, but a good lawyer comes prepared to a meeting. We all know that the key to success is preparation. As we said in football practice, 50% preparation, 50% perspiration.

Since the whistleblower case Jean would bring against the casino had a direct impact on our assault cases against the casino, I was hoping the feds would accept the whistleblower case and do all the hard work for us. When I had basically sketched out the paperwork for each of the cases, I brought Jean into the office to get the fine details.

I met Jean for lunch and then we went back to the office. Poor Jean had to run the gauntlet of my supposedly sophisticated and mature firm members as we walked down the corridor. Our relationship was no longer a secret. I was sure Jean was not offended by the attention, but her blush and mine seemed to provide even more good-natured abuse. I knew that my compatriots were pleased to see me with a new woman, but, "Yo guys! Enough is enough."

We made it to my office and went over all her notes, and even a few DVDs. She had done a good job of documenting her recollection and had been thorough. As a new name came up, I had Angelina come in to do some research on Google and her many other online resources on each name. We had a nice collection of government cronies from Latin America, Africa and the former Soviet Union burying money in investments in the U.S. and the Caribbean in real estate, bank accounts and stocks. Based on our rough estimates, I was sure we were talking well over a $100 million with a nice 30% fee in the casino. The more carefully we documented and detailed each person and his personal stash, the more likely the feds were to accept the whistleblower case. It was after 8:00 p.m. when we quit for the night, so we went to a nice old Italian restaurant reportedly owned by the mob. I knew this reputation to be false, but it helped to draw a nice crowd of tourists and suburbanites. I could almost hear Melissa from Devon whisper to her husband, "Taylor, do you think that waiter is a triggerman?" I think the restaurant even imported a few ethnic-looking Italians to dress up the place. The food though was always good, but I don't think our waiter looked at me once as I gave the order. Jean had his full attention. He was an authentic Italian.

The next day, I dropped our whistleblower paperwork off to the U.S. Attorney's Office. Since I now knew how the game was played, I did not want this case politicized like the Newberry one, so I used a little influence. I called an old buddy of mine from law school on the Organized Crime Task Force. Matthew Macedo was a nice hard-working guy, with good grades from law school. Unfortunately he was Latino, came from a poor family, and wasn't very good looking. None of the firms offered him any starting offer, so he was happy to accept a government job. He was a tenacious investigator and trial lawyer. "Yo, Matt, how you doing these days?"

"Peter, long time no hear. I'm doing fine."

"I can tell. I see you in the newspapers, especially that Russian mob thing."

"Oh, that! We had good FBI work on that. So what can I do for you?" I explained my work on the Newberry whistleblower thing and how the congressman had co-opted the deal. I didn't want this casino thing to suffer the same fate. The FBI is usually above reproach, but the U.S. Attorney is usually a collection of political appointments at the upper levels, the lower levels are filled with bright young people who are very dedicated and a bit too self-righteous. I didn't want this casino thing to go south. I knew Matt would be on board with my request, but he said it would be assigned to the Miami office. He said he would put in a good word with the head of that office – a close friend and a fellow Latino – Herberto Colon. He told me to direct my papers to Colon. I got the message.

I had crafted the paperwork in such a way that my suit against Scuzz, Vargas and the casino would all be brought in the Eastern District of Pennsylvania with a Philadelphia-based judge presiding over the trial as well as the depositions et al. The whistleblower case would be in Miami if either I brought it or the feds did. This pretty much guaranteed that no shenanigans would "interfere" with the two judges' rulings in the case. Do shenanigans "interfere" with judge's reasoning on occasion? Not so much in federal court, but they do occur so why take the risk. A discrepancy between the two judges' actions in the case would draw instant scrutiny. So I let my first shaft of arrows fly and waited. Soon I would get a call from the lawyers for Scuzz and the casino. Much later, I would hear from Colon about the whistleblower. Nothing to do now but wait. What call would come in first? So I settled back in the office and got to work on some of the routine work that had been piling up: Returning calls to clients, preparing briefs, dictating letters.

First, I got a courtesy call from Colon, yes, he would look into it and, no, there would be no outside interference permitted. I got a call from Scuzz' and Vargas' lawyer from their criminal cases, Imperatore. He was representing both in my civil actions, and in his usual bluster, he told me the suit was garbage and he was going to countersue me. This call was highly improper. Where a client is represented by an attorney, opposing counsel may not speak to the client. But this was intimidation, not part of the suit. I said I understood his position, but did he acknowledge at least that Scuzz beat up Jean. He denied it. Did he acknowledge that Vargas attacked me in my own office in front of witnesses? After a pause, he asked me if I was recording him. I explained that it would be a crime in Pennsylvania for me to record our call without his consent. I asked him if Scuzz attacked me in the parking garage. His tone changed slightly. "Look, Stern, (not Peter, not Mr. Stern, Stern) what is this? Do you want a few bucks? I mean my clients got the worst of these fights in self-defense. And you had no injuries. What could this be worth?"

"Ah, Mr. Imperatore, but why was I attacked? In furtherance of some scheme to cover up a murder and money laundering. By employees of the casino. I would say big bucks, and punitive damages. By the way, how are Scuzz and Vargas doing? Have they healed up yet?"

"Yeah, very funny! Yeah, they've healed."

"Well, when can we schedule their depositions? Do I need to compel them or will they appear here in Philadelphia willingly?"

"Hah, no way. File what you gotta. Then come to Miami, on your own ticket."

"You know you pay for that in the end."

"Only if you win."

"Thank you for checking in, Mr. Imperatore, see you in court."

"Count on it." He hung up. I prepared an Order to compel their deposition in Philadelphia and told the court they refused to appear voluntarily. I seem to have gotten Judge Flicker assigned to the case. The judge was part of the wave of small time Republicans now sitting in the local federal district court. A federal judge is nominated by the sitting President, and he usually only approves those from his own party. If there is a Republican senator and a Democratic one, they can horse trade to get a few Democrats in among the Republicans. If there are two Democratic senators, the Republican President lets the judgeships remain vacant until he gets at least one Republican senator. So what we got from the Bush and Reagan years were small time suburban county lawyers appointed as judges. Most of them had no experience in federal court, had a long suffered dislike of Philadelphia county lawyers who were often from big firms, or Jewish or black depending on the case. One good thing though, these small time lawyers were used to appearing in court. On the other hand, they represented a white voter base, came with conservative prejudices and thought that their elevation to the federal bench had raised them to the godhead. They were the boss and they insisted on all the prerogatives of being a federal judge. So you had to kiss their ass, and look like they deserved it. Flicker was no exception. I am sure his suburban, conservative rectitude would be activated by some thugs from a Miami casino attacking a Philadelphia lawyer in his own office or his parking garage. He might overlook some of the niceties and be convinced they were covering up Harry's murder. I felt comfortable in this venue, especially with the blowhard, Mr. Imperatore, offending Flicker's sensitivities at every turn. I felt a mild shiver of shame for tattling on opposing counsel's refusal to produce his clients. But now I was one up on him on the Flicker scoreboard.

One thing about the federal judges, paper doesn't linger long on their desks. In two days, I had an Order to have defendants produced for deposition in Philadelphia within 15 days.

Since Mr. Imperatore hadn't had a chance to object to this motion, he called the judge's law clerk and asked to reconsider since the defendants were residents of Miami. He neglected to tell the judge that they were on bail in Philadelphia for their criminal offenses in Philadelphia and had to return monthly for meetings with the probation department. The judge quickly ordered the deposition to take place in Miami. I was about to object and incur the wrath of the judge for taking up too much of his time on small matters when I got a call from Colon. He wanted me and Jean to meet with his staff in Miami to go over and evaluate the whistleblower case. OK, so problem solved. We could schedule the meeting and the deposition all in the same week. Jean hadn't been back to Miami for some time and would welcome the trip. I had to remember with Judge Flicker not to have prunes for breakfast, he might issue an Order while my intestines might be compromised.

In Miami for Depositions

Scuzz' lawyer thought he had won a minor battle by forcing us to come to Miami to take the deposition of Scuzz and Vargas. All it really did was enable Judge Flicker to issue a makeup Order modifying the one in which he granted me the right to take immediate and early depositions. I didn't mind because it enabled me the opportunity to meet with the Miami office of the FBI to review Jean's whistleblower claim against the casino on the same trip. I had gamed the opportunity to find out from Scuzz and his lawyer what strategy they would use in defending the case before I had to reveal mine in bringing it.

So Jean and I flew down to Miami and stayed at the Langford Hotel – nicely located near the FBI's office and the lawyer's offices near the federal court building. The Langford was a nice old retro hotel but the downtown area of Miami was a revelation. It had turned completely Spanish. Everywhere you turned they were speaking Spanish. Not just Mexican or Puerto Rican, but all the Latin countries, Peruvian, Honduran, with even dots of Brazilian Portuguese thrown in. And at night after dark, from somewhere, homeless men and a few women came out of nowhere to sleep right out on the streets. It had become a third world country. It was late when we got in, so we had a quick hamburger and beer each and went back to the room. Jean stayed in the room while I went to the office floor to prep my notes for the deposition.

There could be a few surprises or none tomorrow. Maybe they had developed an excuse for being in or near Philadelphia at the time of

Harry's death. Maybe they could explain why Vargas was carrying a cooler on the plane to Cuba that Honey had taken to get her new kidney. I wasn't sure at this point whether Scuzz had told his lawyer these facts. Scuzz and Vargas had not been interviewed by the police or that lazy Hackett, so these depositions would be the first to look into what their defenses or alibies might be. How Scuzz' lawyer might play it was still unknown. It was a golden opportunity to ask a criminal defendant questions under oath and on the record.

Jean and I went to the lawyer's office in Miami. Scuzz' lawyer, as part of his Motion, had offered to provide the office which of course was the office for the casino's lawyer. It was a fairly posh, but gaudy office as might be expected for a law firm that represented the casino. The wall had lots of pictures with members of the firm shaking hands with the Florida politicians and a few of the celebrities that appeared at the casino. The receptionist was part of the décor, with a gorgeous figure and a tight red dress and stiletto heels she clicked around the marble floor to take us to the conference room. As Jean walked in, I could feel the tension rise as Scuzz and Vargas saw her on what would be the opposite side of the table. Scuzz had not seen her since he beat her up a few months earlier. Now she was sitting next to his enemy and suing him and the casino. What she knew and might reveal in the lawsuit was still a mystery to him and must be causing him a few sleepless nights. I intended to keep that anxiety at a fever pitch. It is only occasionally that the opposing party sits in on a deposition or even ask questions, but this was a good time for it. Howard Spearman agreed to back off and let me do these depositions. Jean was now dressed up for the occasion in a high fashion black power suit and full glamour makeup. She was ready for battle. I had cautioned her to say nothing since they might try to elicit what she might say. Since her deposition would be far in the future, I wanted to keep them guessing. They just gaped at her. Scuzz' lawyer motioned for Scuzz and Vargas to go to the other end of the room for a short conference. The lawyer had never seen her before and had not realized she would be such a looker. I could hear some loud whispers as the lawyer expressed some anger and surprise at Scuzz.

Soon, the court stenographer was ready and I assembled my notes for the deposition. While the casino's lawyer was present, it appeared that Mr. Imperatore would be representing both Scuzz and Vargas. Interesting? He also objected vehemently to my doing the deposition, but knew the rules permitted it and did not want to bother the judge on this issue.

Before Scuzz was sworn in, I nodded to him and said, "Ah, Mr. Scarramazool (deliberately mispronouncing his name), your nose is healing nicely. Good morning." He of course snarled. He still wore a bandage over his nose concealing several stitches, but the yellow marks still remained from where he had dark purple black bruises from before from my knee to his face. He looked tired, his face was puffy and he now looked all of his 50 some years and his gut was straining his suit jacket. Why had he thought to take on a man in his thirties? Intimidation? Well, that was gone now. His lawyer put his hand on Scuzz' arm, "Now, Scuzz."

The reporter asked Scuzz his name and address and sworn him in. "You may proceed, Mr. Stern."

"Thank you, Ms. Olivedo."

"Mr. Scarramazza, can you give us your occupation and the name of your employer?"

He snarled the answer, "Vice President with the Rock, Roll and Deal Casino"

"Do you know Ms. Honey Horton?"

"Of course, she works as a hostess for the casino."

"Have you now or in the past had an intimate relationship with her?" This question got right to the heart of most of the issues. Most depositions start out with a lot of softball questions about the witness' background, etc., the company structure, etc. This one threw the fat in the fire. I had asked whether Scuzz had in the past or present slept with Honey and were some kind of romantic item. His lawyer of course objected but since the Complaint alleged that the reason Scuzz had helped Honey was because of either a past or present romantic attachment it was relevant. He and I squabbled a bit about things until I threatened to call Judge Flicker to resolve the issue. They backed down and insisted I make my question more specific. Fair enough."

"Mr. Scarramazza, have you ever inserted your penis into Ms.

Horton's vagina?" A huge outburst, Anger. More threats to call the judge. Jean giggled as did the court stenographer who threw up her hands after trying to record the lawyers' simultaneous arguments.

Finally, the answer. "Yes."

Next question, "When was the last time?" More arguments, more threats to call the judge. Finally the answer, "About August."

"This past August?" Nods from his lawyer.

"Yes." Nods from his lawyer.

"Where?" Nods from his lawyer.

"In Miami, at her place." Nods from his lawyer.

"How long has this romantic relationship with Ms. Horton been going on?"

"About 15 years."

"When were you in Philadelphia last?"

"I don't remember." The usual answer of a guilty party.

"Where did you stay?" A glance at his lawyer. It would be pretty obvious from his credit card unless he paid cash. Usually unlikely. The glance was to ask his lawyer if he should again answer that he didn't remember. The lawyer nodded.

"I don't remember."

"Did you charge your stay on a credit card?" Now this stupid deception could end.

"Uh, yes."

"Which your card, yours, the casino's or some other?"

"Uh, the casino's."

"So whatever you were doing in Philadelphia was on casino business?" Ahah. Had 'em. He was now about to admit that whatever he was doing, if it was murder or something else, was on behalf of the casino.

"I don't remember."

"You don't know why you were in Philadelphia?"

"Not now." Of course, I knew we would find out he had charged the casino for a stay at the Waldorf in Philadelphia just two days before Harry's death.

"Have you ever gone on the Northeast Extension of the Pennsylvania Turnpike?" I knew I was getting a bit too close. Scuzz would now be pinned down to a lie which might be disproven, or another inconvenient memory or forgettery as we call it. So he took another rout.

"I plead the Fifth." Scuzz was now embarked on a dangerous cause. In pleading the "Fifth," he was now asserting his right under the Fifth Amendment not to "incriminate" himself. That means two things. First, he might have to demonstrate to the court how his answer, if made, might tend to incriminate him, and two, he was stuck with this answer through the trial. He could not change it. He had now refused to answer my questions and was telling the jury that, if he did, he might incriminate himself. i.e. admit to a crime: in this case, murder. So I now went through every question I could think of which he would plead the Fifth on.

As a tactical matter for him and the casino, this was a disaster. In a criminal case, the defendant does not have to say or prove a thing. That is his privilege and the government must prove every part of the criminal case. In a civil case, the plaintiff must set out a case which it intends to prove and the defendant must admit or deny every fact alleged. If he doesn't deny doing something, then it is deemed admitted. By refusing to answer, Scuzz was now saying that they would not deny what I had said in the Complaint. It would then be deemed an admission or the jury might be instructed that they could make an "adverse inference," i.e. one that was against the witness' interest. Scuzz' lawyer who may have known criminal law, was making a mistake in civil law. The casino lawyer asked for a recess and wanted to confer with Scuzz and his lawyer. He at least understood what Scuzz' non-denial meant for the casino. The recess started at 10:00 and was not done by lunch time so we went out to a local deli.

It was 1:30 p.m. when we returned. Apparently, Scuzz, Vargas and the lawyers had decided to continue with the stonewall defense and refuse to answer any questions by claiming the Fifth. I write this off to their simply not having thought through the case because I had required them to appear for depositions so quickly. They had admitted being in Philadelphia just before Horton's death by using a company credit card before they realized my questions would bring them closer to admitting complicity in a murder. The admission as to the company credit card was vital since it now bound a deep pocket defendant into liability. Some questions remained open. Clearly Honey had remained in Miami and not come north with Scuzz. Somehow, Vargas may have gotten the kidney and managed to get on board the plane to Cuba with Honey with a cooler probably containing Harry's good kidney. There were some holes. At least, we could now prove that Scuzz beat up Jean, and attacked me and Vargas attacked me. They plead the Fifth over what they said, but did not deny that it had something to do with silencing Jean and me over something Scuzz said to Jean he wished to keep unknown. He of course claimed the Fifth on everything having to do with the money laundering for the whales. It might still be unclear that Scuzz had accidentally revealed something which would implicate him in the murder, or something about the money laundering. In either case, his attacks would appear to be related to one of the two illegal activities, and were funded in part by a casino company credit card. We had ample proof of the attacks so the case was looking good. The problem was that, unless we could prove the underlying crimes, it would not get a very large award from the jury. Sure, I was attacked but suffered little in the way of painful injury. In fact, Scuzz and Vargas got the worst of it. We had alleged that we were entitled to punitive damages. That meant the jury had to hear these attacks were related to covering up the larger crime.

My real motive in bringing the suit was to have a platform to dig deeper into the murder investigation. After all, that is what I promised Alicia. These depositions did little for that. We could establish Scuzz' presence in Philadelphia, but why he was there was still an issue.

So some good came of the depositions. One positive was that now the casino through its attorney would be aware of the entire case. A casino license is an extremely valuable piece of business property, and casino commissions are supposed to be very diligent in ensuring that criminal elements do not infiltrate the industry. Upper level executives pleading the Fifth over attacks on a lawyer and an employee to possibly cover up a larger crime is something a commission might well want to investigate further.

I was feeling upbeat as we left for the day so I took Jean to Lincoln Road in Miami Beach. She of course was familiar with this stretch of fashionable shops and nice open air restaurants. For me, it was a first. It was as advertised. One after another restaurant lined the promenade free of automobile traffic. Seafood, Italian, fancy French, Mexican, steak house, you name it was there. Many of the high fashion shops lined the walkway along with a variety of occult vendors and gift shops. The best part was the people had strolled by as we had a drink: of course, the families on vacation, but the South Beach crowd of curiosities came by dressed in a variety of outlandish displays. Women in string bikinis, muscle bound men heavily tattooed, elderly permanent residents, gay couples, they were a continuous parade of diversity. My piña colada hit the spot and I could feel the tension of the deposition slip away. We had an excellent seafood dinner and chatted about the discomfort we must be causing Scuzz and the casino. Tomorrow, we would meet with the FBI and the U.S. Attorney's Office to show Jean's collection of DVDs and notes about the money laundering with Colon. If they took up the case, Jean would get a nice pay day and Scuzz and the casino would be under a heavy dose of government inquiry. In the meantime, we checked out some of the South Beach night clubs. They had great bands – Latin, Brazilian, some interesting Afro-Cuban jazz. There were some great dancers. By now my third piña colada was making me drowsy so we went back to our hotel. On the way in, there was a note from Honey of all people who wanted to see me on my return to Philadelphia. What could that mean? Anyway, a good night's sleep and off to Mr. Colon's office on the morrow.

At the Miami U.S. Attorney's Office

The breakfast at the hotel was meager and expensive so we strolled up to an outdoor café. Jean, a native Californian, had been missing huevos rancheros, but not for long as she wolfed her order down. I had a plain old American breakfast of bacon and eggs, but the coffee was amazing. Somehow these Latino restauranteurs seem to know how to buy great coffee from somewhere in their home country. So refreshed and well fed, we went to the U.S. Attorney's Office, through extensive metal detection equipment and even a brief inquisition as to our purpose there. They even called up to Colon's office to verify. The Miami U.S. Attorney's Office is extremely large and busy. They have drugs leaking through our southern borders, immigrants landing illegally on our shores, as well as the usual federal crimes. We were lead back through a maze of offices to a conference room. We wheeled behind us Jean's collection of DVDs and notes. At the table, Colon himself sat with three other people. A female U.S. attorney sat with a copy of my summary of Jean's complaint with heavy annotation marks and piles of computer printouts. She was Sarah Middleton – a plump middle-aged somewhat frowsy woman in a dark suit. To her left sat Joe Arcona – an older swarthy FBI man with salt and pepper crew cut of an ex-military man, and Hampton Jones – a young black man who never said who he worked for.

I started our meeting by summarizing Jean's background, her prior employment, and what she had heard or learned as she worked for the casino. Of course, it was already in the paperwork I had sent ahead earlier. The others nodded in acknowledgement. About halfway through, Ms. Middleton broke in.

"Mr. Stern, we are of course aware of your claims from your excellent summary and we are interested. May we ask some questions of Ms. Shmedlap?"

"Of course, by all means."

Ms. Middleton opened. "Some of these questions may be a bit insulting, but we must find out if you are a credible and reliable witness. Were you ever a prostitute for the casino or previously?"

"No. I was simply to entertain men with large net worths who came to the casino, and encourage them to gamble."

"Did you ever have sexual relations with any of these men?"

"No. It was supposed to be against company policy to do so, and we were under heavy surveillance on casino grounds. We were not to leave the premises with these men. A few of the girls did, I did not."

"This issue will be heavily contested by the casino if we take the case. Are you prepared for this?"

"Absolutely."

"Did you have any romantic attachments while you worked in Miami?"

"I dated several men. A professor at the University Miami, and a real estate developer. None of these relationships got very far." I breathed a quiet sigh of relief.

"Why did you record all of this information?"

"Ms. Horton advised me to have something to protect myself if the casino ever turned against me. I also sensed that something illegal was going on, and that I could become involved. Some of the men I entertained liked to brag about things and I knew they were illegal."

"Did you participate in any of these illegal dealings?"

"No, the men often would go to meet Scuzz and a team of lawyers and accountants in the company offices. I was never in on that."

"But you heard about it from the men later?"

"Yes. They were very proud of how important they were to receive such attention."

"Were you ever asked to sleep with the men?"

"Not by the casino, yes, by the men. I was offered marriage proposals, mistress arrangements, trips to exotic places. I rejected them. I was making very good money between my salary and perks as well as generous tips."

"What kinds of perks?"

"The usual, health and all, and a free apartment in a complex with the other women who did what I did. They were deluxe furnished condos. I suspect they were heavily surveilled. I never did anything on the premises to warrant their concern."

"Do you now or have you ever done drugs?"

"No. My parents were hippies who grew pot in California and were often stoned. I did the cooking and cleaning for them and my sister from the time I was 12. I have a disgust for my parents and their lifestyle and left the house for college as soon as I could. No, I do not do drugs."

Middleton and Arcona then went down the list of each of the men and the details of each. Jean corroborated my memorandum and added details as they went along. Hampton Jones sat like a stone. He did not take notes, but there was a recorder in front of him. I could not make eye contact with him. The morning session ran until 2:00 p.m. when we all left for lunch. There was a Peruvian fast food place around the corner, so we had some pulled pork, rice and beans. Interesting but not great. We walked around the area which seemed to be filled with small time mom and pop stores – mostly bodegas or delis and a few variety stores. Part of the walk took us past rows of jewelry stores. I found the store selling Brazilian stones the most interesting. It has always amazed me that women want diamonds which come from oppressive, exploitive mining companies, and from a monopolistic cartel that keeps the price of diamonds extremely high. Instead they could have these brilliant colored stones from Brazil. I mean the stones were of all colors, nicely cut and set in exquisite settings. If I were a woman, I would want one of those instead. I mentioned this argument to Jean.

Then I began to feel waves of fear of the "M" word. I mean jewelry was a symbol for dare I say, the "M" word. Fortunately, Jean saved me some anguish. "I don't think expensive stones are very attractive. It says something negative about the woman who needs them." Whoa, where did that come from?

Somewhat relieved, we went back to the U.S. Attorney's Office, went through the embarrassing security gauntlet. After the lengthy trek back to the conference room, we sat. The tone was different. It looked like Hampton Jones was in charge. He had a deep voice and looked at us intensely.

"Mr. Stern, Ms. Shmedlap, we find your information very interesting. I am from the Defense Intelligence Community of the United States. We believe we could put your contacts to good use if you are willing to cooperate."

"What would you expect her to do?" I was a bit nervous about this. It was not the way my whistleblower suit was supposed to work.

"We have marked all of your paperwork and DVDs as classified secret. It may not be disseminated or used for any purpose other than as the property of the Central Intelligence Agency. We would invite Ms. Shmedlap to continue as a hostess for the casino and to extract information from these visitors from Latin America, Africa, and the former Soviet Union. She would be on tape and under heavy protection at all times. She would be compensated very nicely."

"Where would I do this?"

"In the casino where you worked before."

"But I was beaten up by Scuzz. I left there for good, and now live in Philadelphia."

"We would expect you to return to Miami for specific occasions when some targets of our agency are coming to Florida."

"How often?"

"About once per month for several days each. We would arrange for a hotel, and a per diem as well as compensation."

I had to ask, "What about her whistleblower case, and the money she might get from that. And the casino, they are guilty of this money laundering as well. What makes you think they will cooperate in your venture? She wouldn't be safe walking around the casino when some of these thugs learn about all this."

"Mr. Stern, we are well aware of the problem. We expect to confront the casino with our evidence and threaten to discontinue their license to operate if they do not cooperate. Part of this is that they would disgorge all of their fees, and cooperate fully in our operation. They must provide all information past or present and surrender all proceeds under their control. These proceeds would form the basis for Ms. Shmedlap's whistleblower award."

"So this is contingent on getting the casino's full cooperation?"

"Yes. Rest assured, they will be persuaded to cooperate."

"But what about Scuzz and Vargas?"

"They will be arrested, tried and convicted. They will also be persuaded to cooperate to shorten their prison time and the casino will fall in line or lose their license, and their executives will be prosecuted individually."

Jean turned to me, "Peter, can I think about this?"

Hampton Jones assured her, "Of course, can you let us know tomorrow?"

I had to ask, "That's awfully quick. Where could we reach you?"

"Look, my name is not Hampton Jones, and you can't reach me. I reach you. I must have your answer before the information is stale and word of our proposed operation gets out."

"OK, I understand." I turned to Jean, "Let's talk." I turned to Jones and said, "What does this pay anyway?" He handed me a typewritten memo spelling out in detail. Each trip to Miami was to be compensated at a flat rate of $15,000 plus transportation, quarters and per diem. Quarters would be at a "safe" apartment in Miami Beach in a beach high rise. I note that they added that I could accompany her. Someone was keeping us under close scrutiny.

It was not slow to dawn on me the tremendous value Jean's collection would have to the intelligence community. They would have the goods on many of the dictators and their cronies throughout Latin America,

Africa and the former Soviet Union; a treasure trove of blackmail once thought to be safe in the hands of the casino, but now an asset of the CIA.

Of course, it would be tricky to play out. First, the federal forces would have to come down hard on the casino and acquire its files on these whales, while at the same time, threatening the executives with prosecution and causing them to forfeit their fees gained by the money laundering. Yes. A very neat trick. And it would have to be pulled off quickly and neatly before the information leaked out and the whole scheme was exposed. This would ruin not only the lives of the whales themselves but the force of blackmail. Certainly the evidence was there and available, but criminal prosecutions can be lengthy and drag through the court system's thicket of hearings, grand juries and motions. This would have to be a lightning strike on the casino, Scuzz and Vargas before any of it leaked. What's more, Scuzz and Vargas were loose cannons. They would have to be persuaded that they were guilty and would lose in court, but would benefit by prompt and silent cooperation. Hampton Jones' job and that of his fellow agency operatives was daunting.

As to Jean, it was a fairly easy decision. They could collect her whistleblower money either way with the full force of the federal government behind her. The question was whether she would want to accept the risk and the disruption in her life to be constantly in the hands of the agencies listening in on her conversations with these whales. She was a resilient sort, so I suspected she might be willing. The pay wasn't bad, and the cause was just.

But what about the murder investigation. The lawsuit I was so confident of yesterday was now useless. Scuzz and Vargas would be confronted by the feds with the whole money laundering scheme. This would be of far greater urgency than my piddling assault and battery civil suits. Of course, the casino would offer some small amount to settle them as part of their overall deal with the feds. Would I ever be able to pin Scuzz and Vargas down on the major issues involving Harry's death? That whole investigation might be kicked to the curb as this whole spy thing unfolded.

As we walked back to the hotel, I was staring off into space letting these thoughts mull. Jean too was weighing the prospects now offered for her future. She, a spy? Turning upper level corrupt leaders of foreign countries into admitting their corruption? Could she spare the time each month and still pursue a career, have a family. We ate lunch together in silence, knowing we each had many alternatives to weight.

One thought kept popping through my deliberations, what did Honey want to see me for? She was still a wild card. How might she fit into the whole murder thing.

As I was going through the possibilities in my mind I heard Jean say out loud, "Yes, I think I'll do it." I hadn't yet had a chance to discuss the pros and cons with her. I was sort of her lawyer, but also her boyfriend. My God, is that what I was now! But most women dithered about decisions and asked for input, and lengthy conversations. I already knew Jean was a different independent sort. But she was up for it.

Taking my role as lawyer and confident seriously I had to ask why. "I mean I have something of value, I have a skill I have acquired. I'm not a soldier but I am doing some good for the community. And it does give me a measure of revenge of Scuzz, but for most of the time they were good to me. I was hesitating about that. They also made a pot of money because of what I could do. But it would be an interesting side trip in my life. Of course, I would need an understanding employer and husband. But the excitement and the good cause are pretty strong factors. What do you think?"

I was still reacting to the word "husband," but my lawyerly skills of quick absorption of facts sprung to my rescue. "Well, Jean, as you know, it is up to you. It is within your abilities… I am sure you will be well protected and safe… The money's nice… Yeah, I would say go for it. If it gets to be too much for fitting into your life, you can always quit. Besides, I think you should ask for a wardrobe for your new role."

"Yeah, hah! Good idea!"

When we got back to the hotel, there was a message waiting for us from Hampton Jones. They wanted to meet us for dinner at the Brazilian restaurant around the corner at 7:30. Fine. We sent a text accepting. Jean was beginning to imagine herself as a World War II resistance spy. I was wondering who would be watching the kids. Wait! Where did that thought come from? What was I doing? I can't say I was entirely unhappy with the thought.

At the Rodizio

We were to meet Hampton Jones at the local Brazilian restaurant called a churascuria. As we were to find out, it was a very nice place with an immense salad bar where waiters walked among the tables with skewers of fresh broiled meat and sliced off a few slabs for each diner as they requested. The meat ranged all the way from pork sausage up to fine filet cooked anywhere from rare to well.

Before we left I got another call from Honey. After reminding her I was not her lawyer several times, she still insisted on meeting at her apartment in Miami Beach now that she had returned from Philadelphia. She had already been told that Harry's original Will had been probated (i.e. proven authentic) and that she was out of the inheritance whether she had had Harry killed or not. She still wanted to talk. A good lawyer listens, so I arranged to see her the next evening. She specified without Jean. I would have to wait to hear what she was now up to. When we got to the Rodizio, Hampton Jones had been joined by two middle aged white guys – must be his bosses. They welcomed us and introduced themselves. Of course, it didn't matter since these were not their real names. I could not judge Jean's mood, but she was polite without revealing her thoughts. As the meal progressed, it began to appear that the two new players did not totally trust Hampton Jones' scheme and were not too subtly examining Jean as to her ability to handle this job. Jean of course spoke Spanish like a good Californian with several years of high school. Her college transcript, however, showed little in the way of politics, economics, business or banking, mostly art and history. While her criminal record was clean, her parents' were not – a few minor drug possession busts and a DUI. They were aware that her parents grew pot, but in Mendocino County that was not even considered a crime by the local gendarmes, who also reported Jean to be a stellar high school student. They accepted Jean's explanation that she did not respect her parents' lifestyle and wanted her own independent life. Fair enough. They then explained that she would have to attend a few weeks of instant spy school. There was none in Philadelphia, but there was one in Washington, D.C. and one in Miami. She would be paid. OK by her, if she could finish up her college courses at Temple. The spy school had no fixed schedule so they would arrange the dates to accommodate her. She chose spring vacation. They then began to suggest that she might not have a strong enough personality to handle these whales to elicit information from them. After all she was certainly a nice looking woman but this would take some brains.

I could see a fire burn in Jean's violet-blue eyes and her pale white complexion redden. She was in effect being called a passive bimbo and did not like it. She flashed out:

"So you think I can't handle it. You bring three men down to interview me and see if I am stupid. You bring me to a steak house where you gorge on red meat in your middle age with a few beer guts and expect me to be impressed. This red meat is not healthy and you are in a profession that requires some degree of fitness. You never asked where I wanted to eat." The men raised their hands defensively. Uh-oh. Someone stepped on a hornet's nest.

"You think I can't handle men. My job for the past years had been exactly that. I size them up, flatter their male egos, and get them to show off and spend their money. You three are beguiled by a pretty face to think that as a woman I am not capable."

"Can you size up men?" asked the square cut fellow with the gray military crew cut. Could I detect a bit of scorn?

"OK, let's see. OK, you, crew cut. Let's try this. You don't wear a wedding ring so you are divorced. You were in the military and your wife didn't like moving from post to post or serving stretches in battle zones while she was home raising children alone. So now you drink. You like imported beer with a heavy taste – more like a porter, but you also drink heavy local craft beers. Sometimes you mix in a shot. You were not going to get promoted after 20 years in the military so you used your connections to get a civil service job at one of the intelligence agencies to use your military specialty which did not translate into civilian life. I am guessing paramilitary, but you could also be marines. Judging from your gut, I would say you don't work out anymore. You have little respect for women, don't like them and don't understand them. But you like to drink. How's that so far?"

Military crew cut sputtered, "Close, close enough," as his two comrades hid their chuckles behind their hands. She had chosen the elder of the three and the obvious ranking one. She had followed the age old fighting rule when confronted by a group of bullies. Challenge the leader first and hit as hard as you can.

The other white guy in his early forties spoke up. "Look, that was easy. He's obviously military. Not too much insight required there. What about me?" He was a tall, blond in a Dacron, plaid short sleeve shirt.

"OK. You have a Midwestern accent, and your clothes are drab and cheap, probably JC Penney or Sears. Your Rs are hard and probably German. You have a graduate degree from someplace in the Midwest, but are intimidated by your colleagues with Eastern sophistication. You are probably religious. I'm guessing Lutheran. You have a strong puritan streak and put your wife on a pedestal. You could easily be manipulated by a smart demanding woman who was pretty and sexy. Big boy!" She switched into a breathless sexy accent. "Why don't you buy me a champagne cocktail and tell me about how you were all-state in football, even if you weren't." The other two were now chuckling openly. "If you are going out in public you should at least let me pick out your clothes. I might add you like bourbon straight or with soda."

She turned now on Hampton Jones whose smile started to fade. "OK, Mr. Jones. With little ingenuity you name yourself after the college you proudly attended, Hampton University in Newport News, Virginia. You have been trying to get rid of your southern black accent which creeps into your speech every now and then. You too were military. I'm guessing GI bill for college, near home because you were married by then. You insist your wife run a "squared-away" household and are very strict with her and your children. You dress very well and conservatively so that you will out-white the white southern conservatives. You wear very starched Brooks Brothers blue oxford shirt. You drink Hennessey mixed with ginger ale or coke – not very classy. You should step over to red wine, but you have a sweet tooth. Women must be subservient in your world and you have a strong streak of machismo. You must be flattered and then you are a pussycat." Now, chuckles from the other two as their junior officer bore the brunt of Jean's verbal lashing. Jean's eyes were still flashing as she looked over at me and said, "Are you ready to go?"

"Whoa, wait!" said Hampton. "This was a test. A little more than we were expecting. But fine. This will make some good talk around the office." Jean was still breathing in short bursts.

"Look, Ms. Shmedlap, here is a draft of your contract, look it over and let us know if you have a problem with any of it." We sat back and conferred while the three men ordered drinks. Sure enough the drinks came out as predicted. From my point of view the contract was fine, the money was as expected and was terminable by either party at will at any time by either party. Jean spoke up. "What is this clothing allowance, $2,000? Is that a month?"

"No, that's a year.

"You boys have no idea. That wouldn't keep me in clean underwear. If you want me to look like my casino days, I'll need that a month. You should have women doing some of these jobs anyway."

"Can't you wear what you already have?"

"Are you kidding? They are all last year's. You boys don't get it, do you. Do you want a casino hostess or a diner waitress?"

"OK, fine. $2,000 a month. Anything else." I looked at Jean, she nodded.

"Good, I'll get final copies to you in Philadelphia by FedEx." We shook hands. Jean was still breathing heavily. We strolled out into the night air stuffed with a heavy beef meal, walked around the block. Surprisingly, although it was downtown Miami, but homeless men were bedding down on the streets as we walked by. We kept walking in silence.

Finally, I asked, "Jean, I have to ask, did you size me up?"

"Of course. That's what women do. We don't look at chests and butts like you do."

"But… but."

"So you want to know what I thought of you?"

"Well…"

"OK. You have intelligence and culture. You don't drink much and you're Jewish. Jewish men make good husbands. They respect women and listen to their wives' opinions. They believe in a close family life. On the other hand, if they don't agree with something they speak up."

"Okay, so far, so good."

"You are small in stature and resent not having excelled in sports, so you are embarrassingly devoted to sports. You work out religiously. You have a little man complex and respond to challenges a bit too easily, so you carry grudges. How am I so far?"

"OK, I guess."

"You are kind and generous, and will fight for the down trodden."

"Pretty good. How would you manipulate me?"

"Jewish men like to be mothered, like they were brought up. You like to be pampered."

"Oh no, am I that easy?"

"No, it's nice. The best part is that you like your women to speak up, you hate passive women."

"That's true."

We walked some more in silence. "Oh Jean, I have to meet Honey tomorrow afternoon. Are you okay to fly back to Philadelphia the next morning."

"Fine. Beware of Honey. She is very shrewd. I'm sure she knows all about this CIA thing. She got it from Scuzz I'll bet.

"By the way, I do not need $2,000 a month for clothes, and I certainly can wear last years'. I just said that because they pissed me off."

"Oh I certainly got that part."

Enough said. Time to cool down.

Another Meet with Honey

Every time I was to talk with Honey, I was sure I was about to do something wrong. She was a woman of many different levels and had, I was sure, a strong reputation sense of self preservation. But I rang the bell in the lobby to be admitted, and she greeted me outside the hall as I got off the elevator. "Peter, come in." Somehow, I felt lured into something. I could feel a silken web enclose me.

She was wearing some modern engineering achievement which presented her breasts and cleavage in an appetizing array. They rippled slightly to show they were real. I forced my eyes up to her face once again and saw a warm smile. There were a few crow's feet at the eyes but she had a smile that was warming. The costume she had chosen for this performance was a gold and black top with some kind of wing like structure at the shoulders dipping to a delicious vee at her thoracic region. She wore tights in a gold and black pattern which clung to her every curve. Even at her age, (Which was what? Who could guess?) she was exciting.

She had already amazed me with her ability to weave through her criminal trial. She had known all along that her new kidney would not match her old, but that there was no chance of an incriminating DNA connection to her brother, or perhaps half brother, Harry. Yet she let the drama play out.

Now, she had been disappointed as an original Will had turned up after months of a search, and she would lose out on a nice inheritance. Yet she was cheery and happy to see me. I was the one who brought the Will into court, and ended her litigation to be declared the intestate heir. Could she be angry at me? After all, she had sent Jean in my direction. Was that a bribe of some sort? At all times, it was tacit, no understanding that Jean was somehow to compel me to generate my good faith efforts to aid in this lost Will battle. Yet she had never played her cards overtly.

I sat where beckoned on the couch and was poured yet another golden dream. Smack. They were tasty! Again, I was treated to a glorious view of her breasts as she leaned over to pour. I could only guess that this maneuver was more practiced than the solo performances of the great Russian ballerinas. Yes, her breasts were magnificent and real as she nuzzled them against me while readying her questions with innocent round eyes.

"So, Peter, I'm now out of the estate. The Will has been accepted by the court?"

"Yes, we call it probated."

"So the issue of my killing Harry is a closed issue?"

"Hmm. I wouldn't say so. The theory was that you, Scuzz and Vargas planned it for your benefit and the part of the estate that paid off your debts. They could always re-start the murder trial."

"You mean there's no double jeopardy. I can be tried twice." "Well, you weren't "tried" the first time. It was always a preliminary hearing. Not a final trial. You can always be re-arrested."

But no one knows more than they knew before, and now they know my new kidney wasn't Harry's."

"You knew that all along, didn't you?"

"Of course."

"But the question is, did you swap Harry's kidney for your new one?" "Who could say that?"

"Scuzz and Vargas. Vargas was carrying a cooler on the plane to Cuba and that could have held the kidney. And Scuzz was at or near the Poconos on the possible dates of Harry's death. Now, Honey, I have to tell your I'm not you lawyer. What you say to me, I could be compelled to repeat in court." I sensed she was about to make some kind of confession.

"OK, I see." She sucked air in through her teeth. "What kind of trouble are Scuzz and Vargas in right now?" A swift new subject.

"As you know, they each attacked me, and Scuzz beat up Jean. So they have those criminal trials."

"Will they get much time if they are convicted?"

"Probably not. Neither of us was harmed badly and there were no weapons."

"But what about Jean's story about the money laundering with the whales?"

"Oh, you heard about that. Who told you?"

"Please, Peter, I have friends."

"I have to say Scuzz, Vargas, and the casino are looking at some big cases. Millions are involved." I was not going to tell her of the deal with the CIA.

"So was Jean's story very convincing?" She again nuzzled her breasts against my arm and looked at me with wide innocent eyes.

"Oh yeah. Jean was convincing."

"Would I be?" Ah. The question she really wanted answered. So the reason for my invite. She couldn't trust Scuzz or the casino's lawyers. She wanted an honest opinion of her worth in some kind of deal.

"That depends, Honey. Jean wasn't in on it as much as you might have been. And she had kept records and tapes. All contemporaneous and detailed."

"Who do you think taught her how to do that?" Gone was the wide-eyed looks, no more boobs on my arm. She was sitting up and crossed her legs in those gold and black tights authoritatively.

"Aha!" I said. "Very good. You know I have to say that I felt you would be mad at me. I mean you introduced me to Jean as kind of a bribe. And I've never really been on your side. I hope you'll forgive me."

With that, she burst into peals of laughter. Smacking her thighs, she said, "Jean, a bribe to you! Hah, hah! That's good. No, I wanted Jean out of the business. I knew she wasn't the kind of girl for that life. Too smart. She never wanted money or glitz or glamour. She's a nice girl. She wanted kids, and a nice husband. I was setting you up. A nice comfortable lifestyle."

Was that real. Yes it looked like it. Jean certainly was not the sort to hang around casinos duping men into getting drunk and gambling heavy. I could see that. But me, why me?

So of course I said, "Why me?"

"I did a bit of research on you. You were divorced, the right age and a bit of a boy scout. I figured it was time for you. You were ready."

"But how did you figure I would be on this matter?"

"Who else at your firm? You're the only one who isn't a nerd with a stick up his ass."

"So I got to meet Jean. OK. I'm very grateful. She is everything you say."

"I had to get her away from Scuzz before anything bad happened."

"Yeah. I can see that. But Honey, what's going to happen to you?"

'Unfortunately, I didn't get Harry's estate. I am into the casinos big time and my health isn't good because of my let's say indulgences in the past. And now, I'm still looking at a murder rap."

Not good huh!"

"But I got files on lots of people. So I have to know what's that worth. I need to get out of casino debt, I need to clear this murder thing if Scuzz decides to involve me. What do I do?" She was all business now. I still have to admit that I considered Jean a bribe and that I owed her something. And somewhere my inner boy scout was working overtime. Yes I could help her. I was not her lawyer, but she trusted me and she was a damsel in distress. She poured another golden dream perhaps to grease the wheels.

"OK. I got it. A little tricky. First, you prepare a good sample of your files. Then you and a good lawyer go see the feds. You then make what we call a proffer. You, through your lawyer, explain what you have on the casino and its clients. Then ask for a deal. One, the feds get immunity for you on the murder rap. This is tricky because we have to deal with the state prosecutor, not the feds. Hackett may not want to. But, you would have to rat out Scuzz and Vargas' part in the whole deal. At this point, I don't know if you are in on it or not. That's a tricky area. I can't be your lawyer on this. Two, you spill your guts to the feds on all your whales and the casino involvement. You can't leave anything or anyone out. This gives them material they will use for years." (I didn't explain the CIA interest. That would be a conflict of interest with Jean. But I knew the CIA would love her as an undercover agent. But that would come later) Part of the deal would be that the casino would wipe out her debt. Not too tricky. She was a whistleblower in a sense. And deserved a reward for ratting out her employer.

And then, I had an odd thought. I mean Honey was broke and in her what late 40s or 50s. She needed something for her old age. She was still great looking and sexy and knew how to make men happy. I explained that my parents' friend, Sid, was a retired jeweler who lived in Boca Raton in a great condo on the beach. He had done well and was retired in his, maybe late 60s or early 70s. He was a handsome guy, liked to live well and had been single for some time now. I would be the matchmaker. It was the least I could do.

"Oh Peter, this is great. I haven't been able to sleep."

"First things first, assemble your files and I'll get you a decent lawyer. Then I'll treat you to dinner with Sid."

"Tell Sid I'm not a hooker. Only a hostess. I don't want him to get the wrong idea."

"To be frank, then, Honey, I would cover up a bit."

"Oh Peter. I know men. I have the right outfit."

"No French maids or Catholic school girls."

"I was thinking farmer's daughter with braids and freckles."

"Maybe not. Sid's Jewish, he's a city boy." She was giggling like a school girl dishing in the ninth grade. "OK. I got it. Fashion and more fashion. He wants to impress the menopausal women on the Gold

Coast."

"You got it." We got up and shook hands. I was a bit wobbly from the golden dreams and went back to Jean and the hotel.

Honey to Feds Proffer

As I left Honey's apartment and took the taxi back to the hotel, my mind began to clear. Honey with Sid! No way. Sure Sid was a guy who loved fancy things and was definitely a catch on the east coast of Florida, but he was way out of Honey's league. First, he had been married for many years to a very nice lady, Flo, and my parents were close friends of theirs until they retired to the Gold Coast. Then Flo died and Sid became a highly sought after bachelor. He had two decent kids my age and several grandchildren. He was a staunch member of the synagogue and served on several charitable organizations. And who was Honey? The first thing that sprang to mind, now that it was clearing: She might have murdered Harry Horton for his kidney and his estate, she might have hidden an original Will. She was shrewd in a slimy, underworld way after having lived with Scuzz and his compatriots in a mob-like organization for maybe 20 years. She might be a good bed fellow for Sid, but I couldn't see her taking care of him if he got one of those old age maladies. I shuddered at the negotiation for a pre-nuptial agreement as Sid tried to keep most of his estate for his children. Too much baggage. I couldn't subject Sid to all that. Now to undo my fixup suggestion.

But then, I was becoming somewhat sympathetic to Honey. I somehow was reminded of the aging cat in the Cats who sang "Memory." A once beautiful, sophisticated animal now in her declining years with nothing to live on but her street smarts. Of course, she could capture a retired guy of which there were many from Miami to Palm Beach, but then she might end up nursemaid to an elderly man suffering the usual elderly maladies. She couldn't do that. She would flee at the first sign and leave a host of angry children up north. So it might be possible to have Honey become an informant for the CIA as had Jean. I put the reminder on my phone for tomorrow.

The next day I contacted Jean's CIA case officer, Hampton Jones. After my description, he was anxious to meet Honey in her apartment as soon as possible. They met that afternoon, and Honey did not disappoint. He was treated to a flood of golden dreams, and something approaching the dance of the seven veils, or the seduction of Delilah. Perhaps some allusion to Mata Hari was more appropriate. Hampton, or whatever his real name was, was transfixed and wanted to sign her up.

As Honey's uncompensated agent, I had to make full disclosures to Mr. Jones. I described the state of the murder case, and the estate, along with the many other problems that came with Honey. He never blinked. She would be a valuable source. He outlined Jean's deal and added a pension based on results and length of time served. I asked about the murder investigation. He gave a wave of the hand, but did ask: Could Scuzz and Vargas have been involved? She of course said beguilingly, "it is a strong possibility." I had to explain I could not be her lawyer in anything having to do with the murder case, and did not want to hear any sort of confession or admission. Jones understood.

"OK, Mr. Stern. Ms. Horton can provide us a valuable service. I suggest she get a lawyer, and prepare for a meeting with all appropriate law enforcement. She needs to work on her immunity in Pennsylvania, not just in the federal courts." Mr. Jones was astutely advising of a very important issue. While it was true that Scuzz and Vargas might be able to cooperate with the feds on a deal for better sentencing on the money laundering for the casino any such deal would not affect the murder prosecution in Pennsylvania, which would be only a state matter. So they might get a light sentence in federal court, they could be looking at life in prison in Pennsylvania if Honey testified against them. This was a mistake many mediocre criminal defense lawyers made for their clients.

Even now, the casino had been raided with search warrants based on Jean's evidence. Honey's participation was not yet public. The search warrants had reached many casino operatives aiding and abetting the money laundering and included a host of accountants, bankers, and lawyers. As yet, it had all been done discretely in order to keep the casino a viable site for Jean's "hostessing." Hopefully, many of these witnesses would see the light early as the feds put on a dog and pony show demonstrating the overwhelming evidence of guilt. If successful, the casino could be preserved as an appropriate vehicle to extract admissions from the casino whales.

As we explained all this to Honey, she walked Hampton Jones to the door of her apartment, and turned beaming to me. "Peter, you did it." I got a big kiss on the cheek and a long hug. "I knew you were a good guy. I did the right thing for Jean." I too left the apartment and went back to the hotel.

Jean, of course, wanted to know what had happened. This was the first but not the last time, I would have to disappoint her. As a lawyer, I can't reveal confidential communication to anyone. Wives do feel shut out of our lives, but then so do wives of spies and those with secret clearances as well as healthcare people. Our world has now erected occupational barriers which are honored more religiously than religion. Our profession is becoming our faith, for good or for ill. I did warn Jean not to speak to Honey about any of this; it might cause what was now a delicate house of cards to fall. Each step had to be orchestrated by the feds in a careful fashion. Jean shrugged and respected our rules. It had to be a matter of trust between us. Yet another bond. Somehow, I wasn't feeling trapped by these bonds.

Honey's Deal

I had called a lawyer in Miami I had tried a case against years before. He was a smart young guy with a meager start-up practice then, but he tried a helluva case against me. I won but he put me through the hoops. He fought every issue which he had researched well on behalf of a client who obviously could not have afforded to pay him much. I had to respect that. So I called Enrique Rodriguez. He was from the huge Cuban population in Miami. I explained the whole matter to Henry as he preferred to be called when outside of his ethnic enclave. I was very careful to ensure that his going against the interests of the casino would not be a problem. It was not.

I arranged a meeting with him and Honey at his office. Honey needed to exchange her magic beans for many things. She needed of course immunity for the murder charge in Pennsylvania, whistleblower money for her dirt on the casinos and the whales, and a deal to continue "hostessing" the gullible whales who would be stung and set up.

First, Honey had to pass the test of Jones' superiors as a future manipulator of men. She passed this without question. Then, the "defense intelligence community of the United States" had to convince the federal prosecutors in Miami as well as the Assistant Attorney General Hackett and the local detective in the Poconos to drop any future murder charges against Honey in return for her testimony against Scuzz, Vargas and the other thugs who murdered Harry. The Pennsylvania prosecutors were more than eager to let Honey get immunity since they were not too hopeful they could ever win a retrial. Her offer to be a witness against Scuzz et al. was a gift from the gods to them. With her testimony certainly Vargas et al. would fold and do their best to get a plea deal and leave Scuzz as the one holding the bag. Jones did his job weaving through the process and got Honey signed immunity letters as he and Rodriguez shopped her story to those necessary.

About a week later, I got a call from Honey. "Peter, you did it. I'm home free and I got whistleblower money and a job as a spy. You did it."

"So what happened?"

"As you said, Rodriguez was great. He and Jones convinced the feds to accept my whistleblower in Miami. I get paid as they collect, but it could be a few million. And I still work for the casino setting up the whales.'

"That's great. But what about Pennsylvania?"

"Rodriguez went up there with the Jones guy. I'm not supposed to say what I said, so I won't. But they took my affidavit, I mean it's 20 pages long and I explained what I knew about Harry's murder. They gave me immunity. They haven't arrested Scuzz and the guys yet, until the whole deal with the casino is set up. So you did it."

"I didn't do much. But thanks anyway."

"Now, you take care of Jean, she's a good girl."

"I don't think she needs my help, she's pretty good on her own."

"Well, look, I've sent you comps all over Miami and Miami Beach so when Jean has to come down you'll have a good time."

"Thanks, Honey."

"No, thank you."

Result of Casino Conference

I was anxious to hear the results of the meeting Jones and the feds had with the casino, Scuzz et al. After all, Jean's recruitment depended on the casino's willingness to admit guilt, pay off the money it received from the money laundering, and cooperate with Jones' and his agency's further sting operation. After a few phone calls, I was advised that Jones wanted to meet Jean and me in Washington to make things official as he called it. So Jean and I drove down to CIA headquarters in Langley. Jones met us at the metal detector and ushered us through to a large conference room off the entry area. Seated around the table were already three people, two men and a woman and slowly four more drifted in. None were introduced or even spoke to us, but each had a folder in front of them they were shuffling through. Finally Jones introduced us to the group.

"Ladies and gentlemen, as you know, I have asked Mr. Stern and Ms. Schmedlap to come down for a briefing and training. So Mr. Stern has asked what the outcome of our meet with the casino people was. Isn't that so, Mr. Stern?"

"Yes, Mr. Jones. How did it work out?"

"It turned out not to be a problem at all. After our subpoenas and search warrants were served and the documents reviewed, we assembled a presentation for the executives and the lawyers. Ms. Schmedlap's and Ms. Horton's affidavits were flashed on the screen along with the names, bank accounts, real estate holdings, etc. We then started in our proposal for cooperation. The federal prosecutor in his opening sentence seems to have used the magic words "casino license" and "Rico indictment." As you know, the term Rico implies something sinister like the mafia. Racketeer Influenced Corrupt Organization. As any criminal lawyer knows this is a major complicated criminal trial. In any case, the prosecutor got no further than a few lines before the casino lawyers said, "We surrender. What do you want?" It seems that they accurately calculated that the value of the casino and the casino license far exceeded any money they might have to pay for their money laundering. They just wanted a fair calculation of what was due. Figuring just what we had so far, we were talking over thirty million, and looking at in excess of fifty.

"Then I broached the idea of a continuing sting of the foreign officials who might want to park their money in safe American investments. They agreed without a whimper. So what we plan is as follows:

"As each person is recruited to come to Miami for his laundering session, Ms. Schmedlap or Ms. Horton will meet them and shepherd them through the process. We will have government agents posing as lawyers or accountants interview them extensively and relieve them of their funds. At some point, we will confront these men with what we now know and suggest they now cooperate with us to provide strategic information about their countries.

"The casino will provide us with the office space for these transactions at their expense. Ms. Schmedlap will have her own personal hotel room for when she is called in, and will be comped all meals and necessities as well as her contract payments.

"Eventually as the volume of these operations increase, Ms. Schmedlap and Ms. Horton will train others in this operation.

"At present we are completing background checks on both Ms. Horton and Ms. Schmedlap so they will receive the appropriate security clearances. This should taka few weeks.

I had to speak up.

"What about the whistleblower payments?"

"We are reviewing this with our finance department."

"I'm not sure I like the sound of that."

"I can assure you they will be fair with you."

"How about Ms. Schmedlap's personal security?"

"We will have access to the casino's extensive closed circuit system at all times. She will also be assigned a personal bodyguard. Also, she will continue to use a false identity which we will backstop completely."

"Can she quit at any time?"

"We expect at least one year for her to develop continuity in the operation from before. After that, it is up to her."

"What about tips?"

"These men will not be so grateful to her once we finish flipping them. I wouldn't expect any tips."

"What about Mr. Scarramazzo, Vargas and the others?"

"The casino had agreed to cooperate fully against them."

"So they might upset your operation."

"Probably not. They are talking right now about their own cooperation to get a reduced prison sentence."

"Has anything been discussed about a murder prosecution in the death of Harry Horton?"

"That has not been raised or discussed."

"What about my suit and Ms. Schmedlap's suit for their attack on each of us?"

"You may proceed on that. Because of our deal with the casino however, you must drop it as a defendant. Your suit will be against Mr. Scarramazzo et al. alone."

"So they will have nothing to pay us with if the casino is not in the suit and then in jail."

"Probably. But we will still be able to use the suit as a discovery device for a murder conviction."

"So what do we do now?"

"Obviously, we must protect the sting operation. So news of our arrangement with the casino must be kept confidential. Hopefully, the guilty pleas of Mr. Scarramazzo and his gang will pass unnoticed.

Ms. Schmedlap's and Ms. Horton's cooperation will be kept in strictest confidence."

"What do we do now, I mean, right now."

"Go back to Philadelphia. Oh, and by the way, I should add that we have already collected $7.5 million from the casino against their payment of money laundering fees. We have a check for Ms. Schmedlap of $1 million to take back to Philadelphia."

"What, for me!" Jean blurted out. For the first time, the assemblage in the room broke out in broad grins – their first expression of any kind that day. Tears were streaming on Jean's face.

"I… I… don't know what to say."

"You have done a great service for our country. One which will provide us with valuable intelligence for years to come. Thank you."

The people in the room rose and shook our hands as they filed out.

Jean and I sat there. "Peter, I never expected so much money. I won't know what to do with it."

"I will find some safe investment and put it away for you."

She was listening, just sitting there shocked with her hand over her mouth. I gently took her elbow and escorted her out of the room. Jones showed us out and shook our hands again.

Jean didn't say much on the ride back to Philadelphia. "Peter, this is all so new."

I thought about saying the lawyerlike things about money and being conservative. I knew what she was like by now, so I kept quiet and let it all filter through her consciousness.

"I do need a new car. The VW is on its last legs." She looked at the check in her purse. Then, as we drew near Philadelphia she asked, "What are we going to do about Scuzz?"

"I think it's best to wait until he has been sentenced for the casino crimes, then I start back up and see if there's a murder conviction. How do you feel about that?"

"If he did it, he deserves to be convicted."

"Honey may have to testify against him. How do you feel about that?"

"That's up to Honey. She'll have some whistleblower money by then and a steady job for the casino. She can't be threatened by him now."

Jean's Message

We ate dinner in silence. Jean was string off in space, deep in thought. She was humming quietly as she put her things away from her suitcase. We went to bed with little ado – each mulling over the events of the past few days. Then, the next morning, I showered and was shaving. Jean walked in, with a slight smile on her face.

"I'm pregnant," Jean said, with one of those mysterious Mona Lisa-like smiles. It was a not subtle request for my reaction. This message had been given to men probably as far back as the dinosaurs and demanded an unfiltered instantaneous response expressing approval and encouragement, and promising undiluted love for life. I instinctively knew that my time was limited for an answer since any hesitation would mean I was not all-in on a commitment to at least 18 years of family with Jean. Cold waves of fear shot up from my reptilian brain as I envisioned taking on the financial responsibility and incursions of my me-time. Diapers, smells, lugging baby equipment, teenage disputes, college tuitions, and worst yet, assumptions of responsibility. I had been married before, but that was different. Now, parenthood, the most all-consuming infringement on freedom and net worth imaginable, stared at me with the Mona Lisa smile from this wonderful beautiful woman in front of me. My few seconds of time for a happy positive response were running out. Wipe out my fear. Brave face. Come on, Stern, you can do this.

"The… Then, that's wonderful, Jean. When did you find out?"

"Well, smooth talker, I can see why you are such a hot shot trial lawyer. I went to see the doctor yesterday."

I knew certain questions were off-limits. Obviously, she was happy to become a mother. She seemed to enjoy having sprung this on me and my consternation over the sudden lifestyle change it would mean. But this was now to be a full-time, overall commitment. Waves of reptilian flight fear arose from somewhere in my caveman being. No. This was good. Jean was wonderful – a great companion, a clear-headed thinker, - check, check, and check, everything positive. OK. What the hell, give it a shot. Wait a second, not a shot. A full commitment to this little being I hadn't met who would be noisy, interfere with my sleep, wear out my bank account, cut into my leisure time, - wow! Does everyone go through this? Still the brave smile. I moved to give Jean a hug and kiss. Ah! Fatherhood. Now, I was in for it. And I made it all in just the required few allotted seconds, without betraying my fear to Jean. She smiled. She was amused at whatever was uncontrollably crossing my face. She knew I would be happy, and that I would be a bit slow to accept the whole picture. She knew. She gave me a warm hug back and said, "Now, go to work. You have a family to feed." At my bewildered look, she just smiled. She was enjoying my greatest of all male fears. But she had sensed long ago that I would be happy to be with her forever. She hadn't mentioned marriage. I guess women don't these days. But I'm traditional. We would get married. I was ready. Yes. It was time. Time to grow up. The fear was ebbing. My nice condo in the city, walking distance to work, and nice restaurants, would become something in the 'burbs. I would no longer be cool. But I had a sense it would work out. I was still hugging Jean when I realized I had a 9:30 appointment at the office. Time to feed the family! Yes. I had made the change in record time. Slowly my mind stopped racing. I had gotten the smile from Jean – always a pleasant glowing feeling. I had given her reassurance. The embedded request for comfort from the female dating to the cavemen – had been answered by a sign of unalloyed protection. As those sparkling blue eyes of Jean looked back at me, I too was reassured. My heart beat returned to normal, and I began to accept. Yes, I could do this.

My mind slowly returned to rational thought. And I realized I was looking at a tax return filed as married with three exemptions. I am a lawyer after all. It was now November. If I was married by the end of the year, I would save lots on my taxes.

"So, uh… Jean… would you like to get married?"

She still had a slight hint of the sardonic in her smile, "What, and lose my last name, Schmedlap?"

She knew. She knew all along I was good for the long haul. Now, she was just playing. My mind now functioning had me reply, "You could hyphenate, you know. Shmedlap-Stern." Not to be outdone, she said, "You could be Stern-Schmedlap." Well, enough of that.

"So do we have a wedding or something?" I asked.

"Of course. I want the works and before I start to show."

I explained that if we were married before the end of the year, I could get a nice deduction. "Peter, you really are a smooth talker. How can a girl resist that! Sign me up."

And so it was done. We planned a nice wedding with a rabbi friend presiding and a dinner party later. She called her parents who were reluctant to get dressed up and told they could wear bib overalls if they wanted. Angelina was overjoyed. Carmen too. I had to endure the usual abuse from office mates and friends. It was much worse from the meatheads at the gym. But in two weeks it was planned, arranged, and completed. On such short notice, there was no time to plan a honeymoon so we got on a plane and were amply comped at the casino in Miami. We had not told her government employers of her "delicate condition" so they were very happy for us. A passing thought, not uttered aloud, bemoaned the loss of income my new family would experience as she began to show. I mean as beautiful as she was, I could not see her inveigling her foreign visitors with an obvious bun in the oven.

Honey would not be invited, nor of course was Scuzz, but Honey sent an immense bouquet to our room with an effusive wish for our future happiness. I was sure I could hear Scuzz grinding his teeth in the local federal lockup.

Scuzz' Trial

It took several months for Assistant Attorney General Hackett to prepare a murder trial against Scuzz and Vargas, even with Honey's complete statement. He even had brought in a very experienced Deputy District Attorney from Philadelphia to help. He had suffered total embarrassment from his failure to get Honey to trial before and covered every possible error this time. Jean and I were subpoenaed to testify in case we were needed to fill in a few blanks, but we would not have missed this for the world. Jean by now had a small baby bump wrapped in a long black knitted wool dress, but, at least, in my eyes, dazzled everyone she passed in the small town where the trial took place.

Honey, seeing us on the street outside the courthouse, came up to me all-aflutter. She wore a glittering gold rain coat over a black and gold pants suit. Not the dress I would have advised for the star prosecution witness at a murder trial implicating her co-conspirators while she received immunity.

"Peter, Jean, wonderful to see you. I can't believe it will be over. Oh and Jean – don't you look nice, love the fertile look and you're glowing." I had to admit she was. "Mr. Hackett has been going over my testimony for months. It seems so odd, a year ago he wanted to send me to jail for life, now I'm his best friend. Scuzz will now get justice and not me. After all these years of abusing me, finally he will get abused in prison!" Ah! So she was going to play the abuse card in defending herself from the charge that she was the driving force in Harry's murder. She would blame Scuzz for making her cooperate. Neat! Hackett didn't think this up. But she would need some sympathy from this jury.

Judge Tiller, who sat on the previous preliminary hearing, held on to this case like a bulldog. He was basking in the glow of the good press from seeing the flaw in the first prosecution of Honey and was not about to miss it this time around. So he personally supervised the jury selection and started the hearing of endless motions pre-trial by the defense lawyer. As Jean and I sat at the local diner having club sandwiches and Sprites, Honey came by. "Peter, I don't understand. Scuzz wants to negotiate a guilty plea, but Hackett won't talk to him and his attorney. What's going on?"

It was odd. Prosecutors are generally willing to talk plea deals. Was he so confident, he wouldn't consider the possibility of a mistake? Especially Hackett. Maybe he was too stupid or pig headed. Always a possibility. But it was strange, not even to talk. That was a time to pick up maybe a few hints about the defense case. Would he testify? Who were his witnesses? And besides, this was not a slam dunk. There was very little evidence that Scuzz was in the Poconos during the time of the murder, Philadelphia, yes, but the Poconos, no. And Vargas was seen with a cooler on the same plane as Honey going to Cuba at about the time of the Harry's immolation, but not Scuzz. Only Honey could stitch all the loose ends together by a full confession. But she had immunity and the jury would be told that. Could she be credible? Who knew? Better to err on the side of caution, and at least discuss a plea, but Hackett stoned them. No deals! Interesting. Honey didn't mind testifying, she liked the attention and she was getting some measure of revenge against Scuzz. But she was nervous, and wound up. If I were Hackett, I would be afraid of what she might say. Always a risk!

And so it started. Honey was called to the witness stand in front of Judge Tiller and a local jury of mostly rural folk. Hackett had at least listened to good advice and gotten nine women and three men on the jury since Honey – a woman – was the star witness.

Honey's testimony was carefully shaped by someone and revealed more than I could have expected.

She described how she was heavily in debt to the casino, and was on dialysis for a bad kidney for which she desperately needed a transplant.

She described her love affair with Scuzz and her frequent physical abuse at his hands. Copious tears were streaming down her heavily made up cheeks and her mascara was streaking. Nonetheless in a gold silk blouse which displayed as usual an ample cleavage she seemed to be a victim.

She then put on Scuzz the whole plot. She had told him about her brother, her only sibling, who was a lawyer in Philadelphia. It was Scuzz who saw a way to solve her problems – I hate to say it but to kill two birds with one stone. Since she was his sister, his kidney must be able to replace hers. And since he was a lawyer, he must have enough money to repay her casino debts. Honey even suggested that Scuzz had bought up her debts to keep her in his control while he continued to feed her drugs. So it was he that suggested that they murder Harry, take his kidney and inherit his estate. He did the research and it checked out. He even spoke to some lawyer who told him that, Honey would inherit nothing if there was a Will leaving his estate to others. Aha! Locate the Will and destroy it. OK, so things were laid out.

It was decided that Scuzz would come up to Philadelphia with Honey to meet Harry. Honey would ask Harry for a loan to pay off her debts as a pretext while they checked him out. It gave them the opportunity to ask if she was in the Will. At least, he would say if he had a Will. The conversation started off politely, but Harry began to take a dislike to Scuzz who was too blunt with his questions. Since he hadn't seen Honey for many years, it irritated Harry that she would appear, out of the blue, to ask him for money and the distribution in his Will. For some reason then Harry was briefly called out of the office. Scuzz saw a locked file drawer in Harry's desk and was sure he kept his private papers there. When Harry returned, he was curt with them and said, unconvincingly, that he would consider what she wanted. And so they left empty handed. It was Scuzz who suggested that they get into that locked drawer and see if the Will was there. And so they did – Scuzz, Honey and a local handy guy broke into Harry's office suite, pried open the drawer and found the Will. OK. So now the plot was clear. Kill Harry, take his kidney, bury the Will, and leave no fingerprints.

Now the fact that the kidney had been taken obviously had to be concealed so it was determined that Harry's body had to be burned, at least in the middle.

Since this could not happen in Center City Philadelphia, the Poconos in the fall would be ideal. The barbecue could be a great excuse for an accident as the plot was sketched. It was pretty logical, so Honey agreed. Harry was kidnapped in Philly, whacked on the back of the head, taken to the Poconos, and laid out on his back deck. To calm him down as he was burned, Scuzz had gotten some stuff to inject him with. And so he was burned. Vargas grabbed the kidney, took a flight to Miami to meet Honey with the kidney. The Cuban doctors rejected the kidney match, but made a trade for one that did. In Cuba, kidneys are fairly cheap so the doctors were able to make a nice deal with a good profit. Honey recuperated at a seaside resort on the north coast and came back to Miami a week later. It seemed like a well-executed deal. Hackett finished his direct examination with a sigh of relief and Scuzz' lawyer started on cross-examination.

Yes, it was true she had immunity. Yes it was true she had gotten a monetary benefit by ratting out Scuzz to the feds. The defense lawyer was careful to avoid letting her talk about the massive money-laundering scheme Scuzz was running. The judge had earlier ruled that this would be a subject that was out of bounds.

Midway through the second day of trial, everyone went out for lunch again at the local diner. Honey again stopped by. "Peter, what does daily copy mean?"

"Well, Honey, during a trial everything that is said is taken down by the court stenographer who, when asked, can produce a written transcript of all the testimony. Daily copy means that the stenographer goes home after trial, and that night, types up all of the testimony for that day. It's very expensive and not usually ordered, but is available the following day."

"Well, someone is paying for it. Someone from Philadelphia. Hackett told me."

"Someone wants to review the court's proceeding the next day."

"Why?"

"I can't guess. Usually it's ordered after trial, so it can be reviewed for an appeal. Then it can take several weeks before you get a copy."

"Anyway, how did I do?" Every witness asks this. I was clear that I should not coach her while she was still on the witness stand, so I said she was fine. Although I did get this eerie feeling that I was now talking to a cold blooded confessed murderer. Of course, I had a number of my clients make full confessions at various times, and even a few murderers, it was always chilling to look at the face of evil and hear it all said out loud. I could feel Jean squirming next to me. She asked if she could leave for some air, blaming her pregnancy. I knew she was realizing that a woman she had known and been friendly with for several years had killed her own brother with little feeling for her own selfish goals. It also dawned on me that she would get away with it. She would get some whistle-blower money, have a nice job entertaining susceptible foreign visitors trying to launder their money under CIA scrutiny and have a healthy new kidney taken from some Cuban peasant for a fee. It didn't compute.

We returned for the afternoon session, the defense lawyer was doing his best to hack away at Honey, but he had little but blunt strokes and Honey's story was holding up. Then, in walked Alicia Allende with two men in suits and sat in my row. She nodded at me politely. What was she doing here? At first, of course, she was appraising Jean, my choice of bride. She nodded in approval, and then she turned to the testimony. But she had drawn attention. This stately woman in a silver silk blouse, and ash white close clipped hair, was gorgeous and the local folks stared. Even Judge Tiller and the courtroom deputies were open-mouthed for a while. But the trial went on. More blunt force hammering at Honey, now boring and ineffectual. Scuzz and Vargas were looking cooked and ready for a lifetime stretch in the ancient Pennsylvania prisons. As this court session ground to a halt, and the jury panel was escorted out a side door, Honey came down from the witness stand and made for the center aisle. There, Alicia with her two suited companions, stood in front of her as one of the suits handed Honey a large manila envelope. "Ms. Horton, you are served with a Complaint in a civil suit." Without more, Alicia stared down at Honey.

It was a tableau. The lady in a gold suit with a black and yellow print blouse glaring back at this stately beauty in shimmering silver, "What are you doing here, bitch!" the evil side of Honey was coming out. Of course, Alicia had consulted attorneys and figured out that the estate of Harry Horton had a wrongful death lawsuit against Honey and her accomplices, Scuzz et al. Honey had a large whistle-blower claim due her from the feds as they unraveled the money laundering scheme at the casino. This nice pay day would all be scooped up by the estate and eventually become Alicia's. Honey, although with a new kidney, would remain broke in her declining years with a well-publicized reputation as an openly confessed murder. Alicia was holding firmly in her hand the daily copy of Honey's full statement under oath. It now became clear why Hackett would not accept a plea deal. Alicia needed Honey's open court statement under oath to cinch up her wrongful death action. And Alicia had friends in high places. Alicia pointed to the suit papers Honey was now holding. "Harry was a nice man!" she said calmly, turned on her heel and strode out followed by the two suited attendants.

"Whew!" said Jean as Honey seemed to crumple inwardly before her. She resisted the urge to give her a comforting hug, as she pictured Honey looking on as Harry burned. She wasn't there of course, but she had planned it with little remorse.

Now, all her whistleblower money would be claimed by Harry's estate, but Honey's reputation was shot. Her well-publicized testimony of being complicit in her brother's cold blooded murder would be in all the papers. She couldn't "hostess" these money launderers in Miami, but she also was no longer a marriage prospect for a rich Florida retiree. Her goose was cooked.

The news media had gathered in the courtroom from the opening day, but under strict instructions from Judge Tiller, had been quiet. However, in the morning before court and in the afternoon afterwards, the TV cameras tracked everyone's move while the print media lobbed questions at us. We remained inside to avoid all this and sent for takeout lunch each day.

After Honey's testimony, the trial ended rather quickly. Then that buffoon Hackett asked the judge for an hour's recess while, as he put it, "they discussed an alternative resolution." That generally meant a guilty plea was being discussed. And so it was. When the court reconvened, Hackett and Imperatore told the judge they had reached an agreement on a guilty plea. A judge is always happy to hear the sides had agreed on something so he dismissed the jury, swore in Scuzz and Vargas and went through a series of questions designed to show that they understood the meaning of a guilty plea. The men answered gruffly at each question posed. When the judge came to the terms of the deal he turned to Hackett and asked the exact terms that had been agreed on.

"Your Honor, we have agreed in return for a plea of guilty, to recommend to Your Honor, a term of 10 years minimum to a maximum of life on the count of murder, …" There was a gasp from those in the courtroom as Hackett droned on listing all the other lesser included crimes in the offense, all of which would be served simultaneously with the 10 to life term. It was a startling lenient sentence for such a cold blooded, planned out, murder. Judges, however, like to encourage pleas and usually go along with the prosecutor's recommendation. Of course, the judge could always refuse to go along but rarely they did. The deal was an interesting one. The news people could report that the sentence would be life, while they aware of the real implications knew the defendants might serve as little as 10 years, and maybe get parole after 12 to 15 years. So there it was. The judge ordered the men held in jail while he considered the sentence, and banged his gavel authoritatively. We all rose and left looking at each other with puzzled expressions.

Hackett stopped me on the way out of the courtroom as Jean and the rest went out. "Justice is served." He was preening and getting ready to bloviate in front of the media outside. "Please keep out of this. We don't want any appeals." He clearly meant that he didn't want me making him look bad by commenting on the case. He certainly didn't want me to say that he initially was ready to dismiss the matter as an accident until Carmen found some needle marks on Harry's arm. He wanted unalloyed glory for his victory. I had no intentions of saying anything; things had turned out well in that regard.

As I walked out of the courthouse, Alicia, Honey and Jean were gathered in a heated dispute, all in the glaring eye of many TV cameras. Alicia tall and gorgeous in her close cropped white hair and a shimmering silver silk blouse, Honey in her gold raincoat with hands thrust in its pockets so as to expose her golden top and ample bosom, and my Jean, in her black woolen knit with her black shiny curls and flashing blue eyes. I certainly would have to ask for a still shot of the three from one of the camera crew and then I called Angelina at the office to see if there was anything new.

Settling Accounts

I thought this episode in my life was over as Jean and I drove home. The next day I looked for the newspaper reports of the trial. There were no articles that covered the trial. Scuzz and Vargas were, of course, convicted but Honey and her testimony appeared nowhere. The Miami papers, no mention. The Philadelphia papers, no mention. The harm to Honey's reputation detailing her complicity in the murder of her brother was not covered by anyone. I even went online to read the coverage by the local Pocono papers for Carbon and Monroe County. Again nothing on Honey, only the conviction of Scuzz and Vargas, and the excellent work of Hackett and Judge Tiller. Alicia's suit against Honey was also not covered. During the trial, I had counted over 20 reporters from the print and TV media. Had they dropped the ball?

Although I know Honey would still be distraught over being served by Alicia's suit on behalf of the estate, I thought I should at least call her.

I was sure she would be distraught over the lawsuit brought by the estate and Alicia. So I waited a few days. I was more than a little curious over the lack of coverage of her involvement by her in the murder. So I called mid-morning.

"Honey, it's Peter. I was worried about you. How are you doing?" "Oh, I'm alright. I'm back at work at the casino. My shift starts in an hour." She sounded upbeat.

"That's great to hear. I was worried that your testimony at the trial might interfere with your ability to work."

"No… No… The people I work for are used to working with a lot worse than me. They pay me well, and cover my expenses. It's a lot easier without Scuzz around. Of course, I'm on camera all the time and I have a bodyguard. They need me more now than Jean is starting to show. She just can't work like that anymore. They need me to train the new girls. So I'm doing alright."

"That's good to hear. But I checked all the papers about the trial. Your name and your testimony doesn't appear at all."

"Look, Peter, I'm on a recorded phone. Now that I work for you know who you'll have to ask Jones and Alicia about that."

"Wow! I get it. Well, I'm glad to hear you landed on your feet."

"Thanks, Peter. Come down to Miami and I'll comp you for anything."

"Thanks, Honey."

That was interesting. So I should call Jones and Alicia. Let me see, I guess Jones first. I was guessing Alicia might be upset about Honey's survival. At least Jones would be professional about this. So I called the man I knew as Hampton.

"Who's calling, please."

"Peter Stern for Hampton Jones." I heard some papers flipping as the lady was looking through the array of pseudonyms used by the agents.

"Could you hold please, while I see if he's in." I held. I was sure she was asking Jones if he wanted to speak to me, or acknowledge his pseudonym.

"Peter. Yes. How are you?"

"Fine. I had a few questions if you could help me out for a bit?"

"Sure. What can I do for you?"

"I was trying to read the press coverage of the murder trial and found very little."

"Oh, that. Yes. We had to protect Honey's identity so we prevailed on the papers to leave her out. She is a very valuable operative for us, and needs to keep her ability to work free from Internet prying."

"I guess I can see that. I thought she would be distraught about this suit by the estate against her for wrongful death."

"Well, that's been settled. We couldn't have that whole business get out as well. You should ask Alicia about that."

"Okay, then thanks Hampton."

"And thank you, Peter. You have created a whole division in our offices." I called Alicia.

"Hello, Peter. I'm glad to see you're back on the Commission."

"Yes, Alicia, thank you for that."

"Alicia, I just spoke to Honey and she said I should ask you what happened after the trial."

"I have to thank you again."

"I heard you already settled with her."

"Yes, well, this guy Jones called me that night and had a long discussion with me. It seems Jean and Honey are very valuable to him. With Jean starting to show, Honey is the main leverage point in their operation. So they need her."

"I can see that. That's what Jones told me."

"So my suit can't get any press, or appear online."

"I get that."

"So we settled. I can't say I'm unhappy. I got far more out of it than the $1 million I lost from the insurance policy. Honey's whistleblower money is huge. So I made out very well."

"Knowing you Alicia, I am guessing you extracted a few promises from Jones and his boys."

"Peter, what can I say. I'm a political animal. I deal in political favors." "I'm sure of that, Alicia. I'm sure you'll get your money's worth." "Count on it, Peter."

"Nice doing business with you."

"Hang around, I may need you in the future."

"Always happy to work with you."